Praise for *The Oxygen Man*

"Resuscitates Southern fiction ... sparkles with soul and feeling . . . a first novel to be treasured."
—Bill Nichols, *USA Today*

"Deeply felt."
—*Chicago Tribune*

"[A] compassionate, clear-eyed, expertly written first novel. . . . Daisy [is] a figure strong enough to have been limned by Faulkner."
—John Skow, *Time*

"In the finest Southern Gothic tradition . . . laden with symbolism, this novel mixes well the classic elements of the family cycle of cause and effect, hidden and imminent violence, and the long gestation before restitution."
—*Booklist* (named one of the "Top Ten First Novels of the Year")

"Superb . . . abounds with generously detailed characterizations . . . and sharply realized scenes that resonate strongly. . . . A wrenching, compassionate portrayal of wasted lives in explosive conflict."
—*Kirkus Reviews* (starred review)

"Extremely tender."
—*Publishers Weekly* (starred review)

"Original, bold, eerie . . . the pages pulse with a Faulknerian aura."
—*BookPage*

"Compelling."
—*Atlanta Journal-Constitution*

THE
OXYGEN MAN

A NOVEL

STEVE YARBROUGH

SCRIBNER PAPERBACK FICTION
PUBLISHED BY SIMON & SCHUSTER
NEW YORK   LONDON   TORONTO   SYDNEY   SINGAPORE

SCRIBNER PAPERBACK FICTION
Simon & Schuster, Inc.
Rockefeller Center
1230 Avenue of the Americas
New York, NY 10020

This book is a work of fiction. Names, characters, places,
and incidents either are products of the author's imagination or are
used fictitiously. Any resemblance to actual events or locales or
persons, living or dead, is entirely coincidental.

First Scribner Paperback Fiction edition 2000
Published by arrangement with MacMurray & Beck, Inc.

SCRIBNER PAPERBACK FICTION and design are trademarks
of Macmillan Library Reference USA, Inc., used under license
by Simon & Schuster, the publisher of this work.

Manufactured in the United States of America

1   3   5   7   9   10   8   6   4   2

Library of Congress Cataloging-in-Publication Data
Yarbrough, Steve, 1956–
The oxygen man : a novel / Steve Yarbrough.
1st Scribner Paperback Fiction ed.
p. cm.
1. Catfish fisheries—Fiction. 2. Mississippi—Fiction. I. Title.
PS3575.A717O95 2000
813'.54—dc21   00-057370

ISBN 0-7432-0165-5 (Pbk)

For four people who made a difference:

Jessica Green, Sloan Harris, Robin Schorr, and Jonathan Zimbert

Special thanks to Richard Schweid

He knew all the back roads in the south half of Sunflower County, knew where all the curves were, which wooden bridges had planks missing. He could have driven at night with his eyes closed, and sometimes he did, just to see whether something solid might surprise him. So far nothing had.

But other forms—porous ones—sometimes did. One foggy night, out on a pond levee down close to the Sunflower River, he'd come across his daddy. He saw him standing in tall grass near an aerator, wearing gray pants that dissolved at edge and cuff into the surrounding mist and a gray shirt with the construction company's logo over one pocket. Through the fishy odor of pond water, he smelled fresh paint, and just as it had when as a child he walked into the living room and sniffed it in the air, that smell told him that at least for a while his daddy was back.

Daddy, he had said, you're supposed to be dead.

His daddy's lips moved, but no words came out.

After a while his daddy gave up and smiled at him. He didn't know what the smile meant, what the words would have been if he'd heard them. But as his daddy's form faded back into the fog, he said he understood.

I know what you're trying to tell me, he said. Don't you worry, I got it all down.

He'd also seen his momma out there, wearing a pink nightgown that he could look right through. She was squatting at the edge of the pond, her broad back to him, the gown pulled up, exposing her hips. She was doing something with her hands—scooping water out of the pond, trying to wash herself, it looked like. He wanted to speak, tell her the water was dirty, but this time he was the one who couldn't make himself heard. He stood watching her, listening to her slosh water. The pink nightgown became less and less distinct until it was finally just a froth that floated on the surface of the pond. Then it was nothing at all.

They were the only two he'd seen. But one night, he knew, he'd see some other folks too, some folks he hadn't seen in a long time, and the only fear that meeting posed for him was that when it came to pass, they might all lose their voices. And they had a fair amount of talking to do.

1996

Daze Rose was sitting in the kitchen eating an omelet with a little bit of ketchup on the side. While she ate, she read the Jackson paper. Somebody else she'd gone to school with had been convicted. Of a crime this time. He'd soon be coming home, back to Sunflower County, where they would put him to work in the Parchman Prison fields. So many people she'd known had gone to jail. So many more who should have hadn't.

She heard Ned's truck pull into the yard. His door slammed. His work boots crunched the gravel; she knew they did even though she didn't hear it. The screen door closed.

"Hey," he said.

She kept her eyes trained on the paper. Behind her the refrigerator opened and closed. He popped a cap. The cap hit the counter.

He was drinking Beck's these days, and he'd bought himself some new clothes, replacing his old Rustlers with Levis—he'd even bought himself one pair of Calvin Kleins, though as far as she knew he'd never put them on. He'd always wanted to be something he wasn't, and if she'd been what he was she might have felt the same way too.

He drove the back roads in his pickup truck all night. He drove from this fish pond to that one, from that one to the next, lowering a boom into the water, checking oxygen levels. Sometimes he turned on the aerators.

"I've never lost a pond," she'd heard him say.

Out there at night, he also said, you saw the damndest things.

She knew he wanted her to ask what kinds of things, and so she wouldn't. She knew he needed her to ask, and so some part of her wanted to, and because she wanted to she couldn't.

He sat down at the table, stood the cold bottle on the place mat. She couldn't stop herself. Mistress of the gesture, she slowly looked up, let her gaze climb his torso toward his face. He needed a shave. His eyes were bleary. His hair was still more red than gray, but more gray was on the way. The fact that he had aged, and would age further, was a huge mark against him.

He swallowed, though there was nothing in his mouth. He said, "What's in the paper?"

"Kyle Nessler's going to Parchman."

She pulled her bathrobe tight around her, laid her knife and fork on the plate, and stood. She picked up the plate and took it to the sink. Behind her wood groaned as he shifted his weight.

"He killed his little three-year-old daughter," she said, "and buried her on the banks of the Pearl River down close to Crystal Springs." Hot water splashed onto the plate, diluting the ketchup, which began to spread toward the rim. "They gave him life. If you ask me, life's the last thing the sorry bastard deserves."

She turned around slowly then and looked at Ned. As if the weight of her gaze were more than he could bear, he dropped his head.

She got out of the shower and stood in the steamy bathroom toweling off. She handled herself roughly. She rubbed her breasts hard; she made a cord of the towel and ran it back and forth between her legs like she'd once seen her daddy do. He'd been standing in the backyard when he did that. He'd just come home off the road, smelling of paint, and he'd gone out there to wash off. It was fall, chilly, and he'd worked the towel like that between his legs because he was freezing and he wanted to get inside. She was already inside, but she was freezing too, even after a scalding shower.

In her bedroom she combed the tangles from her hair and blew it dry. She pulled on her work clothes: a pair of faded jeans and a loose tee shirt. Then she sat down on the side of the bed, aiming to put on her shoes. And she heard it.

It came, as always, from the room next to hers. She imagined as always a creature with a protruding forehead crouching in a cave, peeping out at a black sky torn by yellow streaks. The ground rumbled, and over all the rumbling came that other sound, pitched somewhere between a groan and a shriek, that sound she heard from the room next to hers, a single sound that was somehow symphonic.

She froze, let a shoe dangle from her hand. She closed her eyes. Head bowed, reverent, she accepted, once again, this offering from her brother.

He turned onto the blacktop road that led to Mack Bell's headquarters.

The headquarters was out behind Mack's house. The house had belonged to Mack's daddy, but he'd died back in '85, and Mack had moved up the road with his wife and kids. It was a big white house with a broad veranda. Rockers stood on the veranda, and every now and then Mack would sit in one of those rockers and drink a mint julep, though he hated anything sweet.

The house had hardwood floors, fancy red tile in the kitchen, and enough bathrooms for a good-sized family to take a leak simultaneously and in private.

There was a spa in the backyard, but Mack had built it under a pecan tree, and pecans were always falling in and clogging up the filters. When that happened, Mack's wife, Ellie, would call Ned. "It's the filters," she'd say, which meant Ned should get in his pickup, no matter what time of day it was, and come and clean out the filters.

Ellie sometimes lay on the deck around the spa and watched him while he worked. She wore a skimpy two-piece, displaying cleavage north and south. Sun had burned her skin the color of a penny. She attended an aerobics class in Greenville four times a week, and all that jumping up and down had made her skinny.

Ned never liked to be around her. She had a deep, slow voice that didn't seem to go with her wiry body, and every time he worked on the spa he had to listen to that voice asking questions. At one time or another, she'd asked him how much Mack paid him, why he liked night work, how come he hadn't finished up at the junior college, and didn't he want kids. She made him feel like he was a potato she'd decided to peel just to see what rotten spots she could find beneath the skin. This afternoon her car was gone—she was probably over in Greenville, he guessed, probably jumping up and down, trying to work off another eighth of a pound.

Mack's pickup was parked near the tractor shed. Ned hadn't even shut his truck door before Mack came stomping out, carrying a big wrench in one hand. When he saw Ned he stopped and stared at him for a minute, his jaw locked so tightly it might have been wired shut. Then he pounded his palm with the wrench. It was clear he wished he could have pounded something else.

"Get in my truck," he said. "Got something I need to show you."

The steering wheel dug into Mack's belly while he drove, even though he'd pushed the seat as far back as it would go. He'd always been big, but now he was nearing fat, mostly because he drank all day long. He kept an ice chest in the back of the pickup truck, filled with beers that Ned had trouble pronouncing the names of. Okocim, Dos Equis, Pilsner Urquell. That was where he'd first tasted Beck's. Mack didn't offer him beer very often anymore. Ned didn't know why, but there was a reason.

There was a reason for everything Mack Bell did or didn't do. Some of the reasons were easy enough to understand. When Ned had asked him why he'd invested thousands of dollars backing two guys who wanted to develop a sonar detector for use in fish ponds, Mack said he'd done it because the time was coming when banks wouldn't agree to loan money against a fish farmer's stock unless the farmer could prove electronically that it was there. That made sense enough to Ned. But when he'd asked why Mack had installed the spa right under a tree, Mack said he'd only bought the thing because Ellie kept bitching about not having one, and he'd put it under the tree in hopes the pecans would keep the spa broken down. And that made no sense to Ned, though it must have to Mack.

"There's been some weird shit going on," Mack said, "and the bulk of it's happening at night."

"Weird shit usually does."

"Yeah, it does, don't it?" Mack said. The question was not a question, but it hung in the air between them, as a question some-times does, for four or five seconds.

"Course, I've seen weird shit happen," Mack said, "in broad open daylight. You know that blacktop road Sam Arnet lives on? Go on four or five miles past Sam's place, and there's a little coun-try grocery on the north side the road. I was driving by there the other day, and I saw six or eight guys standing in a circle near an old overgrown gas pump. I slowed down to see what was going on. About the time I pull up even with the pump, one of them dudes gives a Rebel yell and jumps straight up in the air and comes down with both feet together, and there's the damndest mess of blood and guts spewing through the air you ever saw. Son of a bitches had give a cat a bunch of tranquilizers and laid it on the ground and paid this one fellow to jump on it. Poor bastards was just wasting their money. Guy like the one that jumped on that cat—hell, give him a shot of whiskey and he'd of done it for pleasure."

He turned onto a levee that separated two of his ponds, and they bumped over the ruts. The ponds spread out toward the hori-zon, sunlight dancing golden on the muddy water. Each pond held about seventy thousand catfish, weighing a pound apiece, and those fish would sell for sixty cents a pound.

Mack pointed at the pond on their left. "When's the last time you checked the oxygen level here last night?"

"Around two-thirty."

"How'd it look?"

"Looked fine. Why?"

"When I woke up this morning, it was cloudy, so I went out and checked all the ponds. I come by here around seven-fifteen, and my reading was a little bit low."

Mack parked the pickup near the aerator, opened his door, and got out.

The aerator was connected to the drivetrain of a John Deere tractor that stood parked at the edge of the pond, the rear wheels down in the water. Mack walked over to it. "Take a look at this," he said.

He pointed at the engine. There was a glaze on it, right under a neatly severed injector line.

Ned sniffed the air. "Goddamn."

"I climbed up on the mother this morning and cranked it and went off and left it running. Come back this afternoon to take another reading, and the goddamn place smelled like a Texaco refinery."

"You didn't smell diesel when you cranked it?"

"Fuck yes, I smelled it. You ever crank one of these and not smelled it? I got around here this afternoon to see if the filter was leaking, and that's when I found that cut line. Somebody used a hacksaw on it, and whoever it was knew we were aiming to seine this pond next week. Now we've got several gallons of diesel in the water. The whole son-of-a-bitching pond'll be off-flavor for months, and in the meantime instead of cashing a check from Southern Prime, I'll be writing one to the feed company."

"Who you think'd do that on purpose?"

Mack toed a clump of grass. "Ned," he said, "I don't mind somebody being dumb, but I can't stand it when somebody acts dumber than they are. It makes me start wondering what they're up to. Because normal people—and I put myself smack in the middle of that category—don't want folks to think they're not smart. I see somebody that wants me to think he's a fool, I'm liable to tell him to jump in the lake."

It was one of those moments when setting and suggestion meshed nicely. Ned was standing at the foot of a levee separating two ponds, and he was standing next to a man who, if he chose to, could probably make Ned submerge himself in either one. Mack would have a reason if he gave the order for Ned to jump in the water. *We need to run the cans,* he might say, and Ned would have to slog into the water and run his hand into each of the old ammo cans they'd sunk around the edge of the pond for the females to lay their eggs in—being careful, as he did it, to avoid pissing off the big male catfish that was hovering over the can, fanning the water with his tail and just waiting to fin anything fool enough to disturb the eggs. Or Mack might say, *I dropped my Rolex in the water, get down there and grab it.* Or he might just say, *I want to see you wet.*

"You know fucking well who'd want to make us lose a pond," Mack said. "Any one of several niggers, though I think we could probably narrow it down to three."

He climbed back up the levee to the truck. Ned followed him, shielding his eyes from the sun, which was just going down. They got in and Mack cranked up.

"You think it was done last night?" Ned said.

"Yeah. Because number one, I had that tractor running another aerator yesterday, and I drove it back here late yesterday afternoon, so I know it wasn't done then. Number two, I know it wasn't done this morning because I know where Booger and Q. C. and Larry were, and it was one of them that did it. You know those son of a bitches come to me Monday morning and demanded I raise 'em to six dollars an hour?"

"What'd you tell 'em?"

"What do you think I told 'em? I told 'em to quit dreaming and start working."

"What's number three?"

"Number three," Mack said, "is that in general, a nigger's a creature of the night."

"I guess that's what me and them have got in common," Ned said.

"It's one thing."

Mack pushed the cigarette lighter into the dash, reached into his shirt pocket, pulled a Lucky Strike out of the pack that was always there, and lit up. "You walk around any nigger graveyard in the Delta," he said, "and I guarantee you that for every ten marked graves you see, you'll come across one little five- or six-foot-long depression with nothing where the headstone ought to be. You and me both know who it was ended up there. And why."

He gestured with his thumb at the cooler in the back. "You want you a Heineken, Ned?" he said. "You my right hand and always will be."

Ned checked all sixteen of Mack's ponds once between eight and midnight. He'd plugged a spotlight into the cigarette lighter on the dashboard, and he drove along the levees, shining the light out the window at the dark water, looking for signs of fish along the surface—that was the only evidence they provided when the oxygen was low. Every now and then he'd park the truck, clip the spotlight onto the door, and get out and drop the boom with the probe on it into the water. He kept a notebook open on the truck seat, and when he finished taking his readings he'd climb the bank and write them down.

A thick paste, distilled from midges and mosquitoes, coated the windshield of his pickup. His shirt sleeves were red with mosquito blood and sticky from the repellent he sprayed on his clothes. Midges clogged his nose so that he had to keep blowing it every few minutes.

Once, as he walked down a levee toward the water, he heard a rustling sound in the Johnson grass four or five feet away. Looking down, he saw a cottonmouth as big around as his leg. He ran back up the bank and grabbed the 9-mm. he kept in his truck and squeezed off a shot, but the snake had already slithered off into the grass, where it might well be waiting three or four hours from now when he checked the pond again.

Something was always out there.

The next day was Saturday. He woke up around lunchtime to a house that sounded empty, but the fact that it sounded empty didn't tell him a whole lot. The house sounded empty even when Daze was home. She seldom spoke unless spoken to, and sometimes she didn't speak then. He peeked out the window and saw her car was gone. She went to work early sometimes on Saturday because Southern Prime worked a half-shift that day, and from about twelve o'clock on a bunch of the foremen liked to hang around the Beer Smith Lounge, where she tended bar, and shoot pool or watch baseball on TV. Some of them, he knew, were there to watch her.

One Saturday night about a year ago she'd brought one of them home. His pickup, which he'd parked in the driveway behind Daze's old LTD, had a bumper sticker on it that said, UNIONS AND FREEDOM DON'T MIX.

Ned caught him there because he had the flu. He had it like he hadn't had it since he was a kid—fever of about a hundred and two, runny nose, a throat that felt like a red-hot iron had poked a hole in it. It had gotten so bad that he'd driven by and told Mack he'd have to send Larry Singer out to take the oxygen readings.

He got out of his truck. He slammed his door as hard as he could, then realized there was no need to do that. She'd heard the motor, heard his tires plowing gravel. Daze knew as well as he did that no sound could be ignored, that every one—a top popping, a spring squeaking, a floorboard creaking from this amount of weight as opposed to that amount—signified something particular.

Her bedroom window was dark, but the living room was lit up. He walked up onto the front porch and tried the door. It was locked. He took his key out, stuck it in the keyhole, and twisted.

They were sitting close together on the couch underneath two old framed prints of Pinky and Blue Boy. She had a beer can balanced on one leg. The man was smoking a cigarette, blowing smoke into the air. His free hand rested on the back of the couch, just inches away from her shoulder.

He was a tall man with a long, loose jaw that looked like it could hold a whole pouch of Red Man. He was wearing faded blue jeans that night and a white cotton tee shirt. Ned didn't know his name, but he'd seen him once or twice at the barbecue place out on 82 with a redheaded woman and a little boy who called him "Daddy."

"Hey," the man said.

He stood up, ground the cigarette out in a saucer that was standing on the coffee table, then reached across the table to shake Ned's hand.

"My name's Whitfield Lewis," he said. "Believe I've seen you around town. May even've played ball against you. I'm originally from up in Clarksdale."

"Could be," Ned said.

He ignored the outstretched hand. Daze was staring at the beer can as if she'd like to crawl inside it.

"Can I talk to you a minute?" he said.

The back porch was screened in. It was on the north side of the house, and there was nothing to break the wind. He associated the porch with cold and clutter and the smell of rotting food. When he was a kid, the washer had stood out there, and during the time when his daddy was trying to keep some hogs, the slop bucket had stood there too. Sometimes at night, when the sounds inside the house drove him elsewhere, he had squatted down between the washer and the wall, and surrounded by the sickly-sweet odor of buttermilk and tomatoes and corn and decaying apples, he had hugged his knees and listened to the wind whistling in dead cotton stalks, had wished the wind would pick him and Daze up and set them down somewhere a long way off. But the wind hadn't, not even the tornado that had cut a swath through the Delta in 1973. His daddy had died in that storm, coming home from a job in Pine Bluff, Arkansas. A lot of people had died that year.

There was no washing machine now. It had quit a long time ago, and they'd never replaced it. They washed their clothes in town, in separate washers, at separate times.

The porch was dark—the light had burned out. She stood with her back near the door that led to the kitchen.

"Who the hell is he?"

"I don't know."

"You don't know."

"He showed up at Beer Smith's this afternoon. Look, he's just a body on a barstool."

"He's a body in my living room."

"It's my living room too."

"He's filling the place up with cigarette smoke."

"So what?"

"I can't breathe."

"How come?"

"I'm sick."

"You sure are."

"I've got the fever."

"Try bleeding."

He reached out and grabbed her wrist and held it. She was staring not at his eyes but through them, as if she were trying to see what, if anything, lay beyond.

"The son of a bitch has got a wife and kid," he said.

"He told me he was single."

"What the hell else you expect him to say?"

It was then that they heard the front door slam, and a few seconds later a truck door slammed too. They heard him crank up, throw it into reverse, back up as far as he could before he tore out across the yard. In the morning Ned would find ruts there, grooves as deep as the middles in a cotton patch.

He let her hand go. Spots swirled around in front of his eyes, yellow spots and white ones, spots of different sizes, some perfectly round, others ovular, a few garishly misshapen, all of them orbiting some invisible center that he assumed, for lack of evidence to the contrary, must have been himself.

He drank two cups of coffee, then took a shower and got dressed and climbed into his pickup.

He drove through town and crossed the railroad tracks and then headed east toward the river. Larry Singer lived in a little beige prefab on the edge of Mack's place, right across the road from the biggest of Mack's ponds. Larry's house was the first of several identical houses that stood in a row along a gravel road, no more than twenty feet separating each house from the ones beside it.

All of Mack's help lived right there, except Ned himself. But then, all the rest of Mack's help was black. The houses they lived in were tiny, ugly, and badly insulated, but they'd cost a lot more to build and maintain than the shotgun houses black people had lived in when Mack and Ned were growing up. So Mack bitched day in and day out about the aluminum cans and empty milk cartons and broken toys he saw strewn across the yards every time he drove by.

"You can take 'em out of the cotton patch," he liked to say, "but you can't take the cotton patch out of *them*."

It was on the tip of Ned's tongue to tell him that nobody had been taken out of the cotton patch; the cotton stalks had just been plowed under, a big hole had been dug where the field used to be, and the hole had been filled with nasty water and smelly fish. The people who used to live by the field still lived by it, only now they had as their neighbors the catfish and a few million mosquitoes as well as cottonmouths so big they could eat babies whole if they chose.

But he hadn't said that because Mack wouldn't have liked it, and there were things Mack could say that Ned wouldn't have liked either.

Larry's yard was the only clean one, the only one where the grass had been recently mowed. He wasn't married and didn't have kids, but Ned had heard Q. C. say a woman had moved in with him a short time ago.

Back in the spring of last year, he'd spent a lot of time around Larry late at night, teaching him to take the oxygen readings, and more than once, as they neared some little crossroads juke joint that was covered up in cars and trucks, all of them booming rap, Larry had said, "Ned, let's pull in here for just a second. There's a young lady in that store I need to have a word with." Ned always parked in the shadows, and he never went in, but Larry always brought out something for him to drink and wouldn't let Ned pay him back.

Sometimes Booger and Q. C. came out with him, and the three of them would stand near the truck, shooting the bull with Ned while he drank his beer. One night, he remembered, Q. C. leaned in the window and said, "Tell me one thing, Ned. How come Mack Bell keep raising cotton too if all the money supposed to be in catfish?"

Ned said, "A dog with ambitions don't just piss in one spot. First it pisses over here, and then it pisses over yonder."

Grinning, Larry said, "Diversification."

On those evenings they spent together, they'd crossed a lot of bridges on back roads, little ramshackle bridges that would one day dump somebody's tractor or pickup into fetid water. They'd crossed other bridges too, as many bridges as people like them could safely cross together.

One night every single pond they checked was in the danger zone, so they rode the tractors all night long, driving them from one pond to another, jumping off and wading down into the water with the fish and the water moccasins and hooking up the aerators. They drank both thermoses of coffee Ned had brought with him;

then they passed a warm two-liter bottle of Diet Coke back and forth, swigging it to stay awake. Ned was used to being up all night, but the running to and fro left his feet feeling like they were encased in about twenty pounds of concrete. His back ached, his head hurt, his eyes burned.

"I bet my eyes look like I been on about a nine-month drunk," he said on the way home the next morning.

"They red, all right."

"I like to finished up at the junior college. Wish to hell I had. I had a little more grammar, I could probably do something white-collar, like selling catfish feed for Delta Western."

"Yeah, the white collar's the right collar." Larry worked his shoulders up and down, trying to loosen the kinks. "I ever tell you I applied to Ole Miss?"

"Naw."

"You know Mr. Kenny Baker?"

"The fellow that teaches at the high school?"

"That's him. He talked me into it."

"You get in?"

"Sure did. Even got some financial aid."

"How come you didn't enroll?"

"I didn't like the climate up there."

"By climate," Ned said, "you mean the band playing 'Dixie' at the ball games and the Rebel flags flying?"

"Naw," Larry said. "I just mean the weather, Ned. Oxford's higher and colder than the Delta. Niggers love it sultry."

It was always like that. There were things they could say and things they couldn't say, subjects they could broach but not discuss. At times the water got too deep to stand in.

He'd seen a lot less of Larry lately. Larry and Booger and Q. C. were working days now, driving tractors in the cotton field or working on the irrigation rigs. The few times he'd seen Larry he'd had the impression something was under his skin, that something dangerous and poisonous had worked its way in.

He parked on the side of the road near the mailbox. Larry's pickup, a rusted-out International that sounded like a cotton gin warming up, stood parked in the yard. He walked past the truck and knocked on the front door. It was a long time before anybody opened it, and when someone did, it wasn't Larry.

The woman was tall and big-boned, with caramel-colored skin and shoulder-length hair. She wore a gray UFCW tee shirt and tight black shorts that showed off her thighs. He knew before she even opened her mouth that she wasn't going to sir him, that she never sirred white men, or black men either.

"Yeah?" she said. "You looking for somebody?"

"Looking for Larry. He around?"

She looked him up and down, letting her eyes start their trek at his forehead and travel the length of his body, taking in his nose and mouth, his Adam's apple, his chest and belly, his knees.

"I'm worth about two cents," he said. "Unless you take into account what I owe. Then we're talking negative value."

She never really moved her feet, yet it seemed that she'd come closer. There was energy in the air. Heat. Suffocation seemed suddenly possible.

"You ever had anybody study you like that before?" she said. "Like you was something little with formaldehyde on it?"

"Happens all the time."

"Like you was just a bunch of parts instead of a whole?"

"Like I was something that ought to be cut up and all its tiny insides examined."

"Make a person feel lonesome, don't it?"

"Little's how I'd put it. Makes you feel like a little bitty tadpole."

"You Ned?"

"Ned Rose. Larry at home?"

"Larry?" she hollered. "Man say you at home?"

Larry appeared in the hallway. He wore nothing except a pair of cut-off blue jeans and some pink flip-flops.

"Hey, Ned," he said. "What you up to?"

"Not too much."

"Somebody told me they saw you over in Greenville the other day looking at a used Mercedes."

"Could've been me, I reckon."

"What you want with one of them?"

"Aw, this and that."

"Hope you ain't come out here looking for one—you won't see too many German autos where we stay. We mostly partial to Ferraris and Lamborghinis. A nigger don't like no car that lumbers."

The woman laughed. She turned and walked back down the hall, her hips moving as if she were climbing a Stairmaster.

Inside the house dishes clattered, water ran. A radio came on. "When you are in your hour of bereavement," a voice said over soft organ music, "place your trust in the kind people at Martin's Funeral Home. Our motto is, *Those who are grieving need easing*. 2025 Church Street. Indianola, Mississippi."

"Leota reminds me of my momma a little bit," Larry said.

"In what way?"

"In no way that I can say."

"Your momma left town, didn't she? Seem like I recall she did."

"She's in Dee-troit," Larry said. "She got a little bit tired of cutting fish at Southern Prime. You know they only let 'em leave the line to pee once a day?"

"That a fact?"

"Pee's poisonous. Person get to holding that much pee in their kidneys, sooner or later they bound to turn venomous. Where's your momma, Ned?"

"Dead."

"Dead in fact? Or just dead in your head?"

"Dead like in Dee-troit," Ned said.

On the radio a blues singer was hollering. He sounded as if he had a throat full of gravel.

Ned turned and walked across the yard, back toward the road and his truck. He could hear Larry just a step or two behind him.

Larry was humming along with the blues singer. *When she shake my tree, the peaches start to quiver.*

Ned leaned against his truck. The metal burned him through his thin cotton shirt. "We had us a diesel spill yesterday," he said. "You didn't hear anything about that, did you?"

Larry crossed his arms. His biceps were small, but Ned had once seen him send Booger Merrit sprawling into a road ditch with a stiff-arm. And Booger weighed close to two hundred pounds.

"I may have heard something about that," Larry said. "Can't say for sure if I did or I didn't."

"That's the sort of thing I'd expect you to remember."

"I would if I had any stake in it."

"You work here same as I do."

"You don't have no stake in it either. Least none that I can see." Larry scratched his ribcage. "You ask me, Mack Bell treat you like a nigger too. Why you let him do you that way, Ned?"

The urge to kick something or someone was strong, so Ned concentrated on his awareness of gravity. The ground beneath his feet had been created for him to stand on. Gravity could be escaped, but only at great risk. You could fly right away from yourself.

"Mack thinks you or Q. C. or Booger did it."

"Why'd he single us out?"

"Y'all knew when he aimed to seine that pond."

"You reckon it might be guilt make him think that way, Ned? I bet he's been worrying about paying us too little and making us live out here with the fish. He probably lays over there at night in a big soft bed in that air-conditioned house and frets about that baby of Q. C.'s that's out here getting eat up by heat rash and mosquitoes. Probably he's just been thinking he don't treat us right, and that got him imagining things."

"Mack ain't the kind that feels guilt. But you know that as well as I do."

"What you trying to say to me, Ned? You trying to tell me you think I cut that line?"

"I'm trying to tell you to be careful. I'm trying to tell you not to lose your head, because losing your head may cost you your ass."

"Who's gone take my ass from me, Ned? You worried you might be sent to separate me and it?"

A thin film of sweat had formed on Larry's face, and rivulets were running down Ned's spine. His hands had clenched themselves into fists, and so had Larry's. It was a little like the opening scene of *Gunsmoke*, except that no weapons were involved.

"Larry," he said, "you want to know what you are? Because I've just this minute finally figured it out."

Larry's features arranged themselves into a grin. "What's that, Ned? Don't hesitate. Go right on and tell me."

"You're a goddamn black rationalist."

When he drove off a minute later, he could see Larry in the rearview mirror, standing by the mailbox laughing.

On the way home, he thought about going back and trying to explain himself a little better, but in the end the explanation wouldn't do any good. If Larry wanted to sabotage Mack's operation, Larry would. If Mack wanted to run Larry off his place, Mack could. If Mack wanted to make sure something worse got done to Larry, he could bring that about as well. That was the way it was and the way it had always been, and there was no point in trying to explain it because Larry Singer understood it as well as he did.

Sometimes he thought Larry understood too much. *Why you let him do you that way, Ned?* he'd said. But he was smart enough to know Ned wasn't white in the same way Mack Bell was white. There was a world of difference in their whiteness, and the difference had a lot to do with the fat content of the foods they'd grown up eating, the odor of the toilet bowls they'd grown up using, the number of evenings their daddies had spent at home, the number of evenings their mommas stayed gone, the names the druggist had called out when their mommas picked up prescriptions—*Mrs. Bell, Vonnie May Rose*—and the illnesses those prescriptions were meant to treat.

Why you let him do you that way, Ned? Larry had said, but it was almost as if he were saying something else. It was almost as if he were saying that even though he understood the differences between Mack and Ned, he believed those differences were too small by themselves to make Ned eat the mounds of dirt Mack shoveled down his throat.

It was almost as if he were saying, *You're bound to have a reason, Ned. What is it?*

At six on Saturday evening, 82 was as busy as it ever got. Groups of kids from Indianola Academy, the all-white private school, were starting to cruise, the tops down on their flashy BMWs, the girls' hair streaming free in the breeze, the guys wearing visors that said *Ole Miss* or *MSU*. The only black kids she saw were sitting on the curb in front of Mr. Quik, eating fried chicken and drinking Slurpees from big red cups.

When she was their age, Daze had stayed home most Saturday nights; she'd lain on her bed and tried to read or study, had tried to ignore the sounds of George Jones or Merle Haggard, those sounds that always issued from the record player in the living room. The music itself was intended to drown out other sounds, and most of the time it succeeded.

She stopped off at Wong's Foodland to buy some hamburger meat for supper. Coming out of the store with her package, she saw her boss, Beer Smith. He was just getting out of his pickup. His dog, Bull, a big black lab, was standing in the back, front paws up on the tailgate.

Beer was in his midfifties, tall, gray-haired now. He usually wore nothing but khaki work clothes, but this evening he had on a clean pair of blue jeans and a short-sleeved double-knit shirt.

"Hey," he said. "Everything down at the place in good order?"

"I left Sandy there. It was pretty slow today. Just the usual bunch of sad sacks from Southern Prime."

"It ever seem to you like people around here are getting dumber? Some fucking born-again just sent me an anonymous postcard. It said, *Beer ruins lives.* Sometimes I swear to God I'd love to strike a match and burn down the whole town."

Sometimes she wanted to burn the town down too, but she wanted to burn with it. She was pretty sure Beer hoped to survive the fire he dreamed of starting. He'd survived worse things already. But so for that matter had she.

"You are what you sell," she said.

Beer looked at his watch. "You doing anything entrancing tonight?"

What she planned to do tonight was what she almost always did on Saturday night. She'd go home, eat a silent supper, watch TV until two or three o'clock. Then she'd lock her bedroom door and fall asleep. On Sunday she tried to stay in bed till midafternoon. Ned didn't leave home until then.

"I'm not doing anything entrancing tonight or any other night. What about you and Bull? You aim to drive him around and let him look for Lassie?"

"Bull's like me," Beer said. "He don't have much need-to left in him. Only dish he hankers for's one filled with Ken-L-Ration. I'm fixing to buy him a sack of it now. What say you let me go home and feed him, and then you and me'll drive over to Greenville and eat?"

On the highway a Gresham Petroleum truck was just going by, trailing black ribbons of exhaust. She thought she knew the driver; he'd once asked her for a date. She first said yes, then another driver told her the guy was married. Almost everybody was. Those who weren't, like her and Ned, were generally fire-sale items.

"All right," she said. "Sure. We could do that."

Lee's Steakhouse was close to the levee in a run-down part of Greenville, a dingy white building with a sagging front porch and creaking floors. But she knew, from having heard about it, that Lee's served the best steaks in Mississippi. It was a big deal to go there, the sort of thing she believed people would casually mention on the tennis courts out at the country club.

She and Beer took a table in the corner, underneath a *New York Times* article praising the restaurant. She saw three or four people she recognized from Indianola, but if they knew her they didn't show it, though one of them nodded at Beer. It was all right to nod at him because he owned a bar, but she worked in it, and that made recognizing her a hazardous act, especially in polite company at Lee's.

She didn't care if they knew her or not. There were days when she didn't know herself, days when she felt bereft of blood and bone, let alone mind and soul.

She had her appetite now, and that was enough. She ate a big T-bone and a baked potato, drank two bottles of beer, even had a slab of apple pie for dessert.

"I could double in size here," she said.

"I used to bring my wife to Lee's every month or so," Beer said. He wiped his mouth with a checkered napkin. "Used to bring my daughter here too."

A couple of years back, his daughter, who'd just started college, had been killed in a restaurant down in Jackson—somebody drove by on the street and squeezed off a pair of shots, not aiming at anything, just shooting for the hell of it, and one of the shots struck her in the forehead. A month later Beer came home to find his wife dead. She'd had a heart attack and died with her hand clamped around a glass of orange juice.

"Come to think of it," he told Daze, "seem like everybody that ever walked through the door of this place with me's gone now. Hope that don't mean the old Heavenly Huckster's reserved a hole in the ground for you."

"Sometimes I think a hole in the ground would do."

"You been acting a little depressed."

"When'd you notice that?"

"Ten or twelve years ago. Maybe fifteen."

"Try thirty-nine."

"How old are you?"

"Forty. I was blissful till my first birthday."

"What threw things out of whack?"

"Must've been the air. I think I breathed some bad stuff in and never breathed it out again."

Beer studied his knuckles for a while. They were big, she'd noticed, red and rough. She wondered what he did with his hands that kept them looking like they belonged to a working man. As best she could tell, he hadn't worked much since he quit driving a school bus, and that had been more than twenty years ago, when he made money off a land deal.

"What do you do all day?" she said. "Every time you walk in the lounge, you look tuckered out. Like you just came in from the cotton patch."

"Well, I'll tell you. First thing every morning, I get up and read the paper front to back, every damn bit of it, I mean. The news, the sports, the weather, the TV listings, even read the food section on Thursdays, though I can't cook nothing but canned beans with weenies chopped up in them. By the time I get through with all that, I'm so goddamn wiped out that I have to lay down and take a nap. Then I get up and watch CNN for two or three hours, and after I do that, I spend about an hour working real hard to persuade myself there's verifiable differences between human beings and snakes, and when I get through with that, I usually stop in at the lounge. Does that explain why I might look tired?"

"You still miss Milda and Judy real bad."

"Like couldn't nobody ever imagine."

"I could imagine it," she said.

If her saying so surprised him, he didn't let on. "It's the piddly stuff you miss," he said. "It's not something big, like a wild weekend in Memphis or New Orleans, tearing up the river on the *Delta Queen*. It's stuff like being able to tell when somebody's mad because they slice vegetables with a particular sort of motion when they're pissed. Or you know they're about to cry, even if they don't know it yet, because the dimple in their chin's got a way of quivering fifteen or twenty seconds before the tear ducts open up. That's fifteen or twenty seconds you might be able to stave off the crying if you try."

Outside the air had turned muggy. Mosquitoes fried themselves on a blue light that hung above the entrance to a bar across the street. Somewhere in the distance Daze heard gunfire. There were gangs in Greenville now, she had learned on TV. As a public service WABG had broadcast a roundtable discussion. One of the participants, a high school coach, said things had really changed.

"Modern violence," he said, "is kind of random. It's impersonal. When I was a young man you never attacked anybody physically unless you knew them. You had a personal relationship with whoever you assailed."

In the moonlight Lake Fergusson looked like a big oil slick. And the truth was that folks sometimes dumped dirty motor oil into the lake, along with various other kinds of garbage. The lake, which emptied into the Mississippi about six miles south of town, was also full of snakes and weirdly shaped fish whose ancestors had matured on DDT. A few alligators still remained from the time when the governor had ordered two hundred baby ones set free in the lake in an effort to help preserve the species. And there were bones in the lake, bones from bodies that had been dumped there.

From the top of the levee, where Beer had parked his pickup, you couldn't see snakes or weird fish or bones. You could see the Lady Luck, a casino that floated on pontoons, down at the foot of the levee. Farther out, you could see the lights on a barge, and you could see a few pairs of headlights, which she knew belonged to motorboats. Kids liked to get out on the lake at night, drink beer, and ski in the dark. Every now and then somebody would lose his head to a low-hanging branch in the narrow passageway connecting the lake's upper and lower halves.

"You want to climb out and take a walk?" Beer said. "Me, I'm feeling puffy."

The water pulled her. She resisted. She could almost feel the water in her nose, that burning sensation she'd first experienced in the pond at Hilmer Park. Her momma, never a frequenter of parks or circuses or any of those other places most parents took their kids, had taken her and Ned there for some reason they could neither one fathom. She'd left them at the edge of the pond. While other kids splashed around beneath their mommas' eyes, Daze's momma got into a yellow car with a man and drove off, and when Ned saw her do it he shoved Daze into the water and for two or three seconds he held her under. She wouldn't jump into a pond or a lake again for years. For a long time she refused to sit in the bathtub.

Then, for a time, she learned to love lakes, Lake Fergusson in particular. During the time when her daddy was staying home more and her momma quit meeting men in town and driving off with them or bringing them home, they often came to Fergusson on Sunday afternoon to fish. They'd rent a rowboat, and she and Ned would sit together in the middle, her momma at one end of the boat, her daddy at the other, and her daddy would bait hooks for everybody, and they'd all throw them in. She seldom caught a fish, which didn't matter to her, but if Ned couldn't hook one he'd bawl.

They'd throw whatever they caught in an ice chest, and when they got back home her daddy would clean the fish, and her momma would cook them with hush puppies and french fries. Usually after one of those meals they'd all dress up and go to church, sitting as close to the back as they could, forcing folks to turn around and crane their heads if they wanted to see the Roses. Most folks did.

Then her daddy quit coming home as often, her momma started meeting men in town, and they quit coming to the lake and eating fish and attending church. She learned to hate the lake for not being what it had been.

She opened the truck door and got out, and she and Beer walked down the paved slope toward the water. "You remember the spring of '73?" he said.

For an instant she faltered. She missed a breath or two and had to reach out and grasp his arm.

"Watch your step," he said. "These old cobblestones'll trip you."

"What about '73?"

"You don't remember the flood?"

"What flood?"

"It wasn't technically a flood, I guess, but the levee did start leaking up close to the Winterville Indian mounds. Reason I'm asking right now, though, is I remember my wife and me drove over here one Saturday afternoon just to see how much water there was, and the second we turn onto Washington Avenue, way the hell back down yonder by the railroad tracks, we see the damn marina. It looks like it's sitting on top of the levee. The water was actually that high." He shook his head. "I can still remember hearing my daddy tell about the flood of '27. The whole Delta went under water from here to Valley Hill. Daddy said Grandpa rowed him and my uncle across the cotton patch in a boat. Folks were standing on top of boxcars or sitting on top of their houses—whole families, I mean, just straddling the roofs. You ask me, sooner or later that old river's gone bust the damned levee, and you'll see water like you never saw before."

Standing there holding on to his arm, she imagined the sight: water pouring through the breeched levee in a loud, muddy rush, uprooting trees, washing cars away, ripping awnings off storefronts. All the rivers of the Delta—the Sunflower, the Yalobusha, the Tallahatchie, and the Yazoo—would become a single sea. The Mississippi would stretch from Carrollton to El Dorado, from Memphis to Vicksburg.

"That flood in '27," Beer said, "it left the whole Delta under twelve feet of water."

Twelve feet was two times six feet. Twelve feet was enough to bury everybody twice.

Ellie Bell was three-fourths naked. She walked around the backyard in a sky-blue bikini, a tall pink drink in one hand. Ned could see pineapple slices in the glass and something that looked like a piece of watermelon rind.

"Anything you haven't put in there?" he asked her. She'd stopped prowling long enough to scoop up some blue-cheese dip with a broccoli floret. Ned had been standing near the table where the food was ever since he got here. Mack had phoned him this afternoon and invited him to a party. He'd told Mack he didn't feel too much like a party today, but Mack, whose voice sounded thick, as if he'd had a few already, said the party wouldn't be the party the good Lord aimed for it to be unless Ned Rose was on the premises. "I reckon," Mack said, "you could say I'm instructing you to haul your ass on down here."

Ellie shoved the broccoli into her mouth and worked at it for a minute or two. She was staring across the yard at Rick Salter's wife, who was sitting on the rim of the spa, her legs submerged in the bubbles. Ned couldn't remember the woman's first name—she'd moved here from Natchez, or some such place, after going steady with Rick at State—but he didn't think he'd ever forget the way she looked right now in her bikini. Her skin, tan like Ellie's, didn't have that burned look—it made him think of creamy peanut butter. Her stomach was flat and hard, and her breasts could not be ignored, not even by a man like him who'd rather be found dead than get caught looking.

"Ned," Ellie said, "give me your honest opinion of Stephanie Salter's appearance."

"In how many words?"

"Try to limit yourself to one well-developed paragraph."

"Speaking of well-developed."

Ellie gnawed at her lip. She was drunk, and he'd bet she'd been eating diet pills too. He'd seen her eat whole handfuls of them, like a kid munching M&Ms, and he knew from Mack that she took a lot of Valium. She got too much exercise at her aerobics class, Mack said, and there was something in the Valium that could soak up adrenaline.

"When you look at her," Ellie said, "does she make you think *am* verbs?"

"Adverbs?"

"*Am* verbs. You know. Cram, ram, slam, jam."

"Ellie, I'm not too comfortable with that question."

"Is it the question that makes you uncomfortable or the thoughts you'd have to think to answer it?"

"You getting complex on me. Need to remember you talking to an innocent redneck."

"Sometimes I wonder if you're really all that innocent."

He looked across the yard to see where Mack was. He saw him standing under one of the pecan trees, talking to Rick Salter and Alan Morelli. They were all three holding empty beer bottles and using them to gesture with. The gestures weren't directed at anybody, at least not at anybody who was present. They were violent gestures, the kind that cut through the air and make a swishing sound.

Ellie grasped the watermelon rind and idly stirred her drink. "If you ask me," she said, "I'd say breasts like Stephanie's just get in the way. Mine are no impediment. You don't think mine would impede you, do you, Ned?"

He didn't say he did, and he didn't say he didn't. He just picked up a little strand of vegetable substance and stuck it in his mouth and began to chew it for all he was worth.

"You can start at the top of me," she said, "and you can work your way across the Great Plains and into Death Valley without ever having to cross the damn Rockies."

Ellie and Stephanie were inside. They must have been having a good time—they were making enough noise for ten or twelve people, whooping and hollering like the cheerleaders they'd both been.

The men—Ned and Mack, Alan Morelli and Rick Salter, and a guy named Fordy Bashford that Ned had heard of but never met before—were sitting in lawn chairs out under the pecan trees. They were all drinking beer now, Carta Blanca from white cans. Every few minutes one of them would stand up and spray mosquito fog into the air. The night was full of katydid music, that and the croaking of frogs.

"If she wasn't my wife," Mack said, "*fucking crazy bitch* is what I'd say."

"Man can't say that about his wife," Rick Salter said.

"Not a decent man," said Morelli.

"Not a decent white man," Fordy Bashford said. His arms were about the size of everybody else's legs. He was even bigger than Mack, but there wasn't nearly as much fat on him. Ned remembered that he'd played football at Mississippi State.

Mack dropped his beer can on the ground and crushed it with his shoe. "Speaking of decency," he said, "I been thinking about some things. You know, being born poor don't mean you got to stay poor. Being born out of wedlock don't mean you bound to be a bastard all your life. You can stop being a bastard anytime you choose. Long as you straighten up and fly right."

"Amen."

"Now, much as I hate to say it, I got some individuals working for me that are indecent. And that's a choice they chose to make. I didn't make it for 'em, and neither did Ned. Their mommas didn't choose it, nor their daddies, at least not for them, though I imagine their mommas and daddies may have chose it for theirselves."

"Pretty safe bet," Bashford said.

"But that ain't neither here nor over yonder," Mack said. "Can we all agree on that? Could we put our names to it?"

Bashford and Morelli and Salter said they could.

"And what about you, Ned?"

It was good that they were all sitting outside, and it was good that it was night. They were sitting in a rough circle, no more than three or four feet separating any of them from the one he was closest to. But the dark rendered faces indistinct, and no reflecting surface loomed nearby, like it might have if they were inside. Right now Ned didn't want to be seen too clearly, and he sure as hell didn't want to see himself.

"Hell, Mack, I could put my name to almost anything," he said. "Probably have at one time or another."

"You mean to say you could go out and put your name to a petition that'd make it legal to use little girls in dirty movies?" Fordy Bashford said.

"Naw," Ned said, dipping his head a little, "I reckon I wouldn't sign my name to nothing like that."

"I'm glad to hear it," Bashford said.

"Me," Morelli said, "I'm flat-out relieved."

"Fordy," Mack said, "if you knew Ned Rose the way I do, you wouldn't even think for two-tenths of a second that he'd want little girls in dirty movies." He picked up another can of beer, tapped the top twice, and pulled the tab. "He don't want little girls in 'em, nor big girls neither."

"I'm always with you, Mack." Ned turned his beer can up and sucked about half of what was in it down his throat. One bitter taste can sometimes kill another, but this time it couldn't. Not quite. "Wherever you are," he said, "reckon that's where I'll be. Whether it's hell or Parchman."

"Liable to be hell," Rick Salter said, "but it won't never be Parchman."

Mack sat forward, his forearms on his knees. "They're sending us a message," he said. "Sure as I'm sitting here. That's what these shitty tricks are all about."

It turned out everybody had been asked on Monday to raise wages, and they'd all said no. And everybody had had a diesel spill on Friday morning, and in every case a tractor's injector line had been cut. The spill at Salter's had occurred in a pond he'd planned to seine next week. Morelli and Bashford weren't ready to seine yet, and Bashford's oxygen man had actually noticed the cut line before more than a few drops of fuel got into the water. But as Bashford pointed out, Friday was just the beginning unless somebody put an end to the meanness right quick.

"Why don't y'all just fire a few folks?" Ned said. "Run 'em off."

"And replace 'em with who?"

"Somebody else."

"Got anybody in mind?"

"Not for what y'all pay," Ned said. He said it without thinking, and for a second or two he was glad he'd done it. Sometimes it was best not to think.

"I pay 'em what I can," Fordy Bashford said. "And it's a good bit more than they're worth."

"Ned didn't mean that how it sounded," Mack said. "Did you, Ned?"

"Naw," Ned said. "I reckon I meant it some other how."

He could tell, from the way Morelli and Salter and Bashford and Mack were looking at him, that they were counting up the differences between him and them. At a certain point, however, they looked away, giving up. It would take all evening, and they were too busy right now to indulge. They all knew Ned Rose was Mack's oxygen man, his right hand, and a right hand did what the man it belonged to told it.

"Don't matter who you replace 'em with anyhow," Mack said. "It'd just be more of the same."

He said when the UFCW was getting ready to organize at the Southern Prime processing plant, similar things had happened. Not too many folks knew it, he said, because the plant management was trying to keep it hushed up. But they had all sorts of crazy shit going on.

He said when the union started sending out authorization cards, the plant fired a few workers, no more than twenty or so, as a warning.

"The very next day, two generators went out. Shut down four processing lines right during their peak. I happen to know they lost upwards of ten thousand pounds. And that was just one incident. There was other weird business too. Somebody set off an insect bomb in one of the freezers, and it ruined a few more thousand pounds. Somebody poured some paint thinner into the tanks on some of their live-haul trucks, and they lost several loads like that. That's why the company finally backed off and let 'em hold their goddamn union election, and you know what the upshot was."

"You let a bunch of niggers start singing the same tune," Fordy Bashford said, "and you got you one hell of a racket."

"Need to get one bunch singing gospel," Mack said, "and the other bunch singing soul and all the rest singing the blues. Otherwise, next thing you know we'll be paying tractor drivers fifteen dollars an hour, and it'll cost twenty an hour to get anybody to stick his foot in a pond."

"You ask me," Salter said, "the answer's to rely on commercial seiners."

"Naw, it ain't," Mack said. "Number one, the commercial seiners are being pressured to raise wages too, and whatever cost increase they face they'll just pass on to you. Number two, relying on commercial seiners ain't gone save your ponds at night when anybody that's got a mind to can walk up to one of 'em and dump a few gallons of poison in. That's gone cost you about fifty thousand bucks, Rick, and ain't but one way to make sure it don't happen."

"Yeah?" Rick said. "And what's that?"

"You fuck them like they fucked you," Mack said, "only you fuck 'em a whole lot harder."

Ned shut his eyes to avoid seeing their eyes: four sets of eyes that burned rings in the night, seeking form if not substance in the absence that he was.

He pulled up in front of the houses and cut the engine.

Two of Booger's kids were playing in the yard in front of his house, rolling an old tire around through the mud. They saw Ned, stopped, stared at him for a few seconds, then ran inside. He sat there at the wheel, doing his best to talk himself out of a choice he'd already made. When he realized he couldn't, he got out of the truck and jumped the road ditch.

Larry was home; his truck stood parked before his mailbox. He came out now and stood at his front door, him and the woman Ned had seen the other day, the one who'd asked him if he ever felt like a little dead thing in a jar. Booger and his oldest boy were at home too, and they came out as well, both of them bare chested.

The only house that seemed to be empty was Q. C.'s. The front door was shut, and the curtains were drawn. A pair of muddy work shoes stood unlaced on the doorstep.

Ned walked up and rapped on the door.

"Liable to be taking a nap," Larry hollered.

"Baby be up all night," Booger said. "Heard her crying. I bet they in there asleep."

Ned knocked again.

"Them Supreme Court judges can haggle all they want to about a right to privacy," Larry's woman said. "Black person don't have no right to privacy till they's done dead."

"And maybe not even then," Larry said. "A lot of nigger grave-yards been plowed under."

"Seem like I'm hearing stereophonic sound."

"Liable to hear a lot worse."

"Yeah," Ned said. "I imagine so."

Then the door swung open and Q. C. was there, wearing a pair of old jeans, his eyes red-rimmed as if he hadn't slept for days. His wife stood behind him, and she held the baby in her arms, the baby's head resting on her shoulder, and Ned wished there were somebody who'd hold him in her arms, a long way from Indianola.

"Mack sent me over to talk to y'all," he said. "Reckon I could come in and sit down?"

"Place is a mess," Q. C. said. "What you here for, Ned?"

Ned could feel Larry's eyes on his back, his and the woman's and Booger's and Booger's boy's. It came to him that his personal safety could not be assured, but that was low on his list of immediate concerns.

"You won't let me come in?" he said. "I'd let you in if you walked up to my house."

Q. C. looked over his shoulder at his wife, and his wife shrugged and started to turn away, and Q. C. said, "Naw, you stay." So she walked over to a rocking chair that had stuffing poking out of its armrests and its cushion and sat down. The baby never woke up.

The walls in the living room were bare except for a poster advertising Spike Lee's movie about Malcom X. Rubber toys and baby rattles lay all over the place, and old newspapers were stacked in one corner. A couple of Smirnoff bottles stood on the windowsill, makeshift vases for plastic roses.

There was a vinyl-covered love seat and an armchair that matched it. Gray tape had been used to patch tears in the armchair and the love seat.

Ned sat down in the chair. The cushion sighed. Q. C. perched on the arm of the love seat. The house was hot and stuffy. A fan stood nearby, but nobody moved to switch it on.

"Price of catfish has been falling," Ned said. "Cost of feed's been going up. Market's unfriendly. And so forth. You could probably write the rest of this."

Q. C. laid his hands on his thighs. Small hands for a man his size: the fingers looked delicate, but the nails, Ned noticed, were bitten to the quick.

"Mack Bell wanting to cut our pay?" Q. C. said. "What you here for, Ned?"

"Mr. Bell wants y'all to move."

Q. C. looked at his wife. Again she shrugged. It was as if she were asking him what else he'd expected.

"Move where?"

"He don't much care where. Fact, he don't care at all."

"You telling me I'm fired, Ned?"

"I hate to."

"Must don't hate to too much," Q. C.'s wife said. "Did, you wouldn't be here."

"Might be fairer to say that if I hated to enough, I wouldn't be here," Ned said. "I guess you could say I don't hate to enough—if you had a mind to be fair to somebody that didn't necessarily deserve it."

Q. C. was on his feet now, his big arms crossed before his chest, his broad nose wrinkled as if he smelled something unpleasant.

"That's the thing I hate about y'all, Ned," he said. "Listen to you set there and talk about how this be making you feel. Y'all can't see nothing but the insides of y'all's own guts. Y'all do one thing, it's because you had you a little upset stomach. Do another thing, it's because your belly didn't bother you today. Me, I'm getting tired of y'all's stomach problems turning into my problems. I been living on this place all my life. Don't own a piece of it, maybe, but if there was any justice, a little corner'd be mine."

"If there was any justice, more than a corner'd be yours, Q. C. I'm not here to claim different."

"How come him to settle on me?"

"I think it's got something with that little diesel spill we had the other day."

"Wasn't me put no diesel in the water."

His wife said, "Shut up."

"You know it wasn't me, don't you, Ned? And Mr. Mack Bell, he know it too. He just figure I'll make the best example. Being as I got a baby."

"If you know who did it, go tell him. Then he'll run somebody else off instead of you."

Q. C.'s eyes settled on the baby. Ned could see he was trying to decide who he owed more to—the baby or Larry, if Larry was the one who'd spilled the diesel—and he could see that at a certain point Q. C. determined there was really no choice to make because standing up for Larry meant standing up for the baby too.

A calmness settled over Q. C.'s face. "Y'all just go on and run us off," he said. "We don't have to live with you. But you do."

"He wants y'all out by tomorrow."

"Tomorrow won't be no problem beyond what it always is."

Ned stood up. "Q. C.? I wouldn't waste a lot of time looking around for work with other catfish farmers. I expect they're liable to say no."

Q. C.'s eyes never left the baby. "Y'all got less feelings than them fish, Ned. Got colder-natured blood than a cottonmouth snake."

Booger and his son were standing in Larry's yard along with Larry and his girlfriend or wife or whatever she was. They'd been talking to one another, but their voices hushed when Ned walked out.

They watched him cross Q. C.'s yard, jump the road ditch again, and open his truck door.

"Hey, Ned?" Larry hollered.

"Yeah?"

"I done figured out what you are, man."

Ned rested his chin on the roof of his truck. Sweat was in his eyes, burning them, blurring things, and that was fine. He didn't want to carry off a lot of clear images.

"Yeah?" he said. "And what's that?"

Larry took two or three steps in his direction, as if he didn't want to have to answer too loudly because what he had to say was too disturbing for others to hear.

"You ain't nothing, man. You zero. You just a empty blank for Mack Bell to fill in."

1972

The first time she entered the building, Daisy Rose went through the front door, walking between the Doric columns that looked like they belonged on a plantation manor, someplace with a name like Idlewood or Beauvoir or Tara. Even then she suspected that when she left for the last time, for whatever reason, they'd find some way to send her out the back door. She believed that when that day came she would leave gladly, with her head held high. She'd walk out the back and around the side of the building, through the parking lot and down the shady, winding road that led to the Academy, and when she got to the highway she'd cross it and keep on walking, down Slater Avenue and across Indian Bayou to Cotton Road. Aaron Henry High was about a mile down that street, and Aaron Henry High, she believed, was where she and her brother were meant to be.

The Red and Gray Foundation did not agree. The Red and Gray Foundation had been established by people like Carter Bell, who owned a lot of land, and Russell Gautreaux, who ran the bank, and it had been established for people like her and Ned. Tuition at the Academy in 1972 was six hundred dollars a year, and not every white family in town could afford it. Some of the ones who couldn't afford it would eventually lose their farms and houses for failure to admit segregated education lay beyond their means. That was the thing that struck Daisy as strange: if you said you didn't have the money to send your kids to the all-white school, people who did have the money would send them for you. But if you didn't have the money and you tried to take out loans and send them on your own, either the bank would refuse you the loan or it would grant you the loan and when you got behind on your payments, it would put you and your kids in the road. And once that happened, nobody would care whether or not your kids attended school with blacks. Nobody would care whether or not your kids attended school at all.

She'd been at home the day Mr. Bell and Mr. Gautreaux came to see her momma and daddy about a Red and Gray grant. Her daddy, who'd just come home from a job in Louisiana and was wearing a pair of white painter's pants that had gray stains all over them and smelled of latex, had asked her and Ned in at one point, and they'd sat there listening to Mr. Gautreaux explaining what was right with the Academy and wrong with the public schools. He talked about knifings and underprepared teachers, about disease and drugs, about what he called athletic overkill, in which a boy like Ned, who had average size and speed, might not get a chance to play a varsity sport at all.

"It's important for him to get that chance," Mr. Bell said. "Boy like Ned can accomplish a lot for hisself if he'll play hard and ain't scared to pass a lick."

"Some of those boys down at Aaron Henry," Mr. Gautreaux said, "they hit a kid like Ned and the next thing you know we're facing lifetime damage."

"Got some hybrid types down there that tip the scales at three hundred and run the hundred in three seconds," Mr. Bell said. "They half nigger, half missile."

Mr. Gautreaux, she noticed, never used the word *nigger*, and he never said *ain't*. And his appearance was as neat as his speech. He wore a gray suit, a red tie, and thin wire-rimmed glasses, and he had the softest set of hands she'd ever seen on a man. His daddy had run the bank before he took it over, and when he himself quit, his son would most likely replace him. That was the way those things worked. She was just fifteen years old, but she knew that much.

"There were some niggers at the junior high," her daddy said, "and Daisy and Ned got along all right there."

"I'm afraid that was a very different situation," Mr. Gautreaux said. "Having two junior highs kept folks fairly separate, based on where they lived. The percentage of colored people at Kelly was what, Ned? About fifteen percent? Does that sound about right to you?"

"There were two in my class last year. I liked 'em pretty well."

"That's the kind of thing," Mr. Bell said, "that it's all right to think, Ned, but it's best not to say it." He didn't explain why. For a few seconds he just sat there with his thick fingers drumming idly on the arm of his chair. "Actually," he added, "it's best not to even think it."

"A lot of bad stuff can happen to a boy like Ned at a place like Aaron Henry," Mr. Gautreaux said. "And even worse stuff could happen to Daisy."

Her momma was wearing tight white shorts and a white tee shirt with no bra underneath. She was starting to put on weight, and it was showing on her arms and thighs, but she hadn't noticed it yet. When she did, it would be too late to do anything about it.

She looked Mr. Gautreaux in the eye. "What sort of worse stuff have you got in mind, Russell?" she said.

Mr. Gautreaux turned scarlet, like his necktie.

She was thinking about that day as she filed into the gym for the first assembly her sophomore year. Outside, in the parking lot, she'd seen students getting out of cars, their own cars, flashy little ones she didn't know the names of, and in one case a big long gold-colored car that even she could recognize as a Cadillac. Mack Bell had climbed out of that one, tipping his sunglasses up and then shading his eyes, checking out the girls milling around on the sidewalk in their miniskirts.

The gym looked like most high school gyms in Mississippi. Fold-out bleachers lined both sides of the court, and in the center circle there was a painting of the team's mascot, a skinny old man in Confederate gray. He had a long white beard. He was dribbling a basketball with one hand, waving a sword with the other.

Daisy took a seat up at the top of the bleachers next to Cindy Riggins, a girl she'd known in junior high. Down below, in the second or third row, she could see Ned. He was sitting with Mack Bell and Rick Salter and two or three other guys from the football team. He'd reported for practice three weeks ago. He was just in the tenth grade—the same as Daisy—but he'd played well enough to earn a place on the starting defense.

A green tarp had been spread across one end of the floor. A lectern stood on the tarp, and once everyone had sat down, the principal walked over to the lectern and switched on a microphone.

His name was Mr. Causey, and like most of the male teachers, he doubled as a coach. He was an ugly man with a broad, blunt nose and hair that looked as if it had been the major reason for Brylcreem's success. He began by welcoming everyone to Indianola Academy and introducing the headmaster and the assistant principal. Then he got right down to numbers, proving to her satisfaction that what she'd suspected was true. The Academy was mostly about numbers, about keeping running totals, figuring up how many were here and how many weren't and placing them in separate piles, the ins and the outs.

"This year," he said, "partly because of the efforts of the Red and Gray Foundation, we've got the highest enrollment in our history, one thousand two hundred twenty-three students in grades one through twelve. There are almost four hundred of you sitting here right now, and that represents the third-largest high school enrollment of any private school in the state. We believe we're offering a unique form of education, and we're tremendously proud that we're offering it to more students than ever before. The fact that we're serving so many validates our belief that this type of education reflects a sore need."

Just a look around would have told anybody what type of education this type was. It was white education, and it was education
for the well off. She'd bet a lot of the girls here had spent more
on this morning's makeup than she'd spent on all three pairs of
shoes she owned. They wore clothes that had been bought in spe-
cialty shops, and they looked as if their hair had been profession-
ally done. The boys wore short-sleeved knit shirts and khaki pants
and beige loafers, and if you hadn't known otherwise you would
have thought that this was a uniform, that they were the beige
brigade.

In her homeroom that first day she and Cindy Riggins sat next to
each other, all the way in the back of the room and as close to the
corner as they could get. Neither of them knew anyone else here
except by sight and reputation. They'd seen some of the other kids
around town, and they'd seen their faces in the pages of the
Enterprise-Tocsin, but up until now they'd never sat next to them in
a classroom. Where you went to school determined who you did or
didn't talk to.

The homeroom teacher was a woman named Hanna Taylor.
She was about thirty years old, short and freckled, very trim, with
breasts that everyone in the class would come to know about as well
as they knew her face. She liked to flatten one hand on her desk and
lean forward as she read from a textbook or her lesson plans. Hers
was the only classroom in which the boys tried to sit as close to the
front as they could.

She bent over her desk now, staring at the roster. Cindy leaned
toward Daisy. "She needs to be more careful," she whispered.
"People can see her boobs."

Daisy hid her mouth behind one hand. "She wants people to."

Cindy looked at her as if it were Daisy, rather than Hanna
Taylor, who had just displayed too much of herself.

"Okay, everybody, listen up," Mrs. Taylor said. "We're going to
call the roll. If I butcher your name, just holler."

Mack Bell was sitting right up front, in the first row. "Aw, Hanna," he said, "just looking at you makes a person want to holler."

All the boys in the class laughed, and a few of the girls did too, but Daisy noticed that some of the smiles on the girls' faces looked tight. Hanna Taylor's age placed them all at a disadvantage, though before long the disadvantage would be hers.

"Mack," Mrs. Taylor said, "you better remember to call me Mrs. Taylor. Little boys are not supposed to use a woman's first name." She leaned over farther then, just in case Mack wanted a better look.

He did. He actually craned his neck, and some of the other boys craned theirs, and Daisy thought about her daddy, how he came in off the road and looked at her momma like that, and her momma made it easy for him to do it. He did it knowing full well he was not the only one she let do it, and it always puzzled Daisy, this looking at somebody like they were food and you'd been reduced to your appetite.

She had seen her momma and her daddy making love once. He'd just come back from somewhere, she couldn't remember where, and he'd walked into the kitchen where she and her momma were shelling peas. It was summertime and hot, and he walked right in and looked at her momma, who had taken off her blouse and was sitting there in her shorts and her bra. He looked at her as if he wanted to shell her too, as if he wanted to peel off what little she had on.

"I need some help," he said. "Got to tote some paint out to the shed, and I need you to help me stack it."

Her momma stood up without a word and walked out onto the back porch, and a second later Daisy heard the screen door slam. Her daddy went out the front door; she heard it slam and then the screen door on the front porch, and a few seconds later his truck door too. After that things were quiet for a while. She went right on shelling peas, and when she finished she stood up and toted out the pan with the husks in it.

She always carried them down to the bayou and dumped them there, and she would do that this time too, or at least she intended to. Passing the old smokehouse where her daddy kept his tools, she heard her momma crying and then her daddy crying too, and she knew that it was not suffering she'd come upon, or at least not suffering alone. The wood was full of chinks, and she knew where they were. She set the pan down and pressed her eye to the wall, and she saw her momma lying on top of a paint-stained tarpaulin and her daddy on top of her momma, plunging himself into her, her momma's legs clasped behind his back. Their damp bodies glistened as if they'd just stepped out of a shower.

"Can't nobody do it like you," her momma keened. "Can't nobody, Billy, can't nobody."

What she'd seen them do would invade her dreams for weeks; she would see them there on the hard concrete floor, her momma's body rising every time her daddy's fell, and for a long time afterward, whenever she remembered that moment, she'd feel faint and her legs would turn to cheese. Later still, much later, it would strike her that they'd been moving together in perfect rhythm—doing their business, as far as she knew, the way it was supposed to be done—and getting something right had lent them a kind of dignity they never possessed with their clothes on. It was as if they had to lose control to gain it.

Hanna Taylor, you could tell, was always in control, with or without her clothes on. She'd call out two or three names, and then she'd shift her stance a little, and another part of her body would appear in bold relief. Her dress stretched so tightly over her hips that it looked as if the seams ought to burst.

Finally she got to the R's. When she said "Daisy Rose," a titter passed through the classroom. Everybody looked around to see who the name belonged to. The reaction took Daisy by surprise. Nobody had ever laughed at her name before, though she used to fear someone might.

"Daze," she said. "I go by Daze." Nobody called her Daze except her daddy and Ned, and she'd begged both of them not to.

Hanna Taylor laid her pen down and stood up straight. She smoothed her dress with both hands. A bracelet dangled from one wrist.

Her eyes rested on Daisy. "Daze," she said softly. "Daze Rose. That's a memorable name. I doubt I could forget it. Even if I tried."

"Board drill," Mr. Causey said, "is designed to show us two things."

He stood in front of the seven-man sled, holding a baseball bat in one hand. The bat had been sawn in half, and Ned knew, because Mack had told him, that Causey used the flat side for a paddle. At the Academy the principal could whip anybody about as hard as he wanted to, and there were boys at the school that Causey had beaten blue.

Ned and the other linemen had gathered before him. The backs and receivers were down at the other end of the practice field, running patterns and dropping passes while an assistant coach yelled at them. It was ninety-one degrees. It had rained earlier, during fifth period, and then the sun had come back out, and now steam was rising from the ground. Everybody was already soaking wet from sweating and from rolling in the puddles during warmups. It was three days before the first game, and it was Tuesday, the worst practice day of the week, the day you expected to puke and bleed.

"Number one," Causey said. He smacked one of the pads on the sled with the paddle. "From board drill we learn the width of your wheelbase. By which I am talking about what, Denny Gautreaux?"

"How wide your stance is."

"How wide your stance is. And what is the optimum width?"

"The same as your shoulders."

"*Roughly* the same as your shoulders, give or take an inch. And how wide was your stance during Friday's scrimmage?"

Denny blinked and then looked down at the ground as if he were a slow kid trying to puzzle out the answer. But Denny Gautreaux wasn't slow, at least not mentally, and the answer had already been supplied half an hour ago by Mr. Causey when the team viewed films of the scrimmage.

"My stance," Denny said, "was about the width of my asshole."

"Which is wide enough, no doubt, to pass a sizable turd, but not wide enough to support a butt block." Causey slapped the pad again. "Number two, we discover the extent of your intestinal fortitude. By which I am talking about what, Ned Rose?"

"Guts."

"Guts," Causey said. "And what's the best substitute for guts?"

"There's not one."

"There's not one," Causey said. "There is not a single substitute. To be gutless is to be heartless, brainless, dickless, and dead. Is there anybody here that doubts what I'm saying? If so, you've got my permission to go sign up for band."

Nobody accepted his offer. But Ned could tell, from the way Denny Gautreaux was staring through his facemask at the six-foot-long board which lay on the ground, that Denny would have surrendered his daddy's stock in the bank for the right to shed his pads and take up the clarinet.

"Now then," Causey said, "give me Mr. Ned Rose at one end of the board and Mr. Kyle Nessler at the other."

Ned buckled on his chin strap, inserted his mouthpiece, and walked over to the board. It was exactly one foot wide, and today, because of the rain, it was good and slick. The purpose of the drill was to force linemen to keep their feet far enough apart to support their blocks. It was easy enough to do that when you first fired out of your stance, but when you met good hard resistance and began straining against your opponent, it got a lot harder. Sooner or later, one player's cleats would come down on the board, and when that happened, he'd fall flat on his face. Generally Causey would allow the winner to tromp the loser for a few seconds, stepping on the back of his hand or his fingers or maybe even trampling his neck.

"The immediate result of losing," Causey liked to say, "is supposed to be extreme heartache."

Ned spread his feet out on either side of the board and crouched in a three-point stance. He was about to get hurt, and he knew it. Kyle Nessler outweighed him by forty-five pounds and he was a senior, all-conference last year and sure to repeat. He was quick and strong and, considering how placid he acted on a daily basis, he turned surprisingly violent on the football field, at least until the whistle sounded at the end of a play.

But the prospect of physical pain was one Ned could deal with because physical pain, in his experience, always went away.

Kyle waited now, one hand on the ground, his helmet no more than twelve inches from Ned's. Kyle's momma was a CPA, and his daddy owned a frame shop, and they had never been the subject of gossip or scandal, and Kyle was not the recipient of a Red and Gray grant. And for one all-important instant, Ned ached to kill him and believed he could do it.

"On one," Causey said. *"Down. Set."*

At the first hut, Ned exploded from his stance. White light flashed in his head. Sweat stung his eyes, his right ear was ringing, hog like noises rolled out of his throat.

He clamped his teeth down on the mouthpiece, kept his feet churning, but he was being driven backward. Kyle slugged him in the gut with his fist, and the air left Ned's lungs, but still his feet moved as if of their own will.

The worst thing, worse even than stepping on the board and falling down and becoming a rug, was to let your opponent run you off the end of the board. Ned didn't know how many inches were left, but he knew there weren't many, so he was grateful when his cleats hit pine and he felt himself falling, felt the wood smack his facemask.

Kyle toppled onto him, still grunting, and did his best to burrow into the small of Ned's back.

"Bite him!" Causey hollered.

He let it continue for a few more seconds, Kyle snarling and snorting and clawing at Ned's legs while Ned groaned and did his best to claw back. Then Causey blew the whistle, and Kyle got to his feet and reached down and grabbed Ned's hand and pulled him up.

"Good job, Rose," he said.

Ned still couldn't breathe. He slapped Kyle on the butt.

They watched Mack knock Denny Gautreaux all the way off the board and pin him against the seven-man sled.

"Come on, Mack," Causey hollered. "Quit being sweet. Kick the hell out of him."

Mack took the advice in the most literal way. He kicked Denny in the shin, and Denny began to hop around on one foot. Mack kicked that shin too, and Denny fell backward, over the railing of the blocking sled. He hung there for a minute, his Spot-Bilts dangling in the air.

In a rare moment of hesitation, Mack turned to Causey. "Coach," he said, "I could go ahead and kill him, I guess, but his daddy's got the note on our place."

"His daddy's got the note on my truck," Causey said.

"His daddy's got the note on our house," somebody else said.

More voices joined in. "His daddy's got the note on our car."

"His daddy's got the note on our boat."

Ned was the last one to speak. "His daddy's got the note on me," he said, though he didn't know exactly what he meant.

Causey reached out and pulled Denny off the railing. Blood was running out of Denny's nose and down his face onto his white practice jersey. His mouthpiece had fallen out and was dangling from his facemask, and his chin strap had come unsnapped.

"Denny, the fiscal fears of others are all that's keeping you alive," Causey said. "Your daddy wants you to toughen up, son, and I can see why. Banking's the meanest business in the world."

They scrimmaged for an hour, and then they ran forty windsprints, and everybody puked once or twice. Then Causey called them up and told them a joke about a truck driver whose son had gotten married. "After the son came back from his honeymoon on the Gulf Coast, the old truck driver took him aside and poked him in the ribs. 'Well, boy,' he said, 'did you fuck her?'

"'Why, Daddy?' the son said. 'She ain't never hurt us.'"

Since everybody else was laughing, Ned did too. When the laughter died down, Causey sent them in.

On the way to the locker room, Kyle Nessler fell into step with Ned. "You come off the ball good," Kyle said. "You just need to stay a little bit lower."

"A little bit lower," Ned said. "Thanks, Kyle. I'll remember that."

Kyle pulled his headgear off and shook his damp hair. His hair was red like Ned's but a lot longer, so long it touched his jersey in the back. "You ought to come out Friday night with us after the game and drink some beer," he said. "We got a guy that gets it for us."

Ned pulled his own headgear off. "I might do that," he said, trying to sound like he might or might not. "I just might do that, Kyle."

He parked his pickup at the end of the Bells' driveway.

The pickup was fifteen years old, and it wouldn't do more than forty-five no matter how hard you pressed the accelerator. He'd been working on it every day after practice, bending over the engine, a wrench in his hand, grease on his forearms. He'd replaced the sparkplugs and put new belts on, but it needed a valve job, and while he knew how to do one, he didn't have the necessary hoist.

He'd bought the truck two weeks ago with four hundred dollars he'd borrowed from Mr. Bell. He'd be working for the Bells next year—the money was a loan against his wages. Mr. Bell had lent it to him so he wouldn't have trouble getting home after practice.

Fifteen or twenty cars were already parked in the driveway, one behind another or, sometimes, two abreast. The house was lit up, and you could hear John Fogerty singing "Green River" on the stereo. You could probably have heard him a mile or two away. The Bells had left for New Orleans right after the high school game, on their way to see Ole Miss play Tulane, which was the reason their place had been chosen for the party and the reason the music was playing so loud.

Ned walked up to the front door and rang the doorbell, but nobody heard it, so he pushed the door open and went in.

The living room was empty of everything but furniture, but there was enough of it to make the room look full. Two big overstuffed couches, a big glass coffee table, a couple of antique rocking chairs, two leather-covered easy chairs, lots of wicker baskets filled with magazines, mostly *Field and Stream*. Under everything a cream-colored carpet that must have been three or four inches thick. A deer's head was mounted on the wall above the fireplace. The deer's left eye stared straight ahead, but the right one glanced off at an angle, like something had just captured fifty percent of the deer's attention.

He could hear voices out back, so he walked down the hallway until he found the kitchen. A glass door opened onto the patio, and he saw people out there under a couple of spotlights, everybody drinking beer from cans and bottles, some of the guys with their arms around their girlfriends. The music was coming out of two big speakers at the edge of the patio.

He pushed open the door, and Mack saw him.

"Hey. Ned the knife!"

That was what Causey had called him tonight in the locker room after the game. He'd made a big tackle on the goal line late in the fourth quarter, and to do it he'd played off a double-team block, played it off in the least efficient way. Instead of dropping his outside shoulder and trying to roll out of the double-team as soon as he felt pressure from the tight end, he'd simply put his head down and bulled his way between the end and a two-hundred-twenty-pound tackle and knocked the feet out from under the ball carrier.

"Want a beer?" Mack hollered now. He pushed past three or four people and enveloped Ned in a bear hug. Ned could see all the little pores in Mack's face and smell beer and deodorant on him.

"Sure," he said. "I'd love a beer."

"Give him two beers," Kyle Nessler said. His arm encircled the waist of a senior girl, a blond who was on the cheerleading squad. "Damn it, give him a whole case."

"Far be it from me not to follow the captain's orders," Mack said. He set his beer can down on top of an ice chest, turned and walked over to the carport, which was adjacent to the patio, stooped down, and picked up a case of Budweiser. He walked back across the patio, carrying the case in his arms.

"You've earned it," he said.

While everybody cheered, he walked over, beaming, and presented it to Ned as if it were a trophy. Twenty-four cans of un-chilled beer.

They all stood around drinking and talking, rehashing the game. Denny Gautreaux, who was absent from the party, had been forced to run a play when the second-team left guard lost a contact lens right after the first-teamer left the game with a leg cramp. Denny was supposed to pull and trap the other team's left tackle. He went on the count of one rather than two, and he ran into the quarterback and knocked him over and stepped on his ankle.

"When it happened," somebody said, "did you hear Mr. Gautreaux?"

"What'd he say?"

"He didn't say nothing. He just groaned so loud you could hear him on the sideline. It was like he was the one being stepped on."

"In a manner of speaking," Mack said, "he was. Having a son like Denny hurts business."

"When Denny takes over at the bank," Rick Salter said, "we better all watch out. Some of our money's liable to go missing. The son of a bitch can't tell the difference between one and two."

"When Denny takes over at the bank," Mack said, "some of our money may go missing, but it ain't gone be because he can't count."

"You saying there's mathematical ability in the Gautreauxs' blood?"

"There's that and a whole lot more."

Before long, guys started pairing off with girls in the backyard, and some of the drunker couples french-kissed one another, and some of them rubbed one another, and Rick Salter fell down on top of Carla Tackett in some sticker bushes and they both had to be pulled out.

The music got even louder around midnight, people started dancing and throwing beer bottles at the trees. Mack stomped around the backyard looking worried and begging everybody not to break glass. His daddy, he said, would have his ass when he got home.

Ned stood on the patio by himself drinking beer, cold beer from the ice chest, not the warm beers he'd been given. Before tonight he'd never drunk more than one or two at a time. Back when his daddy used to take him hunting, he'd let Ned sip from his can, treating him, his daddy said, like he was already a man. His daddy seemed to think drinking was a big part of being a man, and for his daddy it surely always had been. He often came home from a job with whiskey or beer on his breath, though you had to get close to him to smell it over the odor of paint. Tonight Ned thought he knew what it was his daddy liked about drinking. Everything looked and sounded different. Noises ran together, shouts and cries and piercing riffs, glass shattering on wood and concrete, the revving of an engine, all of it merged into a dull gray roar. Lines were less sharp, figures less distinct, and nothing seemed to matter quite as much as it did when you weren't drinking. He believed too many things mattered too much to his daddy, things his daddy didn't know how to do anything about, so it was no wonder he seized an opportunity to make them matter less.

Kyle Nessler stopped off to talk to him once or twice on the way to get ice for the whiskey he was drinking from a little plastic cup. He was carrying a half-pint in his hip pocket, and the level of the whiskey was receding fairly fast. "Got Pillow next week," he said.

"They'll be tough," Ned said.

"When you getting ready to play Pillow, the important thing to do is just watch Saturday's NCAA game of the week."

"How come?"

"Their coach gets his plays off TV. Especially the trick plays. If somebody runs a double reverse/statue of liberty/tackle trap tomorrow, you can bet we'll see one Friday night."

Kyle drifted off to talk to somebody else or dance with his girlfriend, so Ned was left there by himself again, standing at the edge of the patio. Once Mack looked his way, and it seemed as if he intended to come over and talk, but then Rick Salter grabbed a wrought-iron patio chair and started running across the yard toward the cotton patch with it. When he got close to the cotton patch, he screamed, "Fuck everybody, now and forever." He threw the chair as far as he could. Mack cussed and took out after Rick, chasing him down the middle of a row, knocking cotton bolls off as he went.

Ned waited around a few more minutes. Then he picked up his case of hot beer and carried it back through the kitchen and down the hall and out to the driveway, and he put it in the back of his truck and cranked up and started for Indianola, driving slow, watching his rearview mirror for rotating lights.

When he got home, the light in the living room was on. His momma's car was the only thing parked in the driveway, but still he walked around to the back door and opened it and entered the house through the kitchen. He could hear the television on in the living room, some old movie, it sounded like, folks with British accents talking. There was no way to get to his room without going through there, so he poured himself a drink of water and opened the kitchen door.

His momma was asleep on the couch. There was a beer can on the floor next to her and a photo album lying open, page-down, across one leg. She was in her pajamas, a pair of thin pink ones she'd had as long as he could recall. She'd fallen asleep with one hand resting on her breast.

He walked into the hallway and pulled a blanket out of the closet and walked back into the living room. He lifted the album off her leg and laid it on the coffee table. He started to move her hand but decided against it—he didn't want to wake her up. He spread the blanket across her and tucked it in under her feet, and she shifted just a little but never opened her eyes.

He turned off the TV. Leaving, he picked up the album. It was still open, so he looked down at the pages. He expected to see some picture of her and his daddy, maybe the two of them at the lake, his daddy holding up a string of fish and his momma making a face and pinching her nose, or maybe both of them on the beach at Gulfport, where they'd gone right after they got married. Or maybe just a family photo, the kind they'd made plenty of when he and Daze were still little, all four of them riding the Ferris wheel in Jackson or just sitting on the porch at his grandmother's, eating a big watermelon.

Instead both pages displayed pictures of a little girl he would have taken for Daze, except the clothes she had on were too old-fashioned to have been worn even in the late '50s. She was wearing baggy pants, and her hair was light-colored, white-looking almost, and she was eating an ice cream cone in one photo and sitting in a swing in the other. Her face was clean and smooth, and her hair was bobbed off, and she was staring at the camera as if the person behind it were the only one in the world she had an eye for, as if that person were the only living creature who could capture her attention and hold it.

Daze hated Fridays.

She'd ride home on the bus while Ned stayed in town. On Fridays, when he didn't have practice and could have ridden the bus just like she did, he'd drive over to Kyle Nessler's house and nap before the ball game, or sometimes he'd go to Rick Salter's. Sometimes, she suspected, he didn't go to anybody's house because no one had invited him. On those days, she imagined, he lay down on one of those padded blocking dummies in the equipment room and took his nap there.

Fridays were the days when she saw what the biggest differences were between him and her. At least once a week, on Friday night, before three thousand pairs of eyes, her brother got to look exactly like Mack Bell and Rick Salter and all the rest. He wore the same uniform they wore, and except for his number you couldn't tell him from them. He could rattle the bones of somebody in a different-colored jersey and show everybody watching he belonged.

She never got to look like most of the other girls. Her blouses might as well have had *Kmart* scrawled across the chest, and she'd once heard another girl refer to her shoes as Goodwill closeouts. She couldn't make an open-field tackle. And if, like Ned, she chose to throw her body around, it would not change anyone's attitude about her; it would merely confirm their suspicions.

Beer Smith drove the bus, so she'd sit up front, close to him and Cindy Riggins, who was his niece, and they'd talk off and on for an hour about something silly, like whether or not Johnny Cash had really done time in prison. Cindy said he hadn't, and Daze said he had, and Beer said that if he hadn't he should have because his music was criminally bad. "You kids never heard Hank Williams," he said. "Compared to him, Johnny Cash sounds like a John Deere."

Beer would let her out at the mailbox and she'd walk across the yard, which was always overgrown unless her daddy had recently been home. Her momma's old Galaxy stood in the driveway, and its presence there on a Friday afternoon was a measure of the changes creeping into her momma's life. There was a time not too long ago when the car would have been standing somewhere else on a Friday afternoon, out in front of a Greenville juke joint, maybe, or behind some little house across the tracks in Indianola, where the men who drove for Sterne Grocery Company or Gresham Petroleum lived. She knew the car had been parked in these places not because she'd ever seen it there with her own eyes but because she'd heard her daddy shouting about it one night and her momma shouting back that she did what she needed to do, and it was all right for him to do the same thing too. And her daddy's voice fell and he said he didn't need to.

The front door was always unlocked when she tried it, which was worrisome when you considered the fact that her momma was usually in bed. She worked parttime four evenings a week at a 7-Eleven and didn't get home until late. Sometimes, even now, when she was putting on weight and dark bags were starting to form beneath her eyes, she wouldn't come home until morning. But whether she'd gotten much sleep the previous night or not, she made breakfast for Daze and Ned, something she hadn't always done. They'd eaten their share of sugar-coated doughnuts growing up, but now they woke to the smell of bacon frying, the sounds of it sizzling on the skillet. Their momma would have it on the table when they walked in, and she'd sit there while they ate it, asking them questions she seemed to think a good momma would ask, like how they were doing in their schoolwork and whether or not they liked their teachers, and Daze would always try to answer them, but Ned would just grunt.

And then, as soon as they left for school, Daze knew, their momma went back to bed and fell asleep, or tried to, and stayed there all day long.

One Friday afternoon in early October, she came home to an unusual sight. Her daddy's pickup truck was in the driveway, parked behind her momma's car. He'd parked it right under an oak tree, and it looked as if it must have been there for most of the day. It was covered with leaves, red and gold and yellow; they were piled up on the hood and the roof.

He'd been working on a job down in south Mississippi, Bay St. Louis or someplace like that, and as far as she'd known he wasn't supposed to be home until the middle of the month. But he was here now, his truck behind her momma's car, and if you'd driven by and seen them both there and you didn't know better, you would have thought this was a normal sight, that everything here was just right: a neat white house, the yard only slightly ragged, leaves cascading down, the air brisk and cool and smelling like garlic from the defoliant farmers had sprayed on their crops. This might have been any house in the Delta, any house where people who might not have a lot of money were doing all right by one another.

But Beer Smith knew better. He hit the lever that opened the door. "Looks like your daddy's here," he said.

"Yeah," she said. "I just hope he didn't get fired."

"He ain't never been fired, has he?"

"Not as far as I know."

"There's a reason," Beer said. "Whatever else you might say about him, he could paint the White House pink and make it look pretty. When he puts a coat of paint on, it stays on a good little while. A contractor don't fire a man like that."

Whatever else you might say about him. There were a lot of things Beer could have meant by that, and as she walked across the yard, she tried unsuccessfully to avoid thinking about them. Her daddy had once been in jail. She remembered going to the police station with her momma, with her momma and Ned and their aunt and uncle, and her momma got into an argument with a policeman, and the policeman said if her momma didn't watch out, she might find herself in jail too. It all had something to do with a car, a gray car that she recalled had a back seat big enough for both her and Ned to stretch out and fall asleep in. It had something to do with somebody taking that car away from them and her daddy going and trying to get it back.

And there were other things Beer could have meant, like her daddy going to the doctor because he was having trouble with his balance. Her daddy believed the problem was his inner ear, but the doctor said the problem was his mouth, which opened too readily and stayed open too long when a bottle of whiskey was nearby. The doctor said that, and her daddy hollered at him, and you could hear it all the way into the waiting room, where she and Ned were sitting with their momma and paging through some Wonder books. Then her daddy came and pulled them out of there, he dragged them almost, and they all drove off in the gray car, which had not been taken away yet, and her daddy told her momma what the doctor had said, and her momma said, *He may have a point.*

And then her daddy said, *Yeah, he just may. Wonder what he'd say opens up too fast on you?*

She expected them to be down the hall in their bedroom with the door shut, but they weren't. They were both in the kitchen. Her momma was wearing an apron, a blue one with an apple-orange-and-lemon pattern on it, and she was standing over the stove stirring a pot of stew. Sweat had beaded on her forehead, but her face wasn't flushed as it would have been if something besides cooking had accounted for the sweat. Her daddy had taken a shower; he wore clean gray work pants and a matching shirt with a red patch on one pocket that said *Roland*, which was somebody else's name. He sat in a stiff-backed chair, smoking a cigarette. A can of beer was standing on the kitchen table near his elbow.

"Hey, Daisy," he said.

"Hi."

She walked over to the back door and opened it and dropped her satchel on the porch.

"We were thinking we'd all do something together tonight," her momma said.

"Like what?"

"Go to town," her daddy said.

Her momma left the wooden spoon propped against the rim of the pot and walked over to the pantry, and on the way there she let her fingers graze his shoulder. And on the way back she ran her fingers through his hair.

"Go to town," Daze said, "and do what?"

"Watch old Neddy rack 'em up."

"The football game?"

"Sure enough," her daddy said. "Why not?"

Why not? she thought later, as she sat in the bathtub soaking herself, resigned to making the trip with them. Her English teacher had said that sometimes the best way to get from one part of an essay to another was to quit worrying about transitions and make a big leap, to jump from A to B and stop looking for a bridge. As long as the distance between those two points wasn't too great, her teacher had said, there was always a chance you'd make it. To Daze, the distance between what her momma and daddy were and what they wanted to be tonight did not seem slight. But one thing she knew for sure: there was no bridge in sight.

"Maybe slow down a little bit," her momma said.

"Sure enough. "

Her daddy was driving the car, Daze sitting in the back seat, her momma up front. A can of beer was clamped between her daddy's legs, and her momma had one between her legs too. In the back seat next to Daze stood a Piggly Wiggly sack filled with popcorn her momma had popped about an hour ago.

There were lots of little mounds of dirt in the blacktop where farm vehicles had slung off mud. Cotton fibers littered the sides of the road. They got behind a picker about a mile from town, and her daddy glanced at his watch and said, "Shit," and tried to dart around the big machine, but there wasn't enough room to pass.

The driver, a black man, looked over his shoulder once and pulled off the side of the road.

Going by, her daddy stuck his hand out the window and waved thanks, and she interpreted this as an encouraging sign, a sign that he was in no mood to start a fight with anybody. Her momma seemed to see it that way too. She slid across the seat toward him and put her arm around his neck, and then she glanced back at Daze and winked.

They parked near the old National Guard Armory, a full three blocks from the stadium. That was as close as they could get. Traffic jammed the streets. People clustered in groups on the sidewalks, some of them wearing red-and-gray sweaters, others black-and-gold. Walking toward the stadium, they could hear the band playing "Dixie," a little too fast and way off key. Moths swirled in the stadium lights; you could see them up there against the darkening sky, spiraling ribbons of beating wings.

"General admission?" the ticket seller said.

"Reserved," said her daddy.

Their seats were all the way up by the press box. Nobody paid them much attention as they climbed up to the fifteenth row and picked their way over people's feet until they found the spaces with their numbers on them. Down below, in a special section where the concrete bleachers had been painted red, she saw Mr. Bell and Mr. Gautreaux and two women she assumed were their wives. They'd brought along stadium chairs.

"Yonder's Neddy," her daddy said. "Number 72."

He was down on the field, huddling with all the others around Mr. Causey and the assistant coaches. None of the players wore a helmet. They all had their eyes shut, and their lips were moving, and they were all holding hands. And then suddenly they all shouted at once and clapped their hands, and the huddle broke up, and she saw Ned and Mack put their helmets on and fasten their chin straps. Then Ned and Mack butted heads, not once but five or six times. After that Ned pounded Mack's shoulderpads, and Mack pounded Ned's, and they both started bouncing up and down on the balls of their feet as if they needed to pee but were doing their best to hold it.

The captains went out for the toss of the coin. She knew that was what they were doing because she could hear the radio announcer say so. The door to the press box was open. Looking in, she could see the announcer, who was sitting at a microphone just a few feet away. Past him, at the far end of the press box, she saw the school guidance counselor sitting before another microphone. He was the one who handled the PA.

"Indianola wins the toss," he said over the speakers, and a few seconds later the radio announcer said the same thing.

Her momma had stuffed the popcorn into her purse. She pulled it out now and asked Daze if she wanted a handful, but Daze said she didn't. Her daddy said he'd take some and stuck his hand in and pulled out a wad of it, spilling several kernels.

"The kids down under the bleachers'll get that," he said.

Daze looked down through the space between their row and the next and saw several little kids, all boys, running back and forth throwing miniature footballs to one another. Every now and then one of them would stop and stare straight up and point at something, and a smirk would appear on his face, and all the others would stop and stare too.

"They're looking up people's dresses," Daze said.

Her momma was jamming the sack of popcorn back into her purse. "Oh, honey," she said, "that's just how they are. They're just little boys is all."

Ned didn't make the tackle on the kickoff, but on the first play from scrimmage he and Kyle Nessler threw the runner for a loss. Her daddy jumped up when that happened and hollered, "How to go, Neddy," and for the first time that night people seemed to notice them. Mr. Bell looked over his shoulder and nodded at them, and her daddy gave him a thumbs-up, and Mr. Bell nodded again and turned away.

"Remember when you used to play?" her momma said.

"I was hell, wasn't I," her daddy said, "to be so little and slow?"

"I used to love to watch you." Her momma looped her arm around his waist. "You were pretty out there, even in them baggy old pants y'all used to wear."

Ned made several more tackles in the first half, and every time he made one her daddy jumped up and hollered, and her momma hollered too. A couple of times she saw Ned get up from a pile and look toward the bleachers, trying to figure out where their voices had come from. Finally, when he was on the sideline resting, he saw them. Her momma and her daddy both waved. He didn't wave back, but at least he nodded at them.

At halftime her daddy said he needed to use the bathroom, so while the band was playing he got up and left. Her momma asked once more if she wanted popcorn. She said no. Then her momma laid her hand on Daze's knee. "You don't like it at the Academy," she said, "do you?"

"Not too much."

"How come?"

"I don't know."

"A lot of them girls out there have some mighty fancy clothes," her momma said. "But they don't look half as good as you, and they know it even if you don't."

"Is looking good all that matters?"

"It's not all that matters, but for a girl it's a big first step."

"So what's the rest?"

"Making a boy feel good about being with you."

"What if you don't care about being with a boy?"

"Oh, honey," her momma said, "who in the world you trying to fool? You trying to mislead your own blood?"

She never answered her momma's question, and it would be a long time before she understood the question the way she came to believe her momma meant it. She wasn't asking if Daze meant to confuse her momma, her own flesh and blood. She was asking if Daze was trying to confuse her own blood, Daze's blood, the blood her heart pumped to the rest of her body. Her momma believed your blood would tell you what did or did not need doing, if only you'd succumb to the rush.

Her daddy, by the time he returned, had succumbed to a brown paper sack. His eyes were bright, and his breath smelled sweet, and the sack was in the pocket of his jacket.

"Had you a little snort?" her momma said.

"Yeah," he said, "you want one?"

"Daddy," Daze said, "not up here. Okay?"

"Sure enough," he said. "I don't want to embarrass nobody."

The visiting team kicked off to start the second half. Ned didn't play much on offense, he just stood near Mack or prowled the sideline, drinking Gatorade and waiting for the offense to score or turn the ball over.

"I saw Burt Hancock," her daddy said.

"Is that so?"

The quarterback threw a long, arching spiral into one corner of the end zone, and Daze heard the radio announcer holler, "Alley oop," his voice rising and then hanging there an instant, holding its note, and the ball fell into the arms of the receiver.

"Touchdown!" the radio announcer hollered. "The Rebels get six more."

The band played "Dixie" again, and the kicker came out and missed the extra point. The teams jogged back upfield to get ready for the kickoff.

"That is for a fact so," her daddy said. "I did indeed see Burt Hancock."

He pulled the bag out of his pocket and screwed the cap off the bottle and turned the bag up.

Daze saw a couple of people looking at him, people she didn't know, people she hoped didn't know her. He put the cap back on and stuck the bag back into his pocket.

"I didn't like the way Burt looked at me," he said.

"How was that?"

"Like he might know a little something that only I ought to know."

"Well, maybe you don't know everything you should."

"Does he know something I don't? Is that what you trying to say?"

"I'm not trying to say anything," her momma said. "What I'm trying to do's watch my son play ball."

The kick was a poor one. It never rose more than two or three feet off the ground. It hit one of the other team's players, and he tripped trying to pick it up, and then he kicked it, and then Ned knocked him over backward. Somebody else in a red jersey fell on the ball.

"Indianola's got it!" the radio announcer yelled.

Some people in the stands started hugging one another, and others slapped backs or jumped up and down. Her daddy didn't say a word this time. He stayed seated, one hand on the bag in his pocket.

The crowd quieted down. "Daze," he said, "you aim to turn out like your momma?"

"What in the fuck," her momma said, "is that supposed to mean?"

"She won't turn out like you have," he said. "She won't go bottoms up for every sorry son of a bitch that leers at her. I know my girl better than that."

She heard the paper sack coming out of her momma's purse, and she knew it was not being pulled out because her momma was hungry, or at least not because her momma was hungry for popcorn. She heard the sack whish through the air, and she heard the paper tear, and then popcorn was everywhere, all over her daddy and her momma, all over her too. The people in the row beneath them were on their feet, a fat man with one gold tooth looking at her daddy, about to speak.

Her daddy stood up, shook popcorn from his hair, and with one hand pulled her momma onto her feet.

"Let go of me," her momma said. "You take your hand off me."

Daze didn't think her daddy would do that, but he did. He let go of her momma's hand, and her momma sat back down, and her daddy turned to the man who'd been sitting in front of them, the one who had a gold tooth. "What would you do," her daddy asked him, "if your wife was a goddamn whore?"

"Here now," the man said. "Don't be talking like that."

Lots of people were staring at them: the Bells and the Gautreauxs, some of the players who stood on the sideline, even Mr. Causey.

"What if your wife was just humping to please," her daddy said to the man with the gold tooth. "Like she thought fucking was a civic duty, the same as voting or paying taxes?"

Her momma stood up and grabbed her daddy, grabbed him by the arm, but he shoved her down.

She tried to rise.

"You stand up again," he said, "and so help me God I'll chunk your fucking ass off the bleachers."

The radio announcer got up and slammed the press-box door.

"If you say any more curse words in front of my wife," the man with the gold tooth said, "I aim to whip your rear end."

Her daddy had a height advantage to begin with, and their row was about a foot higher than the one below. He pushed the fat man, and the man lost his balance and went over backward, falling over the head of a woman in the row below his, and both of them toppled onto the people in the next row.

A policeman had left the sideline; he was bounding up the steps two at a time, and a second policeman had gotten out of the patrol car that stood parked near one end zone.

Her daddy did not try to run. He pulled the bottle out of his jacket pocket and looked at Daze and smiled.

"I better drink it," he said, "before they take it."

He almost managed to finish it off.

Daze woke to the sound of the telephone ringing. Something about the way it rang out, the way its echoes bounced off the walls unaccompanied by the sound of footsteps, made her think the house was empty.

Her momma had brought her home from the game last night, and then she'd left without saying where she was going. Daze hadn't asked. She hadn't much cared. For all she knew, her momma might have gone to throw herself into the Sunflower River, or she might have gone to get her daddy out of jail. Maybe they'd both thrown themselves into the river, or maybe they'd taken her daddy's 9-mm. and shot one another. She didn't really think her momma would have agreed to that, though she wasn't sure about her daddy.

She walked into the hallway. The telephone was there, standing on a shelf her daddy had attached to the wall. She lifted the receiver.

"Hey," a voice said. "Ned around?"

She looked down the hall. His door was closed, and she hadn't heard any noises coming from there during the night. Most nights he talked in his sleep. "Momma?" he'd say. "Daddy? Daze? Uncle Hardy? Aunt Liz?" The names he called out were always those of relatives, as if in his sleep he sought evidence that he and other humans were connected.

"I don't think so," she said.

"Hey," the voice said again. "This is Mack. Could you just check and see if maybe he ain't snoozing?"

She laid the receiver down on the shelf and walked over to the door and tapped on it. "Ned?" she said. There was no answer, so she shoved the door open. His bed had not been slept in.

She'd seen him down on the field last night when they were leading her daddy to the police car. He'd been standing with the defense on the other team's twenty-yard line. Kyle Nessler had his arm around Ned's shoulders; he was talking into the earhole of Ned's helmet, telling him something she'd bet didn't have much to do with football. The other team had come up to the line then and run a play while they were pushing her daddy into the cruiser, and as she descended the bleachers with her momma, her face and ears blazing, she saw Ned grab the ball carrier's jersey and spin him around and throw him down, and then Ned hurled himself on top of the ball carrier, spearing him with his helmet, and the official threw his white flag.

She walked back to the phone and picked it up. "He's not here," she said.

"We didn't see him last night," Mack said. "After the game, I mean."

He paused long enough for her to answer, but she didn't.

"Maybe you saw him," he said.

"No."

"Well—"

"Yeah," she said. "Well?"

"Well, maybe if you see him, you could tell him we were, you know, a little worried about him."

"Yeah," she said. "Okay."

"Me and some of the guys on the team. Kyle, Rick. Folks like that. We're concerned about him's all."

"Yeah," she said. "Well."

Then Mack said something else, she couldn't understand what—it sounded as if he'd put his hand over the receiver, as if he were speaking to somebody else.

"Hey, Daze?" he said.

"Yeah," she said. "What? What is it?"

"Nothing," he said. "I was just . . . Just tell him we were, you know—"

"Concerned?"

"Concerned," he said. "Real concerned."

She made herself a piece of toast from stale bread and sat down on the couch to eat it. A couple of times she started on it, nibbling at the edges, then a few minutes would pass and she'd realize she had quit eating. And finally it was so cold she just set the plate down on the coffee table and forgot about it.

What she couldn't forget and would never forget was what had happened last night. It wasn't the first time her momma and daddy had fought like that or said those things to one another—they'd been fighting and saying those things for most of her life. But last night's bout had been a public spectacle, and the worst thing about it was this: if the police had not taken her daddy away, she believed, it wouldn't have been more than a few minutes before he and her momma made up, and having fought in public, they might have made up in public. They might have wrapped their arms around one another and started whispering there in the bleachers, and then her daddy's hand might have touched her momma in this or that place, and her momma's eyes might have closed and her lips might have formed a perfect ring and said, *Oh.* It wouldn't have mattered who was watching or listening. They'd taken their show on the road.

She was still sitting there when the phone rang again. She let it ring five or six times, thinking it would soon stop, but it didn't. Finally she walked into the hall and picked it up.

"Daze?" the voice said. She knew the voice, a soft male voice that always sounded timid. But she couldn't recall who it belonged to. Whoever owned that voice was somebody you forgot.

"Yeah?"

"This is Denny Gautreaux."

"Ned's not here."

"I was actually calling you."

"What do you want?"

"You know that stuff that happened last night?" he said. "That stuff with your momma and dad?"

She didn't throw the receiver down. She continued holding it, but she felt, all of a sudden, as if her knees could not support her weight. So she leaned against the shelf the phone stood on, and the shelf groaned and fell off the wall.

She stood there staring at it, at the splintered wood, at the ugly scars on the wall where the nails her daddy had driven into the studs had let go. Crumbs of white plaster lay on the floor.

"What's the matter?" Denny said. "Did you hang up on me? Don't hang up."

"What are you whining about?" she said.

The telephone lay on the floor too. She kicked it. The bell jangled. Static crackled on the line.

"What do you want me to do? Didn't my folks entertain you enough last night?"

"I could hang up," Denny said. "I could hang up and call back."

"Call back? What do you want?"

"I just . . ." His voice broke. "I just wanted to say something."

"So say it."

"My folks fight like that," he said. "Listen, you might think they don't, but they do. They can really go at it."

"So?"

"I've seen my dad hit my momma so hard her head bounced off the wall."

"Did I ask you? Did I call you up and ask you to tell me this?"

"He says awful stuff to her too. I once heard him tell her she was so cold her ass must have been on dry ice. He poured hot coffee on her. Down there."

"My momma's ass is anything but cold," Daze said. "My momma's ass is a goddamn firebox."

"Details," Denny said.

That made her laugh.

"Really," Denny said. "You know what my dad tried to make her do once? He's got this reel-to-reel projector he bought in some store up in Memphis, and he tried to make her watch a nasty movie with him while they were both in the bed with their clothes off. The movie was about an all-girl football team. The title was *Tight Ends*."

"How do you know that?"

"She told me."

"She told you that about her and your daddy?"

"My momma drinks," he said. "And when she's drinking, she's liable to say anything. At least to me. I think I'm the only one she talks to."

"So now," Daze said, "you're calling me to let me know that even on Bayou Drive, in that big house you live in, people behave just like common dirt?"

"Sort of," he said.

"Wow, thanks, Denny. I mean it. Thanks a lot. That makes me feel so much better."

"Don't hang up," he said. "Will you please not hang up?" She didn't hang up, and after he understood she wasn't going to, he said, "That's not the only reason I called. I wanted to ask you if you'd like to go to a movie sometime."

"Why?" she said. "Did your daddy quit bouncing your momma's head long enough to loan you his projector?"

"Just a regular movie. At a theater."

She recalled once seeing her grandmother kick a stray dog that had come begging food at her back door. Daze asked her why she'd done it. "Because," her grandmother had said, "that dog reminds me of 1930." Daze asked her why the dog reminded her of 1930. "Because," she said, "I was that hungry then."

She wanted to kick Denny Gautreaux now, the same way her grandmother had kicked the stray dog and for the very same reason. The note she heard in his voice was one she would have sung had she been the singing kind. Which she was not.

"And then after the movie," she said, "we'd drive out into a cotton patch, and I'd show you what all my momma taught me?"

"I could call back."

"Just talking to me, knowing I'm standing here where she's stood and holding the same phone in my hand that she's held—that excites you, doesn't it? You'd like to be my daddy, wouldn't you, and me her?"

"Maybe I better call back. I could call back at a better time."

She said, "We don't have better times in this house."

The house was so silent she could hear her own breathing. It was the only sound she heard now, in this place where she'd heard so many sounds: a headboard banging against the wall, long-drawn-out cries, the grunts of men who'd been introduced by her momma as friends—*This is Bobby, my friend from high school. . . . This is Kenny, my friend from Itta Bena.*

The only sound she heard was the sound of her own breathing. She imagined a time when it would be all she ever heard, this sound that began as motion in her chest, this motion that emerged from her lips as a hiss, this hissing rising falling that kept her crawling, inch by inch, into tomorrow.

They found him on 49, just north of the Sunflower River bridge, around ten in the morning. He was heading south, it was the second time he'd headed south in the last hour, and they were heading north. They were riding in Mack's gold Cadillac. They had their windows rolled down, though the day was not hot, and he had his rolled down, and so when they passed him, even though he turned his head the other way, he heard Mack holler, "Hey, Ned! Hold *upppp*," the last word trailing away down the road in the slipstream.

In his rearview mirror, he saw the Caddy hit the shoulder, Mack making a wide U-turn and coming on behind him. He could travel about forty-five miles an hour in the truck, top speed, and he didn't really want to outrun them anyway. Sooner or later he'd have to face up to what had happened, either that or go to Greenville and see if he couldn't lie about his age and get a job on a towboat. And he didn't want to work on the river. Deep water scared him.

He turned off onto a gravel road and sat there until Mack pulled in behind him, and then he got out of his truck, and Mack and Rick Salter got out of the car.

Mack was wearing sunglasses, which he tipped up onto his head. He and Salter stood there on the side of the road in dry Johnson grass.

Salter was chewing tobacco. He spat out some brown juice. "Shit," he said. "Damn Red Man."

"Red Man's nasty shit," Mack said.

"Beats the piss out of Day's Work, though."

Mack said, "Day's Work's mostly just for niggers."

Salter looked at Ned. "You must have made ten or fifteen tackles last night," he said. "Ain't nobody can quibble with that."

"You may have noticed where Rick was," Mack said. He nodded at Salter, and Rick, as if by prior agreement, hung his head. "You may have seen where he was when you were out there busting ass."

"My fanny was glued to the pine," Salter said. "Sure was. I went in one time, and that was on that last kickoff."

"And what happened?" Mack said.

"Somebody blindsided my ass."

"And you fell where?"

"Fell flat on my face. And like to died of shame."

"Now, Rick's momma and daddy," Mack said, "they behaved just like saints."

"Not a peep out of 'em," Salter said. "For all I know they may have dozed off."

"May have," Mack said. "I've seen 'em sleep in church."

"What we're talking about with my momma and daddy," Salter said, "is well behaved but dull as a gray sock."

"And Rick hisself, he behaved well on the bench," Mack said. "I'm not saying my old buddy here's without value. What I'm saying is you proved yourself a good while ago, Ned, and don't nobody that knows you care diddly shit if your momma and daddy took a notion to pitch a fit."

"You son of a bitches," Ned said.

"We're just sorry well-off got-it-made motherfuckers," Mack said. "I don't blame you one bit for calling us names. If I was you, I might be calling us names too."

"What else would you do if you was me?" Ned said.

"Lordy," Mack said, "I don't know what all."

Ned caught him right under his left ear. It was a blow Mack must have seen coming, but he never moved to block it, never moved to duck. What he did was laugh, and while he was still laughing, he threw his arms around Ned and hugged him.

Salter was somewhere behind, whispering, "Easy, Ned. Straighten up, straighten up."

Ned couldn't straighten up, couldn't do much of anything, because in addition to being bigger than he was, Mack was stronger too, stronger than he'd ever shown on the field or in the weight room.

Mack walked him backward, laughing and saying, "Ned the knife, he's all right," and Ned tried to wriggle free, but he couldn't. So he used the only weapon he had left. He opened his mouth and spat in Mack's face, but Mack still wouldn't let him go; he held on, walking Ned backward and laughing, until the spit dripped off the end of his nose and onto his shirt collar.

Then he did let Ned go. And while Ned stood there panting, Mack dipped his finger in the gob of spit and held it, dripping, before his eyes. He studied it carefully, turning his finger first one way and then the other.

"Ned?" he said. "Buddy, you can take it from me. This has all the characteristics of human spit. A baboon just could not have produced this."

They left Ned's truck in the parking lot behind Piggly Wiggly. It was almost twelve o'clock when they passed the city limit sign on 49, heading north toward the county line. They were going to Oxford. They were going to Ole Miss for no reason at all except that Mack said they might as well go somewhere. He said if he went home his daddy would make him tromp cotton, and Salter said his would make him drive the picker. Nobody asked what Ned's daddy would do because, as far as they knew, his daddy was still in jail.

They ate hamburgers from a sack—they'd bought them at the Sonic. They drank beer from a cooler in the back. Mack was driving eighty, but you couldn't tell it. The car was so quiet there was no road noise, and you couldn't feel a bump when you hit one.

The upholstery inside the car was plush. There were lots of gauges on the dash; the car had cruise control and a good stereo. A set of buttons on the armrests controlled the windows. You could sink all the way into the seats, and you could stretch your legs out. You could close your eyes and fall asleep in a second, especially if you hadn't slept at all, and Ned hadn't. So he closed his eyes and made up his mind to let Mack take him wherever Mack wanted, as long as Mack didn't take him home.

It was after two o'clock when they got to Oxford. Mack turned off the highway and drove down a broad street that led into the campus, which was mostly deserted, as Mack had said it would be, because Ole Miss was playing Georgia in Athens.

Mack said he wanted to see a girl he knew, somebody he'd met when he and Kyle Nessler came up for the last Ole Miss home game. He said she was from Florida, and pretty nice looking, except for her face, which he said was a little bit rough. He'd met her at a Kappa Sig party and danced with her a few times.

"She's living in New Dorm," he said.

They were driving around the Grove now. The light shining down through red and yellow leaves was like gold dust.

"Y'all know what the actual name of New Dorm is?" Mack said.

Salter was sitting in back. "Not me," he said. "You know I'm a State man. This here's an alien nation."

"New Dorm's real name's Whore Hall."

"You're shitting me."

"Spelled H-O-A-R," Mack said. "They named it after some old professor up here, and then after they'd done it, it dawned on somebody that it might not be the best name for a girls' dorm."

He parked the car outside the dorm, which was a brick tower that must have had fourteen or fifteen floors. The parking lot was empty except for five or six cars.

Mack pulled his shades off and laid them on the seat and looked in his rearview mirror to make sure his hair looked okay. "Just y'all sit tight," he said, "and let me see if I can't talk her out."

He entered the lobby, and they could see him standing there, talking to the girl who sat behind the desk. The girl pointed at something behind him, and he turned around and walked over to the wall and dialed a number on the house phone and waited a few seconds and then started talking.

"Old Mack," Salter said. "He's something, ain't he?"

"Yeah."

"If he was just a smidgen quicker, he might could play up here, don't you reckon?"

The truth was Ned didn't think being a smidgen quicker would have enabled Mack to play at Ole Miss. Mack moved about as fast as a continental plate, which was why Causey had started calling him *North America*.

"Maybe he could play here," Ned said. "Hell, I don't know."

"I believe he could. He's doing real good to be having so many problems."

"Mack's having problems?"

"Hell, you didn't know his daddy's in trouble?"

"What sort of trouble?"

"They may have to shut down his line of credit."

"At the bank?"

"Damn straight. He's got a lot riding on this year's crop."

"I thought Mr. Bell and Denny's daddy were friends."

"They are friends. But one of 'em's a farmer, and the other one's a banker, and there's a couple of places friendship can't take you. At least, that's how my daddy puts it. And he had a problem with the bank last year too, so I imagine he knows what he's saying."

"If Mr. Bell's in trouble, how come Mack's got this car? Didn't his folks go to Las Vegas a couple of weeks ago?"

"My folks went to Hawaii last year right about the time the bank was on Daddy's ass," Salter said. "What you can buy or do don't have that much to do with how much actual money you've got, not when you own five or six thousand acres. Hell, my daddy's declared losses every year for I don't know how long. Last time he paid any taxes was back about 1965."

"So what happens to Mr. Bell if he loses out?"

"Oh, they'll probably auction off at least some of his land, maybe some of his machinery, maybe even the house. And then the next thing you know, he'll be buying a cotton gin with money that come from somewhere, and then he'll be buying, I don't know, an implement company or something, and before too long, guess what? They'll be rich again."

"So why in the fuck do they have problems?"

"Would you want to lose what you've got?"

"I don't know—I ain't got nothing."

"Shit, Ned," Salter said. "Sometimes you're hard to talk to."

She was tall, almost gangly, with light-brown frizzy hair. Her face was not one Ned would have described as rough. She had long lashes and a nicely shaped nose. She wore no makeup, and it might have been the absence of it that reminded him of Daze. She was wearing jeans and tennis shoes and a red windbreaker.

Ned and Rick got out of the car. "This is Meryl," Mack said.

"Hi," she said.

"She's the one I was telling y'all about. I met her at the Kappa Sigs'."

"It was the SAE house," she said.

"You swear?"

"That's the only frat house I've ever been in. And I've only been to it that one time."

"When I get up here to stay," Mack said, "we're liable to have to rectify that." He pulled the car keys out of his pocket. "Meryl's gone ride around with us," he said, "and drink a few beers."

"Yeah, but like I told you, you've got to promise to bring me back by four-thirty. I'm waiting on a call from my folks, and that's when it's coming."

Ned got into the back with Salter, and she sat up front with Mack. They drove out of town on the same street they'd come in on, and after they crossed the highway on an overpass, Mack pulled off onto the shoulder and opened the trunk and got everybody a beer. Then they drove on down that road, which turned into a narrow two-lane with lots of dips and curves.

"We don't have roads like this down in the Delta," Mack said. "Ever been down there, Meryl?"

"No. Should I go?"

"It's a pretty interesting place. We have our share of high times."

"I've heard it's awfully flat there."

"As a tabletop."

"Florida's flat," she said.

"Yeah, but you got the ocean all around. You live close to the ocean?"

"Pretty close."

"I love the ocean," Mack said.

"I love it too," she said. "But after a while, going to the beach can get boring. That's one of the reasons I came up here. I wanted to go to school someplace a little different."

She said she was glad she'd left home because sooner or later you always had to. But she missed her parents, she said, and she missed her sister, who was still in high school. And she couldn't totally rule out the possibility that she might transfer to the University of Florida in two years when her sister was ready for college. It would be nice, she said, for the two of them to live together. They'd always gotten along well.

"What you majoring in up here at Ole Miss, Meryl?" Salter said.

"Psychology."

Salter whistled. "You get to run many experiments on rats?"

"Not yet. I'm just a freshman. You do that mostly in the upper-division courses. I've gone into the labs, though, and watched them."

"That seems like a whole bunch of bullshit to me," Mack said. "Tell me what you can learn about old Ned back there from watching a rat."

She turned and looked over her shoulder at Ned and smiled at him. She had a nice face, he decided. Not a pretty face or a cute one, it was actually a little bit longish, but it was a face that didn't hide much. He suddenly wanted to tell her to get out of this car, to tell her she didn't belong here, that she ought to be back in her dorm or maybe even back home in Florida with her momma and her daddy and her sister.

"I don't know Ned," she said. "But I guess maybe there are some things you could learn about him—or you or me or Rick—from watching the experiments they perform on rats."

"Like what?"

"You could learn maybe how a certain kind of pain might affect us over a period of time."

"You mean like if you shocked a rat with a cattle prod fifty times a day for two hundred days straight," Mack said, "and then you just showed the rat a cattle prod but didn't shock him, and the sight of it scared him so bad he peed, it means Ned would pee too if you did that to him?"

"Well, let's say you'd just administer some kind of painful stimulus to the rat and then a minute or two later you'd feed it. You'd see whether or not that rat would come to associate pain—which is unpleasant—with eating, which is pleasant. Maybe after a while the rat might start refusing food."

"Even if you didn't hurt it before you fed it?"

"Even if you didn't hurt it."

"And that'd tell us something about Ned?"

"Or you, or me. Or anybody else."

"You ask me," Mack said, "there's such a thing as finding out too much."

He popped a tape into the stereo, and they listened to Steely Dan singing "My Old School," and Mack asked her what her high school had been like. She said it was a big school in Tampa, one that had almost six hundred students in the graduating class. She said she only knew the names of about fifty or sixty people there, but she'd made seven or eight friends she believed she'd have for life. They wrote to one another all the time and talked on the phone and were planning to spend a lot of time together next summer.

They might even try to rent a cabin together for a week or two in the Smokies and go white-water rafting or canoeing.

"That's how me and Ned and Rick are," Mack said. "You couldn't separate us with a blowtorch."

They stopped again in a few minutes and got four more beers—she'd finished hers before they finished theirs. They drove back toward town, and then around the edge of it on Highway 7, and then Mack turned onto another narrow blacktop and they drove down that for a while.

"Are all of you coming to Ole Miss next year?" Meryl said.

"I'm going to State," Salter said.

"But none of us is going anywhere next year," Ned said, "except Indianola Academy."

"I thought you said you were a senior, Mack," she said.

"Did I say that?"

"I'm pretty sure you did. You told me that at the SAE house. You said you'd be in school here next year."

"Damn, I must have got confused," Mack said. "You know how it is, Meryl. Get to listening to loud music and dancing and drinking and a person can forget their own name, much less what grade they're in."

"What grade are you in?"

"We're juniors," Mack said.

"Tenth grade," Ned said.

Mack glanced over his shoulder.

"Tenth grade?" she said. "You all are tenth graders?"

"Honey," Mack said, "why not think of us as sophomores?"

"It's the same thing."

"Not exactly," Mack said. "You can say somebody's a dago, and it affects folks one way, and you can say they're Italian, and it affects folks a different way. You could say somebody's trash, or you could say he's from a disadvantaged background. I'll bet if you think of me as a sophomore instead of a tenth grader, it'll have a whole lot better effect."

"How old are you all?"

Salter grinned. "We're almost eighteen."

"How close is almost?"

Ned kept his mouth shut.

"Fifteen," Salter said.

She didn't say anything to that, but she did lift up the cuff on the sleeve of her windbreaker and look at her watch.

Mack turned off the blacktop and drove down a dirt road forty or fifty yards and stopped the car and opened the door.

"Four more," he said.

"Not another one for me," she said. "I've got to be getting back."

"Sure thing," Mack said. He got out. He walked around behind the car and unlocked the trunk and raised the lid, and they heard ice shifting. Then he slammed the lid down. He came back and got in and handed Rick Salter a beer, and then he reached over and dropped a can in Ned's lap.

"I've got to be getting back," she said again.

Mack didn't crank up right away. He sat there with his door open, the beer can balanced on his thigh.

"Meryl," he said, "you know ever since that night I met you, I been dreaming about you?" He took a sip of beer. "I been dreaming about you and me winding up someplace exactly like this."

It looked to Ned as if Meryl was starting to understand where she was. They'd passed one pickup truck and one car in the last eight or ten miles. Now they were off the paved road altogether, parked in a thicket which would probably hide the car from the road in the unlikely event that anyone drove by.

Bottles and cans littered the undergrowth. The cool air smelled of moss and mildew.

"I bet you've been to places like this with guys before, haven't you?" Mack said.

"No."

"Hard to imagine."

"Then I guess your imagination's pretty limited. Come on, you guys—take me home."

"Rick back there," Mack said, "hell, he's been dreaming about you too."

"He doesn't even know me. Neither do you."

"I know you well enough," Mack said. "I described you right down to a T, didn't I, Rick?"

"Damn straight."

"Told you she was smart and good looking, didn't I?"

"That's how I remember it."

"And was I right?"

"To a T."

"You guys had better take me home," she said.

"Why be in such a hurry?"

"I just came out to go for a ride. Because I didn't have anything better to do, can you all understand that? I didn't want anything else."

"Bullshit."

"I didn't."

"You wanted it," Mack said, "up until you found out how old we were."

"You may think I did, but you're wrong. God," she said, "just please take me home."

Mack shook his head as if confronted by a level of ingratitude he found stunning. "Rick," he said, "did I ever once say anything to you—one word, I mean, even the hint of a word—about Meryl here having a horse face?"

Laughter exploded from Salter's throat. A few drops of beer trickled down his chin. "Shit, naw," he said, "you never mentioned it. Though now that I've seen her up close, I do notice the resemblance to Trigger."

She opened her door and got out of the car. She stood there for a minute, looking in the door, first at Mack and then at Rick and then finally at Ned. Her lips moved. He was afraid she was going to speak, and he wished he could stop up his ears and not have to hear whatever it was she intended to say.

She never said a word. She closed the door and stood there with her back pressed against the base of a sweet gum tree that was fifteen or twenty miles from the closest town, and Mack cranked up and backed all the way out to the blacktop road, and before he turned around and headed toward town, he stuck his hand out the window and shot her the finger.

"'We're tenth-graders,'" Mack said in a high, squeaky voice, one wrist wagging limply in the air. "What the goddamn hell's the matter with you? You got a brick for a brain or what?"

They had stopped on the side of the road a mile from where they'd left her. Mack jumped out and started around to Ned's side of the car, but Ned was on his feet, waiting, when he got there.

"With a momma and daddy like you've got," Mack said, and then he stopped.

"Yeah?" Ned said. "What about my momma and daddy? Or my sister? What about her? Or my grandparents?"

His throat had started closing on him, and for a moment he thought his windpipe was blocked.

"Ain't none of them descended from royalty," Mack said.

The sun lay low on the horizon, right behind Mack's head, and Ned saw him against a background bloody red, and then he stopped seeing him at all. The features of his face faded, and for the first time he lacked substance.

Salter was there on the side of the road too, somewhere behind Ned, close by. "Easy," he said. "Easy, Ned. Everybody just needs to stay cool."

Gradually Mack's features began to re-form themselves; eyes appeared and a nose, cheeks and lips and teeth. Ned viewed the process with regret.

"Tell him not to haul relatives into it," he said. "He's not a fucking genealogist."

"Let's leave relatives be," Salter said.

"You queer or what?" Mack said. "You a dick-licker, Ned?"

"Mack," Salter said.

"Swear to God, Ned, you don't like pussy, do you? You didn't want her, did you?"

"I wanted her," Ned said, and when he heard himself say it, he knew it was true, knew he had wanted to bury his face between the girl's breasts while she whispered words he couldn't even imagine and so was forced to construe as something besides sounds, as a scarlet velvet fog that enveloped him.

"Well, hell, man, if you wanted her, we could've had her," Mack said. "We could've been balling and squawling. Man, right now we could've been . . . Lord." His voice trailed off in reverent contemplation.

"I didn't know you'd told the damn girl you were a senior," Ned said. "You should've told us."

"I doubt there was much to her anyway," Salter said. "She didn't look to me like she was the type to wiggle her butt."

"I don't give a shit if they wiggle or not," Mack said. "I actually prefer a stationary target."

Salter laughed then, and Mack did, and Ned squeezed a laugh out, and before long it was clear that they'd put Meryl behind them, that what had happened on the dirt road between the trees would not be brought up again today, might not be brought up again for many months.

And then, sometime when they were together, drinking beer at a postgame party or just riding around and telling dirty jokes, Mack would recall what had happened, and he'd poke Rick in the ribs. "You remember that bitch we picked up that time?" he'd say. "The one we left in the woods?"

"Yeah. What about her?"

"Wonder if she's made it back to town yet?"

And then Mack and Rick would grab their sides, howling, and if Ned was there he'd howl too; he'd grab his side and howl like he was dying.

They stopped in Ruleville at the Mecca drive-in and bought some more hamburgers and some onion rings and ate them, and then they got back in the car and drank the last of the beer. It was dark now, nearing eight.

"What you guys want to do?" Salter said. "Go on back to Indianola and cruise 82?"

What Ned wanted to do more than anything else was go to sleep. The question was where to do it. The thought of going home, of walking through the front door and seeing his momma or his daddy, or even Daze, whose face he'd bet grief and shame had turned to plastic, made him want to check into a motel, but he only had two dollars left in his wallet.

"What the fuck's cruising 82 supposed to prove?" Mack said.

"Ain't supposed to prove nothing," Salter said. "But what else is there to do? Go watch a Walt Disney movie?"

"I want some more beer."

"Where you aim to get it?"

"I got my fake ID." He pulled it out of his wallet.

Ned and Salter leaned over to look at it. You could tell the birth date had been altered. There was a scar on the plastic where Mack or somebody else had used a razor blade to scrape the old date off.

"Looks like shit to me," Salter said.

"Well, it ain't been working too well," Mack admitted. "What the fuck. We'll go to a nigger store."

They drove south on 49, and not too far from Sunflower Mack turned off and drove down a gravel road between two cotton fields. You could see the running lights of a picker way out in the middle of one field. An empty trailer stood waiting on the turnow.

"There's a little crossroads grocery down here," Mack said. "Seem to me like I've been in it, but I don't know when."

It was five or six miles off the highway, right in the middle of nowhere. It had a gas pump out front, and there were lots of empty Coke crates stacked up on the porch and a Miller Hi-Life sign in the front window. They could see a black man through the window, sitting on the stool behind the counter and watching a portable TV.

"You ever bought beer, Ned?" Mack said.

"I don't have a fake ID."

"Place like this, you won't need one."

"I don't have but two dollars. How much is a six-pack?"

"Six-pack, hell," Mack said. "What we need's a case." He pulled his wallet out and extracted a ten. "That'll be more than enough. Get Bud if they got it."

Ned took the ten-dollar bill and stuck it in his shirt pocket and opened the door. "What if he tries to ID me?"

"He won't."

"Yeah, he won't, but what if he does?"

"He's a nigger. You're white. Just act like you know it, and you won't have no problem."

Canned goods were stacked up on shelves along the rear wall. There was an ice cream freezer against one of the other walls and adjacent to the freezer two soft-drink boxes. One said Nehi, the other said Coke. No sign of a beer cooler.

"What you looking for?" the man behind the counter said. He never took his eyes off the TV set. He was watching a football game, Alabama and Tennessee, it looked like. He was about sixty years old, short and skinny, and he had a thin mustache. His left hand, which rested on the narrow counter next to an almost empty bottle of Coke, was missing the little finger. There was nothing there but a nub.

"You got any beer?" Ned said.

"Be over yonder in the Nehi box."

The drink box was the old-fashioned type, the kind that was full of cold water. The cans were floating in it, single cans of Bud and Miller, a few Jax, eight or ten brown bottles of Sterling Big-Mouth.

"You don't have no cases?" Ned said.

"Ain't got nothing but what's in the box."

Ned could see Mack through the window, tapping his fingers on the steering wheel. It looked like he was getting impatient.

He gathered the cans up, two by two, and walked over to the counter and stood them, four at a time, near the register. It took him six trips in all, and by the time he set the last four beers down, the man had peeled his attention away from the ball game. He sat there on his stool and studied the puddle of water that had formed on the counter.

"That gone hold you for a hour or two?"

"I reckon."

He pulled the ten-dollar bill out of his shirt pocket and laid it on the counter. The man looked at it, but he didn't pick it up. "I don't imagine you're eighteen," he said. "Are you?"

"Sure."

"What's your birthday?"

"April 14."

"What year?"

"1954."

"You probably do real good in math," the man said. "Wish I could add and subtract like that." He made no move to total up the sale. "I'm gone have to see your ID," he said. "Reason I'm asking, just so's you'll know and tell your friends in that big long car out yonder, is the sheriff's deputies done started bothering my wife and me about selling beer to minors, and we don't need none of that. No sir, we do not. So you gone have to show it to me if you got it— and don't make me no difference if it's real or not—and if you don't have one, you gone have to go back out and get in that car and try to buy it somewhere else, and I'll tell you ahead of time I wish you luck. Far as I'm concerned, somebody that'll be old enough to go in the army in three or four years and get killed is old enough to drink a beer now."

Mack was looking at him through the window and shaking his head, and then he said something to Salter. Ned knew or believed he knew exactly what they were thinking. They were thinking that Ned would fail whatever test this was, just as his momma and daddy had failed the test last night.

For some folks, everything in between the beginning and the end was just a fight for breath, just one long struggle to suck in air or water or food, anything to fill the cavities that threatened to expand inside those folks until they themselves were walking raging nothings that couldn't do much but eat and drink, piss and shit, hurt and moan, that lived to writhe and tingle, kick ass and shoot off, that had a hole they could never fill because the hole was them and they were the hole, the sum of their natures null. His momma was that, and his daddy was, and he knew now that he would be too, that there was nothing he could do to avoid it.

Three or four years from tonight, he might be working in a country store himself, doing his best to watch a ball game while some young asshole who'd gotten out of a big long car tried to make a fool of him. He'd let the little asshole do it when the time came, he knew he would, so it wasn't right for an old colored man to make a fool of him now.

He's a nigger.
You're white.
Just act like you know it.

He turned. And turned again. The man had already looked away, back at the TV set, where an announcer was hollering, "Tide's ball!"

The Coke bottle felt sticky; he didn't know why. It was a big Coke bottle, the king-sized kind. A few drops spilled as he turned the bottle upside down, and the air sang out, and there was a dull sound, a sound that sickened, and for a few seconds, even as blood began pouring from the gash in his head, the man continued to sit on the stool, as if he couldn't quite bear to miss the next play, as if he himself were in Birmingham, sitting in the bleachers at Legion Field, watching all the action live.

1996

Monday morning Daze woke groggy.

She'd felt funny all day yesterday. She'd woken up sooner than she usually did on Sunday, while Ned was still in the house, and she'd stayed penned up in her room, glancing at the Jackson paper without really reading it, even though it contained a follow-up article about Kyle Nessler, who was apt to rot to death up in Parchman. She'd sat there until Ned left, and then she'd gone out and sat in the living room, her feet up on the coffee table, her hand clamped around the Zenith remote. She changed the channels idly. Roy Rogers flashed by several times, Barney Fife did, somebody pulled a hook from the wide-open mouth of a dazed-looking trout, Lester and Earl picked and sang while Uncle Jed and Granny danced rings around the fancy eating table, a Japanese soldier shot John Wayne flush in the forehead, Bill Clinton hugged a woman and her baby and said, *I'm so sorry*. A preacher sat behind a desk, babbling away in tongues, every now and then breaking into the plainest of plainspeak: *Send me a thousand dollars seed money, two hundred, five hundred, three hundred, four. Yabba dabba dabba dabba dabba dabba dee ba.*

"Sold to the fool in the corner," Daze said.

She'd finally gotten up and eaten something—Monday morning she couldn't recall what—then she'd drunk three or four beers and taken two sleeping pills. She'd lain on top of the covers with the light on, and she'd stared at the ceiling. The overhead light went from yellow to white to light blue, the color of the ceiling itself, and once that had happened, it was as if the whole ceiling itself were the light, like the walls were, the floors. Electric current surrounded her; she believed she heard it crackling.

Her mouth was open wide—she thought of the trout. She wore the same dumb look on her face. Somehow her pajama top had come unbuttoned. The pants were unbuttoned too, spread open across her thighs. She touched herself gently and cried.

She was sweating. She kicked off her pants. She sat up in bed, then knelt on the mattress. The springs creaked. Her heels felt rough and hard against her rear. Across the room, behind a row of toilet articles—wintergreen alcohol, Ban Roll-On, Johnson's Baby Powder, a seldom-used can of Clairol spray-net, a bottle of perfume that must have been ten years old—her image trembled: the broad white thighs, the brown patch between them, the sagging breasts.

She was the cast and the audience too. She was all that ever was, all that ever would be, all that had ever been except for an instant, and this wasn't then. She cupped one breast in her palm. It was heavy, it was warm, a heart beat beneath it.

Either Ned had left early or he hadn't come home—his truck was not outside, where it would usually be on Monday morning. Sometimes he slept in it, somewhere out at Mack's, and then went right on to work once more, just as eager as a dog to please his master. That was how she thought of them: as dog and master. If the dog bit you, you couldn't really blame it, because it was doing what somebody had trained it to do. But if it bit you, it was the one you kicked. Which was just what the master intended.

Daze drank two cups of coffee, and then she ran herself a bath, pulled her clothes off, and got into the tub. She lay back, her head against the porcelain, warm water lapping over her breasts, and the drowsiness stole upon her again. There was a moment when she felt her eyelids starting to close, her mouth hinging open, and so she made herself sit up. She grabbed a bar of soap and started scrubbing her armpits, and then she scrubbed her breasts and the insides of her thighs, and the scrubbing woke her up. She got out, put her clothes on, and poured herself another cup of coffee, which she carried with her to the car.

She did most of her shopping on Monday mornings. Most white people shopped at Wong's Foodland now or at the Sunflower store near the Academy, but for her main shopping she still went downtown to Piggly Wiggly. Everything was cheaper there, and she liked knowing that as long as she went to Piggly Wiggly, she would not run into Ned. He hadn't set foot on Front Street in years.

She parked in the lot beside the store, got out, and went inside. Everybody knew her here. As she pulled a cart loose, one of the checkout women smiled and nodded at her. Butch, the black man who'd been sacking groceries here since sometime in the late '50s, hollered out her name.

She rolled her cart along the dairy aisle, picking up a few cartons of yogurt, a quart of skim milk, some reduced-calorie margarine. She liked to watch her weight. Walking appetites, those people, men and women both, whose own hips outflanked them, whose bellies rolled and sagged, scared and disgusted her. The year she died her momma had grown obese; her breasts had drooped down toward her knees as if they yearned for the floor her momma stood on. She drank beer at breakfast with her eggs and sausage, and she'd no sooner finished that than she started frying more sausage for lunch, and she usually ate pork again for supper. Before long she was what she ate—you could smell hog sausage in her sweat, and her skin was always damp no matter what the temperature.

"You're getting awfully big," Daze had told her one morning while her momma sat at the kitchen table, forking syrup-sopped pancakes into her mouth and washing them down with Jax from a can.

"Who cares?" her momma had said.

"I do. I care."

"Yeah?" her momma said. She poured more blackberry syrup onto her plate, soaking her link sausages in it now too. "Well, you can't give me what I need."

"What's that?" Daze said, even though she was afraid to hear the answer, which she expected to be at best euphemistic, at worst downright crude.

There was a bluish streak on her momma's chin where syrup had trickled out of her mouth. She reached up with a bare palm to wipe it away.

"What I need don't have no name," she said. "Lord God, Daisy, it don't have no name."

While she was putting the bags into the car trunk, she sensed a presence across the street. It was always like that, this awareness that came upon her, having nothing to do with sight or sound, some sense far down that told her he was there.

She slammed the trunk lid and pushed the cart over to the sidewalk, and then she allowed herself to glance up. Russell Gautreaux stood there, directly in front of the bank, waiting for a break in the traffic, and when he got it he walked across the street.

His hair was iron gray now, and thin, and he was thin too, thinner than he'd been the last time she saw him. That had been six months ago at his wife's funeral. He'd taken a vacation after that. Rumor was he'd suffered a breakdown.

"Hi, Daisy," he said.

The little handkerchief he liked to keep in his breast pocket was there now, neatly folded, crisp and white.

"Hi, Mr. Gautreaux."

"I haven't seen you for a while. How have things been going?"

He always asked her that, and he asked it in such a way that she knew he really cared about the answer, and so she never lied.

"So-so," she said.

"So-so's not as bad as it could be, is it?"

"No, it could be a lot worse than so-so."

"That's something a lot of folks don't know. They think so-so's about a one on a ten-point scale, when it's really somewhere up around five."

"How are you?" she said.

"So-so minus."

"About a four?"

"Say four and a quarter," he said. "Doing some shopping today?"

"Just a little bit."

"Heat's starting to come on, and that always takes my appetite."

"Mine too. I eat a lot of fruit, though, when it's hot."

"Good for you. That's the best thing to feed yourself anyway."

"That and vegetables."

"Vegetables are good," he said. "I don't eat enough of them. I ought to. I've been eating a lot of TV dinners lately."

"That's no good for you."

"No," he said, "I guess it's not. But I'm sixty-one now. And you know, everything you do in life takes a certain toll on you."

"Well, that's right."

"Walking wears the feet out, eating wears the teeth out, breathing gets your lungs dirty. The water we drink poisons us. And so on."

"Mr. Gautreaux?" she said. "Maybe I should fix supper for you sometime."

He raised his palms as if to fend her off. "Oh," he said, "there's no need for you to do that."

"I'd just like to. I could fix it at your place—or I could just fix it at home and bring it over."

"Maybe sometime," he said. "We'll see. Everybody and his brother's trying to refinance. I've got so much work to catch up on at the bank I can't really accept any invitations right now."

"So maybe when you get caught up, we could do it. I'm not a bad cook."

A liquidy look came into his eyes. Suddenly the Toyota parked nose to nose with her car enthralled him. "I bet you're not," he said. "I bet you could feed a man to his heart's content."

Crossing the street this time, he paid no mind to the traffic. A black man in an old International pickup with side planks on it hit his brakes so hard that one plank rattled loose.

If Russell Gautreaux noticed he'd almost been hit, he never let on, not so that Daze could see it anyway. He stepped onto the sidewalk and walked over to the night depository and stood there a few seconds as if he wanted to make a deposit, but evidently he did not. He jammed his hands into the pockets of his jacket, opened the glass door, and disappeared into the bank.

"Hear y'all had a little diesel spill the other day," Cory Calvern said. "This fish didn't come out of that pond, did it?"

"Nope. This is from another one."

Cory unsealed the sandwich bag Ned had just handed him and took out the catfish. Ned had cut the fish's head off fifteen or twenty minutes ago, but the skin was still on. Cory slapped the fish down on the counter. He picked up a fillet knife and cut the fish in two right behind the body cavity, and then he sliced the fin off. He slid the tail portion into a small paper sack and popped the sack into the microwave oven that stood on the counter and set the oven and punched a button, and the microwave started humming.

"You ever worry about soaking up radiation from that thing?"

"The microwave?" Cory wiped his hands on the bloody apron he wore. The legend on the apron said, *Property of Southern Prime Catfish.* "Can't say as I ever thought much about it," he said. "What I worry about's starving to death."

Cory had never been particularly heavy, but at one time he'd had at least a normal amount of meat on his bones. Now he looked like he weighed about a hundred pounds. Ned didn't know when the change had taken place; it was just something he'd gradually become aware of.

"Looks like you *have* lost a fair amount of weight."

"Fifty pounds in the last two years."

"Goddamn. Are you serious?"

"Afraid so. My wife claims even my dick's getting skinny. Says fucking me's like getting screwed by a Bic fine-point."

"You got a stomach problem or what? You better go see a doctor and have an exam."

"Don't need no exam. Problem is I ain't got any appetite. You wouldn't have either if you'd tasted a quarter of a million fish samples last year."

The microwave beeped. Cory opened the door, pulled the piece of fish out, stuck it in his mouth, bit off a tiny portion, and tossed the rest into a tall trash basket lined with a plastic bag. He closed his eyes, and his jaws moved, and then he opened his mouth and spat the fish into the trash basket.

"Zero," he said. "Y'all can go on and seine it." He walked over to the stainless-steel sink and washed his hands and dried them on a paper towel, and then he picked up a form from his desk and signed it and handed it to Ned. "By the way," he said, "you still interested in finding you an old Mercedes to restore?"

"Yeah. Why?"

"I was over in Leland Sunday, and I noticed one sitting at a used-car lot out on 61 South. Looked like it was in pretty good shape. Might ought to take a look at it."

"What color was it?"

"I forget—seem like it was either white or cream-colored, though."

"Thanks," Ned said, "I'll check it out."

He walked into the hallway, then turned around and stuck his head back into the kitchen. "Cory?"

"Yeah?"

"Don't rule out radiation. You might better go have yourself checked."

Cory was sitting on a tall stool, glaring at the trash basket full of fish samples. He puckered his lips. "I hate fucking catfish," he said. "Damn if I don't hate them all, male and female, the grown ones and the baby ones too, the ones that are on-flavor and the ones that are off. This job's taking all the joy out of life for me, Ned, but I keep right on showing up every day. Can you understand that?"

"That's pretty much what I'm doing too."

"Can you tell me why we do it?"

"We're bound to have our reasons."

"I guess we do. I reckon my reasons are named Kenny and Mary Kay and Lu. What about yours?"

"I don't believe my reasons have got a name. I guess they're just kind of out there."

He gestured in the general direction of the parking lot, but in his own mind the gesture took in the highway beyond the parking lot and the town that lay across the highway and the fields and ponds that surrounded the town, and beyond those fields and ponds the hills that formed three of the Delta's boundaries and the river that formed the fourth one.

The Delta had once been an inland sea, and there were times when he felt it was somehow separate from everything outside it, like what went on here and what went on out there, beyond the hills and the river, were different from one another in some basic way. There were times when he felt like he was living in a lake or a pond that was sustaining itself but getting smaller and smaller, just like Cory Calvern.

Ned intended to leave the form inside Mack's screen door, but Ellie opened the wooden door while he was stooping down.

She wore a white terrycloth bathrobe. The sleeves weren't quite long enough to hide a purple bruise on her forearm. There was a bluish-purple ring around her right eye as well. She didn't look like there was much jumping up and down left in her.

He handed her the form. She stood there holding it, looking down at it as if it were some mysterious document the likes of which she'd never seen. It occurred to him that she might be on something—tranquilizers or muscle relaxers, something to get her numb.

She finally looked up at him, and when she did a strand of hair fell across her forehead. She reached up to brush it away. Her robe opened up just enough for him to see one of her breasts. It was small and burned looking, the nipple irregularly shaped.

He could tell she knew he'd seen her breast, but she made no move to pull her robe closed. "It happened the other night," she said, as if he'd asked a question. "After you and Rick and them were over here. I was asleep, and it was dark. I didn't even know he'd come in the bedroom. Lots of nights he doesn't, he sleeps in the guest room. I woke up and I felt this sticky stuff on my skin, and I didn't know what it was, and that was when I heard him."

"Heard him doing what?"

"Heard him breathing. And then my eyes got used to the dark, and I could see him standing there over the bed, holding something in his hand and shaking it over me, and I could feel this stuff dripping down, and I jumped up and turned on the light. And God, Ned, you know what it was?"

She reached out and laid her hand on his forearm, and he let it stay there, connecting them, just as whatever it was Mack had done to her the other night connected them too.

"It was a bottle of ketchup. One of those big thirty-two-ounce bottles of Heinz, and it was all over me, all over the bed, this thick red stuff that I swear to God I was afraid was my blood, even though I knew it was ketchup. And then he grabbed me and started shaking me, and you know what he said? You know what he said, Ned?"

The welcome mat was green. It was green, and it was made of something that looked like Astroturf, and the word *welcome* was scrolled on it in white. All the letters in the word *welcome* were lowercase letters, even the first. The *l* and the two *e*'s looked almost identical.

But you couldn't study a welcome mat forever. "Something about a fish," Ned said. "Something about you and a fish."

"He said if I ever did anything like that again, I was liable to wind up floating face down in a fish pond. But he didn't say what it was I'd done. Can you believe that, Ned? Can you believe it?"

For a moment Ned stood there with his hands in his pockets, knowing he ought to do something but not sure what. Finally he did the only thing that he knew for a fact needed doing. He took his hands out of his pockets and reached over and gently pulled her robe closed.

"Yeah," he said, "I can believe it."

"Next time you find yourself over around Amarillo, be sure and stop in at Slim Lacy's Truckstop. Six miles west of town on Interstate 40. Take a good hot shower and eat a slice of the best apple pie your momma never made."

He left the *Charlie Douglas Roadshow* on while he drove the pond levees, stopping now and then to get out and turn on an aerator. The afternoon had been overcast—tonight almost all the readings were low. He'd stay on the road nonstop; there wouldn't be an hour or so where he could pull off onto the shoulder and take a little nap. By five or six A.M. he'd be feeling like he couldn't take another step. But he'd keep taking steps, all right, at least till nine or ten o'clock. Because in the morning they had to seine that pond.

Twice he crossed the highway, driving from one set of ponds to another, trying, as long as possible, to avoid the big pond across the road from Q. C.'s house. But there was a limit to how long he could put it off. You could lose a pond in half an hour if the oxygen level dropped too low.

He drove down the road in front of the houses at a quarter after ten. All of them were dark. Somebody had removed the curtains at Q. C.'s place—the house was already empty. Larry's truck stood near his mailbox, but Ned didn't see Booger's old car anywhere.

Probably he was out at a crossroads dive getting ripped, maybe even drinking with Q. C.

Ned tried to imagine what sorts of things they might say to one another. He guessed they'd use the word *they* a lot, *they* and *them*. He bet they'd speculate about how *they* could possibly sleep well at night, and he wished he could be there with them to tell them not to worry, that he couldn't sleep at night, at least not in the way a person was supposed to sleep, which was the main reason he didn't even try.

He pulled up in front of the headquarters at seven-thirty. Mack was sitting on a section harrow, smoking a cigarette, his shotgun clamped between his legs. About thirty feet away, at the edge of the cotton field, lay an overturned fifty-five-gallon drum that had once contained spindle oil. The drum was rusty looking. It was also full of holes, and the holes looked like they'd been made by buckshot.

Ned got out and walked over. "Been having some target practice?" he said.

"Little bit. You got a problem with that?"

"Naw, I ain't got no problem with it."

Mack tossed the cigarette butt onto the ground and stood up. "Good," he said. "Because if you had a problem with that, I reckon I'd have a problem with you."

He leaned the shotgun against the section harrow. "Come on over here," he said. "Take a look at this."

Ned followed him over to the shed.

They kept the seine there. When it was stretched out, it was about as long as a football field and five feet wide, with a line of cork floats along the top edge and a line of lead sinkers along the bottom. Right now it was wrapped around a big wooden spool that they'd anchored to a two-wheeled flatbed trailer.

Mack grabbed a hunk of it. "Look at this."

There was a jagged hole in the mesh—probably three and a half feet across.

"Ain't no point in trying to pull this son of a bitch through the water," Mack said. He let go of the net. "You know what did that?"

A knife had done it. And a hand had held the knife. And Ned had a pretty good idea whose arm that hand was attached to. But he bent over anyway and pretended to examine the seine.

"Look to me like it may have been a damn gar," he said.

Behind him Mack snorted. "Gar my loving ass."

"Be careful with that goddamn seine. It belongs to Mr. Salter. Ours has got a hole in it. I didn't know better, I'd think somebody didn't want me to seine this pond today."

They were sitting on the tailgate of Mack's truck, which stood parked on the pond levee, watching while Booger and Larry and two other black men who lived on the place played net off the spool.

Gnats and mosquitoes kept buzzing around Ned's eyes and ears, and he kept slapping at them, and every now and then he'd cuss them. It was hot, almost a hundred. His shirt was already soaking wet, and Mack's was too. The others had taken theirs off. Their dark skin glistened in the hot sunlight.

"Your daddy helped me and Ned and my daddy dig this pond, Booger," Mack said. He reached into his ice chest and pulled out a can of Tecate and popped it open and took a big swallow. "He ever mention that?"

"No sir," Booger said. "I don't believe he ever talk about it."

"You wasn't no more than a foot long then," Mack said. "Just a little bitty old Fudgesicle."

"Everybody got to be a foot long sometime," Larry said.

"That's a fact," Mack said. "Everybody got to be." He sipped his beer and watched them work, sweating and grunting, their muscles rippling. "Your daddy was something else, Booger," he said. "Wasn't he, Ned?"

"Yeah."

"You know what he could do? He could control the speed of his heartbeat."

Booger strained against the crank on the side of the spool while Larry and the others pulled at the seine.

"Turn the motherfucker," Larry said. "Come on, Booger, we ain't got all day."

"Say your daddy took a notion he wanted to go to town, Booger," Mack said. "Say it was a Saturday when my daddy wanted him to work. Your daddy, he'd head out to the field and get up on the tractor, right out there in the hot sun, and he'd just start driving that thing and singing gospel songs, and you could hear him roaring about Jesus and chariots swinging low and coming for to carry him home, and it was one of the prettiest things you ever heard in your life. I mean you could hear it all over the place. He could flat-out *project*.

"Well, long about the time you got used to the idea that he'd be singing all day, you'd quit hearing it, and then the tractor noise'd stop too. You'd take a look out the window at the field, just to see what was up, figuring maybe he'd run over a root or something and tore up the cultivator, and the tractor's standing there nice and quiet and your daddy's slumped over the wheel.

"And my daddy, he'd go tearing ass out there, and sure enough your daddy'd be gasping and clutching at his chest, and my daddy, he'd say, 'Preacher, what is it?' And your daddy'd tell him, 'Mr. Bell, my *heart* done seized up.'"

"Reckon he thought them old chariots had swung down for him," Larry said. "Reckon he felt relieved."

"And my daddy'd stand there and take his pulse, and sure enough old Preacher's heart'd be hitting about three beats a minute. So Daddy'd put him in the truck and head for town, and they hadn't no more'n got to the hospital parking lot before old Preacher'd claim he was starting to feel better. My daddy'd grab his wrist and feel his pulse, and his heart'd be beating just as nice as you please. And your daddy, he'd say, 'Mr. Bell, you reckon since I'm in town I could *remain* and pick me up some snuff and Dr. Peppers?'"

Mack got down off the tailgate. The truck springs groaned.

"Yeah, old Preacher, he loved town like a hog loves slop. Lot of folks would've run him off, I guess. But the kind of man my daddy was, he never could get too mad at him. Could he, Ned?"

One sour note might spoil the entire composition, and it suddenly seemed important to play it. "Seem to me like I recall he boiled over," Ned said. "But just once or twice."

Mack turned and looked at him as if he'd voiced opposition to federal crop subsidies.

Ned was driving one red-bellied Ford tractor, and Mack was driving the other. Normally Mack waited down at the far end of the pond, where they always left the old wrecker they'd fixed up with a hopper for scooping fish out of the water and dumping them in the live-haul truck. But today Mack had told Booger, who usually drove the other tractor, that he'd been driving too slow—"dragging," as Mack put it. He'd jumped up on the Ford himself and ordered Booger to strap on his waders.

The seine was attached by nylon rope to the tractors' drawbars. Ned and Mack drove along the sides of the pond, barely creeping, while Larry and Booger and the other men, all wearing hipboots, waded behind the seine, clinging to the mesh and making sure the mud-rollers crawled along the bottom.

The tractor Ned was driving had a metal seat with little round holes in it, and the cushion was missing. He didn't know what the holes were there for, unless it was drainage, but they were starting to cut into his skin. He'd have red rings on his ass.

When he climbed onto a tractor, especially if it was a miserable day like this, he thought about his grandpa on his daddy's side of the family. He'd been a small farmer who'd finally lost his lease on sixteenth-section land when Ned was four or five years old. Before that happened, Ned's daddy had worked with him, and they'd owned three tractors, one of them a red-bellied Ford just like the one he was driving now. He remembered how he used to get up early in the morning and run out to the shed and climb up onto that tractor and pretend he was driving it. He'd sit there for half an hour sometimes, making revving noises, glancing down on either side, just like his grandpa and his daddy did, to make sure he kept the wheels in the middle.

One morning he'd run out to the shed and climbed up on the tractor and then realized he'd worn his tennis shoes. And without thinking much about it, he hopped down and walked back in and put on his boots, and then he went back to the shed and climbed up onto the tractor and played make-believe again.

A real tractor driver never wore tennis shoes. A real tractor driver had to climb down off the tractor in knee-high cotton, which might lie close to a bayou or a drainage ditch, and use a file to scrape mud off the cultivator blades, and a cottonmouth might strike him as he did it. It didn't matter that there were no cottonmouths there in the shed, or that he never climbed down to check the cultivator anyway because there was no cultivator attached to the towbar, or that the tractor stood silent. A real tractor driver wore boots, so he did too.

It had taken him a while to figure out that what he'd done that morning didn't prove he was a stickler for detail, and it didn't prove he was a down-to-earth, realistic sort of fellow. It just proved he didn't have shit for imagination. And in the end, that was a big reason why he'd become what he was.

"Hey!"

Feeling the seine grow taut, Ned stepped on the clutch, throttled down, and looked across the pond.

Mack had stopped his tractor. He was pointing at the surface of the pond, just in front of Booger. "Look like there's something down there," he hollered. "Maybe an old tire."

Booger looked over the float line, his eyes searching the muddy water. Then back at Mack. "I can't see nothing down there, Mr. Mack," he yelled.

"Maybe *you* can't, but I do. Get over there and see what it is. We don't want to rip a hole in Mr. Salter's net too."

Booger glanced once more at Mack, then looked across the pond at Ned. Ned didn't know why, but his legs had tensed up almost to the point of cramping. Holding the clutch down, he watched while Booger pushed down on the float line and raised his right leg. He stepped across the seine, stood balanced for a second on one leg, then pulled the other one over too.

Mack pointed once more at the surface. "Yonder!" he hollered.

Booger bent down, reaching into the water, groping. Ned was watching him when the tractor he was sitting on shuddered, and the seine tore loose from Larry and the other three and moved forward. Booger disappeared beneath the muddy surface.

Mack's tractor had lurched forward four or five feet. He stopped it fast enough, but by then Booger was tangled up underwater, thrashing about.

Ned killed the engine and jumped into the water and sloshed toward the middle of the pond. Larry and the others were sloshing forward, hollering Booger's name.

Larry got there first. He reached into the water, found Booger's arms, grabbed both of them, and tugged. Booger came up spitting water and shaking his head. Gasping, he threw off the seine.

Ned had gotten there by then. He reached out, intending to lay his hand on Booger's shoulder, but Larry turned around and glared at him and slapped his hand away.

Booger caught his breath and wiped the water out of his eyes. Then all five of them—Ned and Larry and Booger and the other two men—stood there in the muddy, fetid water, looking up at Mack. For the longest time Mack sat on the tractor without saying a word or moving a muscle.

Finally he killed the engine. "Foot slipped off the clutch," he said.

Larry let go of Booger and sloshed through the water like he aimed to climb the levee and tear Mack off the tractor. Mack stood astraddle the seat, smiling, relishing the prospect.

In his head Ned heard the roar of an outboard motor, heard the sound of churning water, then a dull thud. He lunged after Larry. He caught him from behind and pinned his arms at his sides. Larry struggled, doing his best to break free.

"Easy," Ned whispered. "Easy. You don't want to do it, I swear to God you don't."

Larry's elbow dug into his ribs. Ned's breath whooshed out of him, but still he held on.

Finally Larry realized Ned didn't aim to let him go. He stood there panting, glaring up at Mack. Gradually some of the coiled-up tension drained out of him.

Still standing on the tractor, the sun beating down all around, Mack crossed his arms over his chest. "Guess there wasn't no tire down there after all," he said.

Larry and Booger and the other men were standing in a tight circle on the levee at the end of the pond. They were talking in low voices. Down below, in a detachable portion of the seine that acted as a holding tank, forty or fifty thousand catfish were swimming about, wondering what was up.

Ned wondered too. Mack was standing beside his pickup, talking on the cell phone and looking pissed off. Ned walked over to listen in.

"Yeah, I know I said nine, but we had a problem with the seine." Mack listened while the other person talked. "You son of a bitches have fucked me up, Henry," he said. "You tell Clyde Sweeny he can forget them box seats I promised." He threw the phone down and slammed the truck door.

"What's the problem?"

Mack wiped his forehead on the arm of his shirt. "They told me they'd try to come get 'em today, but now they say it'll be in the morning."

"It generally is."

"Yeah, and that generally don't matter. But what it means now is I'll have to sit out here all night with a goddamn shotgun to make sure nobody fucks with my fish."

Larry stepped away from the other men. They stood behind him as if to show that whatever he aimed to say he would say for them too.

"Gone be lots of mosquitoes out here," he said. "They liable to eat you up."

Without ever taking his eyes off Larry, Mack reached into the ice chest and took out another beer. He tapped the can twice and popped the top. He took a swig, wiped his mouth on his shirt sleeve, set the can on the tailgate.

"You know what?" he said. "Them mosquitoes mess with me, it's gone be the last sad act of their little lost lives."

The Beer Smith Lounge was a windowless room with a concrete floor, bare lightbulbs dangling from the ceiling. Oak tables claimed the space in front of the stage where country-and-western singers played. The pool tables were lined up against the back wall, and a shuffleboard stood by the door.

The bar, part of what Daze called the Beer Smith Complex, stood about a hundred yards from the Beer Smith Truckstop, behind which was the Beer Smith Trailer Park. Directly across the highway from the truckstop was a run-down motel, a place where ragweed reigned in the parking lot and half the bulbs on the sign were burned out. A few months ago Beer had bought it too—mostly, he said, because a couple of professionals and far too many amateurs were turning tricks in the rooms. He'd closed the place, but he aimed to reopen it one day, as soon as he had the money to tear everything down and remodel.

A pair of truckers who drove for Southern Prime wandered in, ordered a couple of beers, and started playing pool. The butts of the cues tapped the concrete floor, there was talk of the Grapevine, a grade in California that one of them said had been closed off last week.

"Damn tanker turned over on the mountain and spilled oil. Slicked the pavement up so bad you couldn't do nothing but spin your wheels and slide back down."

"One day I'm liable to kill somebody on that thing. Seem like ever time I go out there some little pussy in a Porsche whips past me and makes it a point to shoot me the finger."

"Ain't nothing in California but Porsche pussies."

"Man, you tell me. Crying shame you can't separate all that white sand out there on them beaches from all the assholes that lay on it."

"I wouldn't live in that fucking state to save Jesus from the Romans, but I can't imagine not ever seeing it."

Daze never worried much about what other folks had seen that she hadn't. Whatever it was, it wouldn't have been the same thing if she herself had seen it. Inside everybody's head was a funhouse mirror. Outside was something nobody could see, at least not as it really was, and she thought it possible that outside there really was nothing at all. At times she hoped this was so. If it was, then nothing mattered, and right now there were still too many things that mattered way too much.

Around two o'clock, Beer Smith walked in. The truckers had left after one beer, and the bar was completely empty. She didn't know why he made her keep it open in the afternoon unless it was just to give himself an excuse to pay her for a few more hours' work. That was the sort of thing he might do. He'd had a certain amount of financial good luck, and he always tried to spread it around.

Back when he offered her the job, she'd been working at the 7-Eleven, working nights just like her momma, and he'd come in one evening just before midnight and bought himself a candy bar and offered to hire her. "You stay here," he'd said, "and sooner or later you'll get shot." He nodded at the parking lot, at the highway beyond it. There had been a rash of shootings at convenience stores in the Delta. Two clerks had died in Greenville. One had died in Shaw. "Shot," he'd said, "or kidnapped."

"Kidnapped," she'd said, "might not be so bad."

He climbed up onto a barstool now. "I just saw old Ned down yonder at the red light. I thought he worked nights and slept days."

"He does, unless they're seining, and then he works days too."

"Mack must be paying him a shitload of money to work him so goddamn hard."

"I think he likes to hang around rich folks."

"There's easier ways to hang around rich folks than working twenty-four hours a day. He ever think of trying to marry money?"

"I doubt it."

"You ever think of it?"

She squirted some dishwashing liquid into the sink and turned on the hot water. He had a way of stepping onto ground that wasn't his. She didn't know if he was searching for the plots she'd roped off or if he just blundered onto them.

"Why?" she said. "Are you proposing?"

His face did something she'd rarely seen it do: it changed colors. "Me?" he said. "Hell, I don't have no money."

"All the beer these assholes drink adds up to something."

"Adds up to a bunch of hate mail," he said to change the subject. "I've got three anonymous postcards in the last week alone. Look what came today."

He reached into his shirt pocket and pulled out the card. It was a plain white card, the kind you could buy at the post office with a stamp printed on it. It had been postmarked in Indianola on Saturday. In black ink someone had printed, *Alcohol is the cause of many a broken family. Stop pouring, Beer.*

"Can you believe it?" he said.

She handed back the postcard. "You know," she said, "I've always wondered something. How'd you come by your first name?"

"My daddy used to make home brew," he said, "and everybody knew it. Everybody called him Beer Smith, so when I come along he decided to name me that. I never thought too much about it till now. I got a good mind to do a mass mailing to all the churches. Get me some flyers printed up claiming the brew I sell's less intoxicating than the stuff the old Huckster and his little helpers peddle. Reckon they'd consign me to the flames if I did that?"

"They might."

"Excuse my vulgarity, but there's times I'd like to take me a cane pole and insert it into an orifice or two."

"That was graphic," she said, "but not vulgar. A vulgar person would've said he'd like to ram a cane pole up their ass."

"Well, rumor has it my family's got Tidewater roots."

"So you're incapable of real vulgarity."

He ducked his head and stared down into the bowl of peanuts that stood before him on the bar. "I was wondering if you'd want to go out and eat again. I kind of enjoyed your company the other night."

She turned the water off and started picking up the mugs that had been left out last night. She stood them upside down in the sink. Three rows of four.

"I've got to work tonight," she said.

"I'll ask Sandy to come over from the truckstop."

She picked up a sponge and started washing the mugs. "Where do you want to go?"

"We've already done Greenville, so how about Greenwood? There's supposed to be a good Italian restaurant over there."

"In Greenwood?" she said.

"Downtown," he said, "somewhere close to the Yazoo River."

"Did you ever notice you can't get away from water in the Delta?" she said. "Has that ever occurred to you?"

"By rights, water ought to be all over the Delta. You know there wasn't much solid land here a hundred years ago? Reason it took Grant so damned long to win at Vicksburg was he was scared to march an army through here and come in from behind. He believed his soldiers would mutiny if he tried it. Wasn't nothing here but swamps and snakes and mosquitoes."

"There's not much more than that now," she said.

He thought she was stalling, looking for a graceful way to say no. But she couldn't say no, not to him, and she was far from certain she wanted to.

She told him she couldn't go to supper tonight looking like she looked. She was wearing jeans and a tee shirt and a pair of sneakers, and they wouldn't let her through the door like that, not if it was such a good place.

He slid down off the barstool. "You got the afternoon off," he said. "Go on home and put on a dress, or whatever. I'll draw the assholes their beers."

She didn't need any more urging. She finished washing the mugs and laid down her sponge and dried her hands on a dishtowel. Then she told Beer good-bye and walked through the door into the sunshine. When the heat hit her, her knees almost buckled. She'd reached the age, she guessed, when she couldn't tolerate high temperatures very well anymore. She was fit for lukewarm water, mild days, and cool nights.

Ned had come home around lunchtime and tried to sleep, but he couldn't. He kept thinking of that moment when Booger had disappeared under the water. How Larry and the others had immediately rushed to help him. How he himself had jumped down and slogged through the water, letting his instincts take over. He kept wondering why your instincts helped you in one situation and deserted you in another.

After a while, he gave up trying to sleep and got out of bed. He made himself a pot of coffee and drank two cups of it, black and bitter, and then, because this was a perfect time to inflict a little more misery on himself, he went out back and got his tool chest, then carried it around front.

He'd just stuck the tool chest into his truck when Daze pulled into the yard. He watched her get out of the car, an eighteen-year-old LTD that looked and sounded like it had been put together out of several different makes and models. Mostly it was green, but the left front fender was cream-colored. It had a busted ring, so it smoked like a paper mill and stank like one too. He could have worked on it and made it run and look better, but she'd warned him not to ever touch it.

She started across the yard to the house. It didn't look like she even aimed to say hello.

"Hey," he said.

"Hey."

She was climbing the front steps.

"Home early, ain't you?" he said.

She stopped and turned around real slow. She always did it like that, taking forever to face him, giving him time to dread the moment when her eyes would rake him over.

"Am I?" she said.

He felt the big clot that formed in his throat whenever she deigned to speak to him. "Seem like it," he said.

"You pay a lot of attention to my coming and going," she said. "But then, there's nothing new about that."

"I just noticed it's all," he said. "Hell, I just—"

She turned and went inside. The door slammed behind her.

The used-car lot was on the outskirts of Leland, across the road from a sheet-metal shop. Twenty-five or thirty trucks and cars stood lined up a few feet from the highway. The lot was gravel, and there was no fence around it, just cotton fields on three sides, and on the fourth, the one next to the highway, a road ditch that looked as if the dealer had dredged the bottom to make it deeper.

A gravel road with a culvert in it led into the lot, and there was a gate across the road that the dealer probably locked at night. If you wanted to, Ned supposed, you could hot-wire one of the cars and drive off across the cotton patch. But it was doubtful that anyone would go to such trouble for any of the heaps parked here.

The one exception he could see was the white 300 D. It stood by itself next to the cinderblock building that served as an office. Unlike the other vehicles, this one had no price scrawled across the windshield in white shoe polish. The absence of one was generally an ominous sign.

Ned slowed down to about fifteen miles an hour. The dealer, who wore khaki pants and a white short-sleeved shirt, was standing in the office door, smoking a cigar and watching a young black couple. They were examining an old green Accord. Other than the couple and the dealer, no one was on the lot.

Ned drove on past, and in a few minutes, after he'd left the city limits sign behind, he turned off the highway onto a gravel road.

The road ran between two cotton fields. There weren't many catfish ponds in Washington County, just row crops, mostly cotton, some soybeans. The cotton was about a foot tall now, and the fields were relatively free of the red vines and tea weeds that had broken many a hoe hand's heart. Nobody was working in the fields nearby. They looked like they'd just been plowed.

He went on for a mile or more until, off to the right, he saw the remains of a tenant shack. Part of the chimney was still standing, but otherwise the site was just a pile of bricks and boards overgrown by Johnson grass. He parked his truck on the side of the road, removed his tool chest, and jumped the road ditch.

He left the tool chest in the grass, next to a mound of beer cans and liquor bottles. It wouldn't have been safe to stash his tools here at night—ruins like these often functioned as a rendezvous, a place where folks not mated on paper paired off in the dark—but the tools would be all right for the next half-hour. Hardly anybody made love in a cotton patch in open daylight.

"You got German blood?" the dealer said.

Cigar smoke wreathed his head. The smoke smelled like angel food cake.

Ned had disliked him even from the highway. "Naw," he said, "I got equal measures of Rankin County and Tunica County in my blood. I imagine some of Sunflower County's worked its way in there too, just by virtue of me living my whole life there."

They were standing in front of the Mercedes. The dealer thumped ashes off the end of his cigar. "I don't like the sons of bitches," he said.

"Germans?"

"Mercedes."

"How come you trying to sell one?"

"This is the only one I ever had a chance at that checked out. This son of a bitch don't just run, it pure dee eats the road up."

"What you asking for it?"

"Thirty-two hundred dollars."

Ned walked around to the door and pressed his face to the glass. The odometer said 92,588.

"For a Benz," the dealer said, "we're talking low mileage in the extreme."

"What year is it?"

"1980."

"You know anything about the original owner?"

"Bought it from a woman lived over on Washington Avenue."

"She the first owner?"

"You'd have to ask her that. And you can't."

"How come?"

"She passed on."

The car was clean on the inside, and the paint was intact except for one spot on the rear quarter panel about the size of a nickle. Touch-up had been applied to the hood in one or two places, but you'd never notice them unless you looked hard. If there wasn't too much wrong with it, it was exactly what he wanted—it was even the right color, he wouldn't have to repaint it.

"Any problems with it?"

"Wouldn't be sitting here if there was."

Ned knelt and looked under the car. He could see a few drops of fluid on the automatic transmission, and there was a spot of oil about the size of a half-dollar directly under the engine. It was probably leaking from the rear seal.

"Now, a diesel's just got to leak a little," the dealer said. "You may as well just make up your mind to live with that."

"Reckon I could take it out and drive it a few minutes?"

"Don't see why not."

The glow light stayed on for fifteen or twenty seconds, but when Ned turned the key the car cranked right up. He sat there in the lot, listening to the engine. The valves were sticking, clattering like machine guns.

The dealer dropped his cigar butt and kicked gravel over it. "Just needs to warm up," he said.

"Wonder how it'd sound on a cold morning?"

"Car like this was *made* to run good in cold weather. It may hem and haw a little right when you first crank it, but this son of a bitch was designed to take care of business on a February morning in them Hannoverian Alps."

"Didn't know they had no Alps around Hanover."

"Oh, they got 'em, all right," the dealer said. "Some of the worst ones in the world stand right there."

The transmission hesitated when he went from first to second, and a few minutes later, when he turned off the highway onto the gravel road and tried to gun the engine, the clutches slipped and spun out. The clattering under the hood never let up, and the needle on the temperature gauge was already rising toward 100 Celsius.

By the time he parked the car near the spot where he'd left his tools, the gauge read 115. Either the radiator was plugged up or the water pump was shot. Leaving the engine idling, he reached under the dash, popped the latch, got out, and raised the hood.

He grasped the upper radiator hose and gave it a squeeze. He couldn't feel any pressure surge when he let go. The water pump was most likely finished. He didn't know what a new one would cost, but he knew it wouldn't come cheap.

The engine had been steam-cleaned—it wasn't as dirty as a diesel should have been. But a couple of high-pressure hoses were bleeding, and fuel was leaking out around all of the injectors. Oil had seeped out at the rear of the valve cover. At the very least the gasket was shot. He suspected the story was a lot sadder than that. He cut the motor off and walked across the field and got his tool chest.

He pried off the throttle linkage, pulled a ratchet handle out of the tool chest, and attached an extension and a socket. He removed the nuts from the valve cover. Then he wrapped a couple of old rags around his hands and lifted the cover off.

The engine operated with an overhead cam. The lobes all showed wear, and a couple of them were almost flat. At some point somebody had starved the car of oil.

Standing there alone at the edge of the road beside a car constructed half a world away, he stared at the Mercedes and shook his head. It made no sense that he could see, buying this kind of machine and refusing to do the minimum to help it remain what it was meant to be. There wasn't much, he guessed, that neglect couldn't destroy.

When he pulled into the lot, the temperature gauge was redlining. He turned the car around and backed it up and cut the engine.

The dealer was standing right where he'd left him, smoking another cigar, one thumb locked around a belt loop. "Make me an offer," he said.

Ned opened the door and got out. "This car's falling apart," he said. "What'd you use to roll back the mileage?"

"Most folks'd use one of them little high-speed hobby motors if they aimed to roll it back," the dealer said. "But that's unscrupulous, and as you can probably tell, I'm a scrupulous man."

Ned walked around to the trunk and unlocked it and lifted out his tool chest.

"You an authorized Mercedes mechanic, I guess?" the dealer said.

"I got about as much business working on a Mercedes as you got trying to sell one."

He slammed the trunk lid and laid the key down on it and, carrying his tool chest, walked across the lot toward his pickup.

"Hey, Mister?"

The dealer was sitting on the front fender of the Mercedes, one foot down on the ground. He was grinning, and the grin had real depth. Far too much of his personality was presently on display.

"I'll sell this car," the dealer said. "This time next week, this car'll be out cruising the streets, maybe here in Leland, maybe over in Greenwood or down in Yazoo City or wherever it is you came here from. Somebody'll try to drive it all over whatever town he lives in, make sure everybody that knows him sees him behind the wheel.

"Yes sir, I'm gone sell this car," he said again. "Gone sell it to trash that's consumed by illusions."

Ned set the tool chest on the ground. He walked toward the dealer. As if it had just dawned on the asshole that he'd gone too far, the dealer shrank away, raising his arms to block the blow he thought was coming.

Ned reached down and snapped off the silver hood ornament. He pulled open the dealer's shirt pocket and stuck the ornament inside.

"Now trash don't want it," he said.

There was a roadside park between Leland and Indianola. The tables were made out of concrete, and so much birdshit had accumulated on them that you couldn't have gotten it off without a sander. Aluminum cans bleached white by the sun littered the ground around the garbage bins. You could smell the restrooms from the highway. Nobody ever ate here, as far as he could tell, and nobody with any self-respect would have pissed here either.

It was five o'clock when he pulled up under a tree and killed the engine. He lay over on the front seat, pulled his knees up close to his stomach. Within five or ten minutes it was so hot in the truck that his shirt was soaked.

Birds sang, the sun sank a little lower. He lay there bathed in his own sweat. He knew he needed to get a little sleep before he went back to work, but too often sleep tired him. He'd go to sleep and wake up feeling like he'd just played a ball game or run an 880. He'd wake up thinking it was '72 or '73, that he had those years to live through again, and he knew he wouldn't make it this time. He knew he wouldn't want to.

He wished he had a woman to hug him. He wished his momma were here with him, here beneath the trees, bathed in sweat like he was. She'd been sweating the last time he saw her. She'd lain in the hospital bed, her arms stretched out on either side of her, needles piercing both wrists, drip and painkillers flowing into what remained of her veins. She wore a lime-colored hospital gown that couldn't quite hide the ruin she'd turned into.

Her body, which had been her main source of pleasure, was now a source of pain. She shut her eyes against the pain, but you could see it pulsing there, underneath the papery lids.

"Neddy," she'd said, "lay your head on your momma's old breasts."

He was in the room alone with her, there for what the doctor had said would probably be the last time. He'd reached out to touch her just as she spoke, but after hearing her request, he flinched, and as he did he became aware of her odor, which reminded him of his own back porch, of rot and decay, of the slop he'd toted out every day that year his daddy had tried to raise hogs.

He backed away from her bed.

"Neddy?" she said. "Neddy?"

At sundown he stoppped off at a country store and bought himself a six-pack. He drank two beers while he was sitting in the parking lot. Then he started making his rounds.

Bumping over one of the levees, he spotted Mack's red pickup. He'd parked it down at the end of the pond where the fish were trapped in the sock. Ned could see him sitting in the cab, his cap pulled down over his eyes. When he got a little closer, he could see the gun barrel too. Mack held it clamped between his knees, the muzzle up close to his chin.

Ned pulled up beside him. "That's a stupid-ass way to hold a shotgun," he said. "You got a death wish or what?"

Mack tipped up the bill of his cap. He wasn't used to hearing this kind of tone, hadn't heard it from Ned in an awful long time. "I may have a death wish," he said. "But it don't involve me dying."

"Who you expect to catch out here?"

"Don't expect to catch nobody."

"So how come you sitting here?"

"So there won't be nobody to catch."

A big mosquito lit on Ned's forearm. Idly he mashed it. It left a bloody spot. He watched the blood run, becoming lighter-colored as the sweat on his skin diluted it.

"You ever wonder," he heard himself say, in a voice that even to his own ears sounded far away, "how many buckets of blood you'd have if you started filling 'em up with all the mosquito blood you ever spilled?"

"Naw, I never. I got more pressing things on my mind."

"Tell you the truth, sometimes that kind of shit gets to pressing on my mind pretty hard. Gets a good bit of pressure built up. All of this you ever did, added up with all of that. Just imagine all the water you ever drank in your life—I bet you it'd fill ten or twelve catfish ponds. Stack up every slice of bread you ever ate, and sure to God you'd have a regular whole-wheat tower of Babel. Add up every lie you ever told, everything you ever stole, every mean, nasty act you ever committed. Everything you should've said or done but didn't."

"Sound to me like you're a little bit nervous," Mack said, eyeing him.

"I'm calm as can be."

"Sound strung-out to me. You need a night off or what?"

"Naw, I don't need no night off. I need to be out here keeping my eyes peeled, watching. Need to keep my ears tuned up, listening. That's what you hire me for, ain't it?"

"I reckon."

"So there you've got it."

"Got what?"

"Got yourself an oxygen man," Ned said. He threw the truck into reverse and started backing up. "Got yourself a walking monitor."

"Hey," Mack hollered, "you going apeshit on me or what?"

"If I do," Ned hollered back, "you gone be the first to know."

Mack had climbed out of his pickup. He was holding the shotgun halfway down the barrel, resting the stock on the ground. He watched Ned back down the levee.

Before he turned the truck around, Ned stuck his head out the window. "Just imagine," he yelled, "every shit you ever took piled up in one heap. You could call it Mount Brown. The Mack Bell National Monument."

In the twilight a flock of cormorants settled in the shallow water near the edge of a pond. They stood there plucking fish out of the water with their long, hooked bills, and while the fish did their best to flop free, the birds swallowed them whole. You could lose a lot of stock that way. He'd heard of folks losing the better part of a pond.

Cormorants were on the endangered species list, so it was a federal offense to shoot one. You were supposed to try to run them off. Some farmers fashioned scarecrows out of tin plates that could make a fair amount of noise, especially on a windy day, but the birds were brazen and didn't scare easily. Mostly what the tin plates did was upset the fish.

Ned himself had experimented with boom boxes, car alarms, police sirens, and coaches' whistles, but none of them really worked. The birds would rise from the water, fly off a short distance, circle around, and then, as soon as the noise stopped, they'd fly right back to the pond they'd just left and go fishing again.

They were stupid beings just trying to get by, but for reasons he didn't fully understand Ned hated them. He opened his truck door now and got out.

The cormorants had occupied one whole corner of the pond. Except for an occasional squawk, they went about their business in a quiet way—sticking their heads into the water, pulling them back out a few seconds later with slithering catfish clamped between their jaws. A few of the birds looked up at him, but not for long.

He reached into the truck and pulled out the 9-mm. He walked down the bank a few feet until he was standing no more than ten yards from the closest of the birds.

He raised the pistol and looked down his arm at the bird. It stood there dirty and dumb and unconcerned, a filthy thing that simply took what it needed, when it needed it, that could live off trash if it had to, that felt at home wherever it was.

He squeezed the trigger; there was a sharp crack, and the bird skittered sideways, beating the muddy water with its wings, its webbed feet splayed out in opposite directions.

The flock rose, deserting the struggling bird. They banked and headed north, toward someone else's pond or another one of Mack's.

Crickets chirped. Katydids sang.

In the water the thrashing soon subsided. The cormorant floated, its breast barely moving.

A red slick began to form on the surface. Ned stood there watching, his own breast as still as the bird's, until gradually the blood faded into the rust-colored water.

The road between Greenwood and Indianola was a long, straight stroke through the heart of the Delta. There were fish ponds on both sides now where once there had been cotton fields. Wind rushed in Daze's open window, bringing with it the odor of fish and fetid water.

She hadn't traveled this road very often in the last few years, but there had been a time, back when she was eight or nine, when for several days in a row she'd driven the road in the morning with her momma and they'd come back late at night. Ned stayed with their grandpa, their daddy had started painting houses and was always on the road, and her momma told her grandparents she was going to see the dentist. Her momma met a man named Bobby who took them out to lunch every day at a place called the Crystal Club—you had to stick a special card into a slot in the door, and then the door would open. You couldn't eat there unless you were white and had the money to buy the card.

Afterward she'd play in a tree-shaded yard behind a big white house that stood next to the house where the man accused of shooting Medgar Evers lived. While she played, her momma stayed inside with Bobby, who really did seem to be a dentist because there was an office in his house with a dental chair in it and lots of drills and other instruments, though Daisy never saw a single patient. Sometimes she heard laughter coming from the upstairs windows, her momma's laughter or, less often, Bobby's. Sometimes they left her there by herself and drove off in Bobby's car, and when that happened she'd go inside the house and handle Bobby's dental instruments, or, if the door to his office was closed, she'd sit alone in the living room, in a big easy chair that was covered with some sort of white fur, and she'd watch old shows on TV—*Jack Benny, The Three Stooges, I Love Lucy, Donna Reed*. She wondered if maybe she was going to live in the big house for good, if maybe her momma was getting ready to leave her daddy and move in with Bobby.

Once she asked her momma, one night when they were driving home on the same highway she was traveling now. Her momma threw her head back and laughed so hard and so long that Daisy was afraid she'd lose control and steer them off the road.

"Lord, no," her momma said. "Baby, you got a thing or two to learn."

"So go on and teach me," she said.

"It's impossible to teach you. You got to learn 'em on your own."

In the end, what she'd learned that summer did not have much to do with why she and her momma could not move in with Bobby. It had much more to do with the accused killer who was living next door.

There was a jungle gym in Bobby's backyard, left there by his own kids, who no longer lived in the house with him. One afternoon when she was climbing on the jungle gym, she heard the man next door moving around in his backyard, picking up garden tools and laying them back down, humming the melodies of old hymns—"Washed in the Blood" was one she recognized, that and "Standing on the Promises." She'd heard Bobby tell her momma he knew damn well the man was guilty of the killing, but a jury had just said he wasn't.

The man climbed a ladder to change the bulb in the spotlight he'd attached to his garage, and he happened to look across the fence and see her.

"Hi," he said.

"Hi."

He smiled at her. She believed she could tell who did and did not like kids. Bobby didn't, but this man did.

He was wearing a baseball cap that had a smudge of white paint on the bill. The cap itself was green.

"My name's Delay," he said. "What's yours?"

"Daisy."

"Daisy," he said. "That's a right pretty name."

"Thank you."

"You welcome."

He went back to work then, removing the old bulb and screwing in the new one, humming "Just as I Am." On his way down the ladder, he looked at her and waved.

She never saw him again that summer, though she'd seen his face many times since then, in the newspapers and on TV, and she'd heard they'd even made a movie about him. Now, almost thirty years later, he'd been retried for the crime. This time around he'd been found guilty. When she saw him on the news after the verdict was announced, he'd acted crazy.

But he still had the face of a man who liked kids.

For a few seconds, the figure on the seat beside her did not belong to Beer Smith, it belonged to her momma, and Daze was not riding in a fairly new GMC pickup but in an old Ford Galaxy, a moving mass of creaking metal that held her encapsulated in a time she would never escape from, just as Byron de la Beckwith could not escape from it.

"That was good spaghetti tonight," Beer Smith said. "Had half a mind to eat some of the fancy stuff, but I was scared it'd harm my self-image."

"Which is what?"

"A weathered son of a bitch with an upper lip that's stiff as steel. Like most folks' self-image, mine's about as accurate as the TV news, but I do my best to hang on to it."

"That's probably wise."

"What about you?"

"I guess I try to hang on to mine too."

"Yeah, but what is it?"

She started to give him a frivolous answer or say she didn't know, but then it dawned on her that both he and she deserved more honesty than that.

"I kind of think of myself," she said, "as a historical figure."

"Somebody that lived in the past?"

"Somebody that lived, if she lived at all, in the past."

"You ain't been messing around the junior college, have you?"

"Why?"

"Generally folks don't start talking like that till they've had some exposure to higher education."

"My education was of the lowest kind."

"Meaning?"

"Meaning low, like below the belt. You remember my momma and daddy. They thought everything really worthwhile took place between their legs."

"Seem like I recall having thought that way from time to time," Beer said. "Don't you reckon most folks do? From time to time, I mean?"

"My momma and daddy thought that way all the time."

"What about you?"

Wind whipped through the window, stinging her eyes. "I suppose I thought like that," she said. "From time to time."

Normally he drove with both hands, but he'd taken one off the wheel now. He rubbed the side of his face with it, massaging his jaw like it hurt. Then he quit rubbing his face and laid his hand on the back of the truck seat so that it rested just inches from her shoulder.

"My wife was a pretty woman all her life," he said. "But back when she was young, she could really strike you blind. Me and her went to high school together up in Linn—believe it or not, the place had its own schools back then, we didn't have to go into Ruleville or Drew or wherever it is they go now. Anyhow, we had us a little fling when we was teenagers, and then she took up with a fellow that had just come back from overseas, and eventually they up and got married, which is why I didn't get her back till I was almost thirty."

His fingers grazed her shoulder.

"Man, when she took up with that other fellow," he said, "it like to killed me."

She crossed her arms over her breasts and leaned toward the dashboard as if she were cold. Which she wasn't.

"I guess having to imagine somebody you love fooling around with another person's pretty hard," she said.

"Wasn't no imagining to it," he said.

The dashboard glow lit his face enough for her to see a smile dart across his lips.

"Year we graduated from high school," he said, "me and her got kindly red-hot. Her momma and daddy lived just up the road from us, and I used to go on upstairs at our place and get in my bed, and then along about midnight, after I heard Daddy start snoring, I'd slip down the stairs and walk up the road to her house, and she'd let me in the window. They had an old beagle named Lester after Lester Flatt, and he'd raise hell when most folks set foot in the yard, but he never done nothing but wag his tail when he saw me.

"Then me and her had a spat about something, I can't remember what, and she pitched a fit and told me to get lost. So I sulked around for five or six days, but come Friday night, something got the better of me. One of them below-the-belt hankerings.

"In the yard, outside her window, I tripped over a wire. The moon was out that night, but I hadn't seen that wire till I hit it. Looked like it'd been strung between two old pecan trees about a foot off the ground. It crossed my mind to wonder how she'd explained the need for that wire to her momma and her daddy, and I can't say I wasn't a little spooked. Her daddy had a piss-awful temper and was a damn good shot, but you know how it is at a time like that. Knowing what I was doing might cost me my life just made me want to do it even more.

"So I said hey to Lester—he'd come out from under the house, and he never acted like they'd turned him against me. I went over to the window. It was down but not locked. It slid right up when I pushed it.

"She was doing something she hadn't done for me—that's all I aim to provide in the way of description, except to say that the army guy was standing about a foot or two from the window, and in the moonlight I could see the son of a bitch had a gorilla tattooed on one hip.

"He wasn't in no shape to notice that the window had been raised, and if she noticed she never let on. It wasn't nothing the two of us discussed at a later date." He began to laugh then, but the laughing soon turned to something else. A glaze appeared on his cheek. "Man, I hurt for so long. All the way through my twenties I wasn't no more useful than an empty cotton sack. I just hung around."

"That's about how I feel now," she said. "As useful as an empty cotton sack."

"Ain't no reason for you to feel that way. You're not that much older than I was when me and her got married. Assuming somebody don't shoot you one day just for the hell of it, you got a lot of years left to live, and assuming somebody does plan to shoot you, you owe it to yourself to quit living with so little. Because once you're dead, it's pure dee over."

Off to the left Moorhead slipped by, dim lights clustered in the dark. There had once been a traffic light here, where the road to Moorhead intersected 82, but so many people had died running the light that the highway department finally took it down. It was as if somebody had decided that not only was there nothing nearby worth dying for, there wasn't even anything worth stopping for.

Beer's hand was still lying on the back of the seat. Once or twice he'd drummed his fingers on the vinyl.

"Beer?" she said. "Mind if I ask you something?"

"Go ahead."

"Lately you've been sending me funny signals. Are you wanting things to change between you and me? Is that what you're getting at?"

"I been thinking about it," he said. "But hell, I must be fifteen or sixteen years older than you. If you didn't have no better sense than to get interested in me, I'd up and die on you."

When he said that, she knew what it was that had drawn them together, why it was they got along so well. They'd both been left with precious little. In his case, a few pictures that he probably kept under lock and key and almost never looked at because he couldn't bear to, a smoldering anger for his maker, a bunch of recollections that he clung to: his wife on her knees before a man who had a gorilla tattooed on his ass, his wife on her knees before him, his wife on the couch, dead and cold, her eyes wide open, a glass of orange juice standing by her hand. The way his palm had started sweating on the receiver when they told him someone had shot his daughter, Judy. How Judy had looked as a baby, how she'd looked at her high school graduation, how she must have looked when the bullet tore into her forehead. The sound dirt clods made when they struck a metal casket.

And as for her: the moans of her brother, the way Ned cried when he finally fell in on himself and went to sleep. An occasional encounter with an old man on the street, a man who used to try to make his wife watch dirty movies, who'd once poured hot coffee between her legs because, he said, she was cold as dry ice. A certain sort of sickness that crept over her when she was near a body of dirty, stinking water. The absolute impossibility of forgetting that it was her own palms that caressed her aching nipples, always her own palms, her own fingertips that probed her tender dryness.

"A young man could die on me too," she said. "Young men do die. Goddam if they don't."

Her voice must have sounded as strange to him as he did to her. He let off the accelerator. His hand rose off the back of the seat, moved toward her.

"What you getting at, Daisy? What you wanting to say?"

Ned read the oxygen level on a small pond not far from the Sunflower River. It was low. He entered the reading on his clipboard, noted the time, and switched on the aerator. He climbed in his truck, backed down off the levee and into the road, and headed toward 49 again and crossed it, and it was then that he saw the set of headlights.

Somebody was driving across a pond levee about eighty or ninety miles an hour. It was near the pond they'd just seined.

He stomped the accelerator, his tires heaved up a storm of dust and gravel, and he almost slid off the road into a ditch.

The levee ran into the road about two miles from Mack's headquarters. The racing set of headlights and the pickup truck they belonged to reached the intersection a few seconds before he did.

Mack fishtailed into the road, headed toward home, with Ned on his rear bumper. In the glare of his headlights, Ned could see that Mack was driving with one hand, holding his truck phone in the other.

When he reached the turnoff to his place, he threw the phone down and gripped the wheel with both hands and spun into his front yard. Gravel showered Ned's windshield, cracking it in several places.

Mack jumped out of his pickup, and Ned jumped out of his, and Mack ran across the yard, his big work boots barely clearing the ground, so that he looked almost as if he were on rollerskates. He held the shotgun while he ran, and a few feet away from the front door he pointed the barrel straight up and squeezed off a shot, straight up into a pecan tree.

"What the fuck?" Ned bawled.

The front door opened, and Ned saw Ellie. Her face was drained of color.

Mack pushed past her. She started to slam the door in Ned's face. He stopped the force with his palm. She let him in then and shoved the door closed and turned the deadbolt.

"Will somebody tell me what the fuck's going on?"

Mack was moving through the house, heading down the hall, the shotgun held at port arms. Ellie pressed her back to the door and hugged herself and sobbed.

"Son of a bitch!" Mack growled.

Ned crept down the hall. He found Mack in the kitchen. The light was off in there, but he could see Mack crouching at the windowsill, looking out the window into the backyard.

Something was on fire there. Orange and yellow flames burned in a ring.

"They've set the motherfucking spa on fire," Mack said.

Using the butt of the shotgun, he smashed a windowpane out. And then, as if this were a Western and he was the Duke, he started firing, his shoulder jerking from the recoil. The odor of cordite filled the air.

Every time he fired, Ellie moaned, and when Ned looked back at her in the hallway, he saw a dim figure in ghostly white. Her right hand was in her mouth, and it looked like she was biting it, like she might even mean to eat it.

When the shotgun was empty, Mack laid it down on the tiles. He rested his back against the wall and wiped sweat out of his eyes.

The fire in the spa was beginning to burn down now. The flames weren't quite as high.

"You reckon you hit anybody?" Ned said.

"Fuck, no. Because there wasn't nobody to hit. Them son of a bitches was gone before we ever got here."

Ellie was in the kitchen now, standing by the door. "Somebody threw some rocks through the bedroom window," she said. "That's what woke me up. And then I looked out and I could see a couple of folks running, and it looked like they were carrying cans."

"You see who it was?" Ned said.

"I couldn't tell. It was too dark."

"It was too dark," Mack said, "and they was too dark."

There was a phone on the wall next to the stove. Ned knew, without really knowing how or why he knew it, that it was important to pick that phone up and call the sheriff and demand that he get out here right now. A lot was riding on that phone call being made, though he didn't know exactly what. He opened the refrigerator door to give himself some light and lifted the receiver.

"What the fuck you think you're doing?" Mack said.

He started dialing.

"You trying to call the fucking sheriff?" Mack leaped up and jerked the receiver out of his hand. He hung it up. "We don't need any goddamn sheriff."

He reached into the refrigerator and took a beer out and opened it. He leaned against the counter and took several big swallows.

When he quit drinking, he looked at Ellie, who still stood near the door. She was wearing a sheer nightgown. You could see a lot through material like that.

"Go get some fucking clothes on."

She looked at Ned as if she expected him to say something, but he didn't. She turned and disappeared into the hallway.

Mack drained the rest of the beer and slammed the bottle down on the counter. Then he leaned over the sink and ran cold water on the back of his neck. He tore off about two feet of paper towel, wiped his neck, balled the paper towel up, and tossed it into the trash basket.

"They probably used coal oil on that spa," he said. "Let's go see what they've used on my catfish."

"Toxaphene, I'd say."

The flashlight beam revealed thousands of white bellies floating on the surface. A sharp, acrid odor hung in the air.

"There lays about fifty thousand dollars' worth of dead stock," Mack said. "And that's a whole lot more than I can afford to lose." He switched off the flashlight. "Yes sir, they done made fish farming a mighty unprofitable business. And you and me's fixing to give it up."

"Give it up?"

Mack jammed the flashlight into his pocket. In the darkness his face looked gray. "We gone quit seining catfish," he said. "Gone start seining black fish."

1973

That spring was the wettest on record.

Behind their house, a hundred yards or so away, on the other side of the pen where their daddy had tried to raise hogs, lay Beaver Dam Canal. Its status as a canal was open to question if by canal you meant it had a bank on either side and in the middle water that was moving, on its way someplace else. The water in Beaver Dam Canal rarely moved. Beavers did dam it up from time to time, but the real problem was that it provided drainage for farmland that lay to the north, land owned by people like the Salters and the Morellis. The drainage commission had dug ditches to convey runoff into the canal, and while those ditches were dredged regularly, the canal itself wasn't. So when its waters did move, they moved up and over the banks rather than south toward the Sunflower River.

A three-inch rain would bring the water of the canal into the backyard. A four- or five-inch rain, and the house would turn into an island. You'd hear the water lapping at the floorboards, and you'd look out the window, and waves would be rolling in from the soil bank across the road, or what had once been the road, and the tires of her momma's old Galaxy would be completely submerged. More than once Daze stood on the porch and watched snakes slithering in the water just a few feet away. Ned liked to sit in a lawn chair on the front porch, with the screen door open, and shoot them with his .22.

Her daddy had called the drainage commission. They'd said they'd see about bringing a dragline up the canal on a barge and dredging out the channel. But the Salters and the Morellis, people who mattered in a way her daddy didn't, were happy enough because the water was running off their fields fast. Her daddy was gone all the time, so he couldn't stay after the commissioners about it, and she believed he didn't much care if water surrounded the house or not. As long as they were unable to drive out, he must have figured, her momma would have to stay home. But he'd underestimated how badly her momma wanted to be out and gone. She could not part the waters or make them recede, but she was not of a mind to let them swallow her up.

The head of the drainage board was a man named Park Luttrell. Daze knew him by sight, but she'd never spoken to him. His daughter was a cheerleader at the Academy, but Daze had never spoken to her either. His son was on the football team, one of the guys who sat near Denny Gautreaux on the bench and never got to play—Denny would have said never had to play—until IA was ahead by at least thirty points.

The day her momma phoned Park Luttrell, the water was all the way up to the front steps. Rain was still falling, had been falling off and on for forty-eight hours. It was supposed to stop the next day, but toward the end of the week another front would be coming through. These were things you knew in 1973, when everybody's mind was on the weather.

Daze was sitting on the couch in the living room, flipping through an old copy of *Redbook*, when her momma walked out of her bedroom and into the hall and picked up the phone. Ned was outside in a raincoat and a pair of hipboots, slogging around in the water with a fishing pole in his hand. Last week, when the road was covered for a couple of days, he'd worn the raincoat and the hipboots and waded out to the main road and caught the bus to school.

Spring practice had started, and even though it was raining, the team was working out in the gym. Daze told him he was crazy for wading out, but he said he'd won a position and didn't aim to let a little water make him lose it.

Her momma was wearing a pair of blue jeans and a sweatshirt. The top two buttons on the jeans were undone—you could see the pink fabric of her panties. The jeans were too small now, but her momma would not admit it.

She picked up the phone and dialed a number. One of the Luttrell kids must have answered.

"Can I speak to your daddy?" she said.

Daze didn't know yet who she'd called, but the request to speak to somebody's daddy caught her attention.

"Hello, Park," her momma said. "This is Vonnie Rose."

Evidently Park Luttrell expressed surprise.

"Yeah," her momma said, "I know you told me not to, but this is a special situation."

Daze could imagine him standing in his den, which she believed would have a brightly polished floor, a big color television set, maybe even a fireplace where a small flame flickered. He would be pressing his lips to the mouthpiece, hoping his wife would not wander in from the kitchen where she stood fixing supper, hoping whichever kid had answered would not say, *Daddy, who was that woman?* as soon as he hung up.

"This doesn't have anything to do with that other stuff," her momma said. "At least, it doesn't have to."

Her momma stood there a few seconds, not saying anything, listening to whatever it was Park Luttrell said. While she listened, she bounced the phone cord up and down off the palm of her hand, like a little kid playing with a Slinky Linky.

Apparently what Park Luttrell said amused her. She grinned. First at the wall and then at Daze. And then she winked.

"I can't really wait and discuss it with you in Greenville tomorrow," she said. "The problem is I can't get to Greenville tomorrow. The Holiday Inn's outside my boundaries right now. See, that's what I'm calling you about. Everything's outside my boundaries. My car—you remember my car, don't you, Park, that green Galaxy with the ripped covers on the back seat?—it's standing out in the yard in about three feet of water. I think maybe my husband called you about this drainage problem once or twice already."

Again she listened and bounced the phone cord.

"You'll have to speak up," she said. "I can't hear you. You whispering, Park? Got you a little sore throat?"

Daze closed the magazine and got up off the couch and went over to stand by the front door. She pulled up the door curtain and peeked out. Ned was standing out there in the dusk. He no longer held the fishing pole. He stood with his back to her, looking out over the soil bank. There was water almost as far as you could see. She knew it wasn't deep, maybe two or three feet, but the wind drove waves toward him. The waves broke against his legs, licked at the folds of his raincoat, and she almost called out to him, begged him to come back before he disappeared into the murky, stinking water.

"Well, to start with," her momma said to Park Luttrell, "I want somebody to get out here tomorrow morning and get me and my kids and my car to dry land. And we'll need someplace to stay till it gets dry enough for y'all to send a dragline in here to dredge that damn canal out."

It was silent again then except for the rain drumming down on the roof. Ned was still standing in the yard with his back to Daze, and it looked to her as if he thought that by holding his ground and braving the waves, he might somehow will the water away.

"Yeah," Daze heard her momma say, "the Travel Lodge'll be just fine, long as it's either you or the drainage commission that pays for our stay.

"And Park?" her momma said. "We'll each need our own room."

The next morning Park Luttrell came himself, along with one of the men who worked on his farm. Daze heard the tractor droning and looked out the window, and there they were, Mr. Luttrell on the seat behind the wheel of a big John Deere, and the other man, who was black, standing behind him on the towbar. It had quit raining during the night, but the sky was still gray, and both of the men wore raincoats and hipboots.

The water had receded a little. It still covered the road and the yard, but you could tell, from looking at the doorstep, that it had fallen. The top two steps were uncovered.

Ned had intended to walk out again this morning, but her momma had told him not to, and for once he did as she ordered. He even dragged her old suitcase with the broken latch out to the porch, and then he helped Daze with hers. He didn't have one of his own, though he'd thrown a few clothes into the duffel bag he carried his football equipment in.

Park Luttrell pulled the tractor around in front of her momma's car and backed up and told the black man to get down and chain the car to the towbar. He himself did not dismount, just sat there in his yellow raincoat, gripping the steering wheel so tightly his knuckles blanched, while the black man got down on his knees in the cold water, soaking himself, and attached the chain.

Her momma walked out onto the porch and smiled and said, "Why, good morning, Park."

All Park Luttrell did was grunt. He grunted at Daze too, but he had a few words for Ned. "Coach Causey told the Lions Club you've been busting butt," he said. "You got a future, boy. I'll tell anybody that."

Riding out, she sat up front with her momma. Ned sat in the back. Park Luttrell had told her momma not to crank the car, just leave it in neutral so the wheels would roll, and she'd damn well better keep her window closed unless she wanted the car to fill up with muddy water.

A brisk wind swept in across the soil bank, sending small waves rippling over the surface, and a few of them broke over the hood and splashed onto the windshield. You could feel the water sloshing under the floorboards.

"This is probably the last time we'll get flooded," her momma said.

"Why's that?" Ned said. "You think it's never gone rain again?"

"It'll rain," her momma said. "But I think it's safe to say Park's finally understood the importance of keeping things dredged."

To Daze's amazement, her momma pulled a can of beer from her purse and opened it and took a sip. The black man riding on the towbar saw her do it. He leaned over and said something to Park Luttrell. Park turned around and glanced at them. Her momma raised the beer as if she were toasting him. He shook his head in disgust.

"When your daddy bought the place," her momma said, "the Caldwells claimed they were selling it so cheap because that older boy of theirs had shot the other one in the living room when they were messing around with a gun. That may have been part of the reason they sold it, but the water had a lot more to do with it. The place was already starting to flood even then."

"Yeah?" Ned said.

"That's right."

"So how come you let him buy it?"

His tone was accusatory. For a long time now it had seemed to Daze as if he blamed all their daddy's mistakes on their momma.

"Back then," her momma said, her eyes on the rearview mirror, where she must have seen Ned, "I didn't give a shit. Back then he wasn't always gone. I didn't care if I got stuck at home for three or four days with my husband and my daughter and my son. I thought a big rain might be a lot of fun."

"Some fun," Ned said.

"Well, it could be," her momma said. "You got a thing or two to learn about fun, son. Busting heads ain't the only pleasure life offers."

Park Luttrell pulled them all the way out to the main road. Then the black man got down and unhitched the chain, and this time Park Luttrell got down too. He walked over to the car.

Her momma rolled down her window. Park Luttrell squatted down by the side of the car.

"Y'all registered at the Travel Lodge," he said.

One of his front teeth was chipped, Daze noticed, and all of them were stained. He had heavy black eyebrows, and a little piece of toilet paper was stuck to his throat where he must have cut himself shaving. She wondered how old he was. Forty-five, she would have guessed. Maybe a little bit older.

She wondered too when and where her momma had done whatever it was she'd done with him. She wondered if her momma had liked it. It disturbed her to think that she had, but not nearly as much as it disturbed her to think that she hadn't.

"Y'all got three rooms," he said. "Two on top and one on the bottom. Best I could do. There's two or three construction crews holed up at the motel waiting out the rain."

"Who's picking up the tab?" her momma said.

"You're not. So don't worry about who is."

"Okay," she said, "I won't worry. But when you aim to start dredging the canal?"

"Soon as the water gets low enough for us to get a dragline in there."

"That's good. Because if we get back out here three or four days from now," her momma said, "and it starts to raining and we get flooded again, you'll have to come out here and tow us a second time."

Park Luttrell looked past her at Daze, then cut his gaze into the back seat, where Ned sat. Ned flushed and turned his face to the opposite window.

Once more Park Luttrell shook his head. "Put Ned and that girl of yours in the second-floor rooms," he said.

"How come?"

"Them construction workers liable to start raising hell and carousing," he said, "and you wouldn't want that going on right above your kids' heads. Sure to God you wouldn't want it. Not even you."

The Travel Lodge stood just across 82 from the Academy. The motel was shaped like an L, with rooms on two floors, front and back. Her momma, for reasons of her own, had taken Park Luttrell's advice and assigned her and Ned the second-floor rooms.

Daze's had a double bed and a dresser with a color TV on top of it and a small table that stood by the window with two chairs nearby. A framed reproduction hung on one wall. Blue waves crashed against rocks along a rugged coast, breaking up into white spray and froth. California, she felt sure, though she didn't know why she thought that.

From her window you could see the parking lot, which was almost empty that first afternoon when she got back from school. The sky had cleared, the sun was out, and either the construction crews had gone to work or else they were out doing whatever a construction crew could do in Indianola when there was no business to attend to. It crossed her mind that her momma might be involved. Her car was nowhere to be seen, and she wasn't due for work at the 7-Eleven until evening.

Daze dropped her books on the bed and walked into the bathroom. She pulled off her sweater and bra and her skirt, and then she opened her suitcase and took out an old blue sweatshirt and her blue jeans and put them on. She turned on the TV and lay down on the bed, intending to watch *I Love Lucy*, but in just a few minutes she'd fallen asleep.

It was a sound that woke her—sounds always did. Someone was knocking at the door, knocking tentatively, little taps that kept getting weaker.

She got up off the bed and opened the door, and there stood Denny Gautreaux.

"Hi," he said.

His fist was raised to knock again, and he held it there in front of his face for several seconds. He looked like a department-store mannequin.

"Hi," she said. "How'd you know I was here?"

He unclenched his hand and stuck it in his pocket.

"I heard Ned telling a couple of guys in the locker room that you all were staying at the motel for a few days."

She looked at her watch. It was a quarter till four.

"How come you're not at practice?"

"Because I'm here."

"Causey'll crawl your ass."

"Nobody misses me. I'm just cannon fodder."

"You've got a tendency to put yourself down. Did you know that?"

"I don't give a shit about football. Now, if I thought I lacked good looks, had bad taste, and needed to start applying algicide to my teeth, I'd be worried."

"But that's not the case," she said.

"That's not the case," he said, but his voice broke when he said it, as if he harbored strong doubts.

It was not the case. He was an inch or so taller than Ned and far too slim, she thought, to be a lineman. His eyes were big and round and brown, and his hair had grown out in the last couple of months so that now it lapped over his collar. He never made anything other than straight A's, and he always carried books under his arm, books that were not assigned in class. He was a Civil War buff. Someday, he'd told her, he aimed to write a book himself.

"Well," he said, glancing at his watch.

"Well?"

"Well, I've got my daddy's car."

"I don't have anything of my momma's," she said. "Just in case you're thinking I do."

His cheeks began to turn red. It was amazing to her that you could say a few words, in a certain tone of voice, and cause somebody to change colors.

"I'm not thinking that," he said. "I wouldn't think that about you."

"Good. At least we've got that settled. What about your daddy's car?"

"I've got it. It's out there."

He gestured at the parking lot.

She saw it down below. He'd driven it to school before, so it was easy to recognize now. It was a big convertible, brand new, the hood so brightly polished you could see yourself reflected on the surface. The top was down now.

"What kind of car's that?"

"A Mercedes," he said. "280 SE. The kind of car only an asshole would own."

"Are assholes the only ones who drive them?"

"Generally speaking. But every now and then you'll see a sensitive, generous type at the wheel."

They were outside now, on the landing, moving as if by mutual consent toward the stairs.

"You're coming down?" he said. "You're coming with me to go for a ride?"

"No," she said. "I'm going down there because we're up high, and heights make me dizzy. Shut up, Denny. Don't talk."

She liked the way the seat felt. It was covered with soft black leather, and there was so much room you felt like you were sitting on a big, comfortable couch. There were lots of gauges on the dashboard, and the trim was polished hardwood, and something—

the floor mats, maybe, or some sort of hidden fragrance stick—gave off the odor of wild cherries. When Denny cranked up, the engine roared.

He backed out and pulled into the highway and headed toward the stoplight at the intersection of 49 and 82. They crept along at about twenty miles an hour, past the truckstop and the John Deere dealer.

"What do you want to do?" he said. "I mean, it's really up to you."

"Aren't these cars supposed to go fast?"

"They can if you want 'em to."

"I think I want it to. Don't you?"

He didn't answer her question. But as soon as the light changed and they passed under it, he stepped on the accelerator. The car leaped forward.

At first he looked surprised. Then he seemed to accept the idea that he was driving hard. His mouth set in a determined line, and he scooted around an old GMC pickup, and then he shot past a big semi. Daze almost choked on diesel fumes.

They roared by the city limit sign, her hair streaming.

"How fast you think we could make Moorhead?" Denny hollered.

"There's no reason to go there," she yelled.

"Got to go somewhere. Can't stay still."

They made it in under five minutes, and they made it without running into or over a single soul or attracting the attention of a single potbellied highway patrolman or deputy sheriff. They made it with faces chapped red by the cool rushing air, their minds reeling with images of the flooded fields they'd flown by, the eighteen-wheelers they'd left spitting in their slipstream.

That first afternoon they drove around on back roads near Moorhead, passing the County Farm four or five times. It was too wet for the convicts to work. They lounged around on benches outside their barracks, all of them wearing zebra stripes, and every time the Mercedes passed, they'd all look up, shade their eyes, and then a few of them would look at one another and shake their heads. She supposed they were agreeing that it must be nice to be the other half, the ones who were out and free and driving fast, nothing save the wind in their faces. And they were right, it was nice, even if you knew it couldn't last.

In her own way, she believed, she was a convict too, and so was Denny Gautreaux. They'd both been convicted at birth. When people looked at her, they saw the daughter of a certain sort of woman, and they knew without doubt that the blood in her veins and her momma's was the same. They expected her to behave a certain way, and whether she did or did not, they would always think she had. When people saw Denny, they saw the son of a certain sort of daddy, and they believed what flowed through his veins was green, that there was no difference whatsoever between him and his daddy's money.

"You like beer?" Denny said. "Want me to go in somewhere and try to buy some?"

"What makes you think I want beer?"

"I didn't say I thought you did. I just asked."

"You wouldn't stand a chance. Nobody'd sell it to you."

"Probably not. But I'd try if you wanted me to."

"I don't want you to."

"What about a burger? You hungry?"

"I'll never let you buy me anything," she said.

"So what can I do?"

"I don't know. But whatever you do, you'll have to do it without money."

He slowed down then and pulled off onto the side of the road. They were near somebody's field. It was still laid out in last year's rows. In the middles, water lay six inches deep, the sunlight on its surface a burnt-orange sheen.

"I like your hair," he said. "Your hair's great."

"It's just brown hair. What's special about it?"

"It's on your head."

"What's special about my head?"

"What do you want me to say?"

"Jesus, Denny," she said. "I don't want you to say anything. I want you not to ever say anything, ever again, for at least the next five minutes or maybe even the next ten."

Denny Gautreaux closed his eyes, and for a moment she believed his lips would actually move, that she would see him mouth the words *Dear God, please.*

Instead it was his arm that moved, the arm nearest her. It moved around her shoulders, and when it was locked securely there, it pulled her gently.

The gearstick grazed her belly, and she would never know if it was that contact or something else which made her shiver. Her teeth and Denny Gautreaux's collided.

"Ouch," she said. "Goddamn."

Denny pressed his lips against hers, pressed his chest against hers, engaging in contact with the kind of fierce determination that eluded him on the football field. He smelled of Right Guard and cold air. His fingernails dug into her back. His tongue probed her mouth, and her tongue probed back.

"What if Ned comes?"

He stood by the window in his underwear, peeping through a slit in the curtains. It was dark now, and the motel room was cold, and he was hugging himself. His arms were much thicker than she would have guessed.

She was sitting on the side of the bed. She'd removed the last of her clothes. She could tell he knew it but was putting off the moment when he'd have to turn around and acknowledge it.

She got up and walked over to stand beside him. She looped an arm around his waist. This time he was the one who shivered.

"He won't come," she said.

Light from the neon sign in the parking lot turned his face pale green.

"How do you know?"

"He's not worried about what I might be doing. He's worried about what Momma might be up to."

"What might she be up to?"

She wrapped both arms around him now and, using all her strength, turned him away from the window. When he felt her nipples against his hairless chest, his eyes rolled toward the ceiling, and then he did mouth the words *Dear God, please*. His arms dangled at his sides, for the moment utterly useless.

"My momma," she whispered, "might be up to damn near anything."

"I can make any surface look new," his daddy was fond of saying. "All it is is a question of the right kind of paint, the right number of coats. Don't matter much what used to be. What is can be made to look shiny."

His daddy said all that and more the afternoon he showed up at the Academy to watch spring practice. It was two or three weeks after Ned and Daze and their momma stayed at the Travel Lodge. It had quit raining, then started back, but this time the roads didn't flood because Park Luttrell had floated not one but three draglines down Beaver Dam Canal, dredging out the channel and in the process, Ned figured, clearing his own life of a certain amount of dirt and debris.

Now the skies were clear too, and spring practice was in its last days, and he was starting both ways, playing left tackle on defense and right guard on offense, next to Mack, who'd moved up to first-team too.

They were practicing goal-line offense when Ned noticed his daddy standing on the sidelines, wearing clean khaki pants and a white windbreaker that Ned had never seen him in before. He had on a pair of tennis shoes that looked new too. A quiver ran through

Ned's stomach as he remembered that evening last fall when his daddy had started the fight in the bleachers.

He could never think of that night without feeling sick. That night had been followed by the next night, and the next night had changed everything forever. He didn't know exactly how it had changed things, but he knew it had, knew he would never be the same again, and Mack wouldn't, or Rick. The three of them, especially him and Mack, hung around together a lot now, never mentioning that night, though it was always in Ned's mind and he believed it was always in their minds too. He caught them staring at him a lot, in the lunchroom or in the corridors at school, and when his eyes met theirs they'd look away. He stared at them too, watched them off and on throughout the day. Sometimes he phoned their houses, and if one of them answered he hung up. The same thing happened to him: the phone would ring, he'd answer, the line would go dead. His momma always believed the calls had been for her, and maybe some of them had. Her life and his were full of dark corners, unlit angles where only sounds mattered: the rapid, stabbing breaths he knew men drew from her, the dull thud of thick glass on bone.

"Pick it up, pick it up, pick it up."

They broke the huddle and lined up. The play the quarterback had called was 32 Blast. Ned and the center would double-team Denny Gautreaux, who was impersonating a noseguard, Mack would kick out the defensive tackle, and the fullback would blast the linebacker, leading the tailback through the hole.

On the second hut, Ned exploded off the line. Denny had learned that the safest thing to do playing noseguard was to lie down as soon as the ball was snapped, so Ned and the center just fell on him, and the tailback waltzed through the hole, crossing the goal line standing up.

"All right, Neddy," he heard his daddy holler. "That's the way to roll 'em up."

They ran another five or ten minutes' worth of plays, then Causey put them through their windsprints and sent them to the showers.

Ned's daddy was waiting for him on the sideline.

"Hey," Ned said. "I didn't know you were home."

"Well," his daddy said, "I wasn't supposed to be. We had a little disagreement on that job down in Vicksburg, so I'm back for a day or so. I've got another one starting Wednesday."

"Where?"

"Crosset, Arkansas."

"The town with that stinking paper mill in it?"

His daddy laughed. "Half the towns in Arkansas have got stinking paper mills in 'em," he said. "It's a stinking state."

Causey was walking off the field by himself, a clipboard in his hand. He glanced their way. "Hey," he said. For a moment Ned was afraid he wouldn't say anything else, wouldn't crack a joke or make a comment about the weather like he would have with one of the other dads.

But Causey reached out and shook hands with his daddy. "If we had ten more like Ned," he said, "we could play in the SEC."

In that instant Ned would have tackled a two-row picker if Causey had told him to, and he knew from looking at his daddy's face that his daddy would have too.

Causey chatted another minute or two, then said good-bye and walked on toward the gym. They watched him disappear into the locker room.

"I wouldn't have minded playing for him," Ned's daddy said. "He's tough."

"Good coaches always are."

He jammed his hands into the pockets of his windbreaker.

"Son," he said, "I've been wanting to talk to you. What say you and me grab some beer and ride around?"

They rode with the windows open, even though the day had turned chilly. The fields had finally dried out enough for the farmers to start planting, but they were doing it late, and a lot of them had decided to turn cotton acreage into soybeans. The rigs were in the fields now, throwing up little clouds of dust. Some of them would probably run all night.

Ned's daddy kept a Styrofoam ice chest in the pickup truck. It was filled now with ice and Budweiser. One can was clamped between his legs.

"You can have farming," he said while he drove. "You can take it and throw it in the river. There's too much about farming that's beyond a man's control."

He lifted his beer can and sipped from it and smacked his lips and said, "Lordy, that's good." He stood the can back between his thighs. "Painting," he said. "You got a little more control over that."

"You can't paint a house when it's raining, though. Not the outside."

"Naw, you can't paint the outside. But you can paint the inside."

"What if you already painted the inside?"

"You go paint the inside of another house—hell, you paint the inside of two more houses, or three or four—and then when it quits raining, you go back to that first house and you paint the outside. What I'm saying is that in my current line of work, there's places you can go where the elements can't find you. That's the point I'm trying to get across."

Ned sipped from his own beer and looked out the window at the fields that had recently been flooded. All spring he'd been aware of the weather in a way he never had before. A big part of it had been the flooded roads and his fear of missing practice, of losing the starting job he'd won. But that wasn't the whole story. The rest of the story was that he'd been feeling like there was some force out there— something big and overpowering, something *elemental*, if that was the way you wanted to put it—that had the potential to come and sweep everything and everybody away. Him and his daddy and his momma and Daze, anything or anybody that got in its way. A few days of spring sunshine hadn't been able to chase away that feeling.

"Work's important," his daddy said. "There's some things you can do something about and some things you can't. But if you can find a job you like, chances are you'll do it well."

"I guess I'd like to play football for a living," Ned said.

"You and about ten million other boys. Trouble is, you weigh about one-eighty, Neddy, and that's just big enough to be a water boy in the NFL. You're not even big enough to play college ball, son—that's just one of those limitations you're gone have to live with. It don't mean you can't enjoy playing the game now."

They were driving north on 49. They passed through Sunflower, and a mile or so later his daddy turned off onto a gravel road that ran east. When Ned realized what road it was, he felt as if he'd been poked in the chest with a cattle prod. He put his hand over his heart. For a second he couldn't breathe.

"What's the matter?" his daddy said.

"Nothing."

"Heart skip a beat?"

"I guess so."

"That used to happen to me after running a bunch of wind-sprints," his daddy said. "I wouldn't worry about it. The kind of exercise you're getting's good for the heart. It's just a muscle, and working it hard strengthens it."

He clapped Ned on the leg. "How's that beer doing?" he said. "Beer's good for the heart too. Beer may be the best heart medicine in the whole damn world."

The gas pump was gone now—Johnson grass had grown up around the slab where it had stood. Part of the porch had caved in, and the windows were boarded up, and all the soft-drink signs had been removed. A piece of rusty tin siding hung off one edge of the roof, like a stiff wind had torn it loose and made it buckle.

His daddy paid the building no mind. "How you getting along with your momma?" he said.

"All right, I guess."

"Wish I could say the same," his daddy said. He reached into the cooler and pulled out another beer. "I can't, though."

This was not a conversation Ned wanted to have, but avoiding it would have been a betrayal. And his daddy, he believed, had been betrayed too many times already.

"What's wrong?" he said.

"Beats me," his daddy said. "Thought maybe you might know."

"Why would I know?"

"You're around home more than I am. Thought maybe you might know what it is that's going on."

"There's not much going on now that wasn't going on before," Ned said. "May even be less of it now."

That was when his daddy said it. Before he said it he sighed and looked out the window, then back at Ned. "I can make any surface look new," he said. "All it is is a question of the right kind of paint, the right number of coats. What was don't matter. What is can be made to look new. That old store we just passed? I could make that thing look like it was built yesterday, and you'd believe it was till you stepped on the floor or leaned against the wall, and then the whole thing might damn well fall in. I'm a painter, not a carpenter. I can put a bright face on things, but fixing structural damage is just way beyond me. Truth is, it don't even interest me."

It was a big statement for his daddy to make, and for a minute or two he seemed embarrassed. Ned believed no more would be said, and the relief he felt was mixed with something that might have been sadness. He'd come close, he felt, to the core of his daddy, closer than he'd probably ever come again.

But his daddy was not content to let it stop there. Later on it seemed to Ned like his daddy had known it was time to sum himself up, to put whatever he was into words.

"Staying on the road," he said. "That's how I handle it. When you think about it, it makes sense. Every few days a different place.

They're like layers. You put Lake Village on today, this time next week you put on Yazoo City, put it on over Lake Village, I mean. Two or three days later you put on Biloxi or Pass Christian. It's not that different from what your momma does. If you think about it long and hard."

"I think about it," Ned said. "Long and hard. You bet I do."

He knew his daddy was looking at him now across the truck seat, but he didn't want their eyes to meet.

"You blame me?" his daddy said. "For working away from home? You think things would be different if I didn't stay gone?"

"I don't know. Yeah, I guess they'd be different. But I don't know that they'd be better."

"If I stayed at home," his daddy said, "one of us would end up killing the other one. That's how it is between me and her."

He shook his head.

"Yes sir," he said. "One of us would sure enough wind up dead."

They crossed a plank bridge over a drainage ditch. The ditch was still swollen with muddy, swirling water. Tin cans bobbed along toward the Sunflower River, and various other forms of refuse were headed there too: the sideplank off an old cotton trailer, a bicycle tire, some coiled-up baling wire, the body of a possum. A moccasin slithered near the surface.

There were different kinds of dead—you could be dead while your heart was still beating. Dying didn't always happen at a specific moment in time. You could die over years or decades, and some people were dead long before they were born.

Ned wanted to say those things to his daddy, but something—he'd never know what—kept him from doing it. His daddy said no more to him either except to make a few idle comments about the weather and spring practice and his need for some new truck tires. They drank more beer, and when the ice chest was empty, they went on home.

That night, as he lay in bed, he heard his daddy's footsteps in the hallway.

"Vonnie?" his daddy said.

Ned heard him knock on the bathroom door. In his mind he could see him out there. He'd be standing close to the door, his forehead pressed against the wood. His eyes would be closed.

"Vonnie? Hey, Vonnie, are you in there? Open up."

His daddy knocked again. But his momma never answered.

It happened sometime late on a Friday night, probably while she and Denny were out in the cotton patch, their bodies glued together in the back seat of the Mercedes. There was enough room back there to do whatever needed doing, even if what needed doing tended toward the gymnastic.

"I'm a better athlete than Causey'll ever know," Denny liked to say.

She never disagreed with that assessment. Denny was athletic in the back seat, his biceps rippling while he pumped up and down, his thighs turning into steel cables, the band of muscle across his back growing taut just before he came. He growled like he was making a tackle.

Then, having died the small death, he reposed on top of her, his dark hair damp from all his sweating effort, and while she ran her palms over his shoulders and he stroked her own damp hair, they talked. He told her about the books he'd read and the ones he hoped to write, about what he'd seen when he went to Europe a few years ago with his momma and daddy, what he'd seen in places like Mexico and the Bahamas.

"You can learn a lot," he said, "by traveling. Big things and lit-tle ones too. I never liked coffee until we went to France, but I loved it there. I'd go to these cafes in Paris by myself and sit there and drink two or three of these little tiny cups."

"How old were you?"

"Thirteen."

"And they let you go out in Paris by yourself?"

"Daddy *made* me go out by myself. He was back at the hotel trying to get Momma to hang upside down from the light fixtures so he could fuck her while he stared out the window at the Eiffel Tower. He was really into atmospheric sex."

For an instant the word *atmospheric* made her imagine Mr. Gautreaux and Mrs. Gautreaux as skydivers. Mrs. Gautreaux fell spread-eagled. Mr. Gautreaux clung to her back, pumping up and down, as gravity worked its magic.

"So tell me," she said, "what's so special about French coffee."

"It's just got a lot better taste than Folger's. I don't know—I can't quite describe it. You'd have to taste it to know what I mean."

"I'll never taste it."

"You might. You and I might go there."

"When?"

He grinned. "Soon as we're eighteen."

"I've never been anywhere," she said. "Memphis is as far as I've ever gotten."

"Every place is different, but every place is the same, because you carry yourself with you wherever you go."

"I hate to hear that."

"Why?"

"I was hoping I could go someplace and leave myself behind."

"Your self is just fine."

"Maybe it's my baggage I ought to leave behind," she said.

"Baggage should always be left behind. Travel fast and travel light."

That seemed like a wildly smart thing for somebody Denny's age to say, and she told him so. And so he said it at every opportunity. Baggage should always be left behind. Travel fast and travel light.

He'd said it, she believed, that Friday night, but with a worried edge to his voice that she hadn't heard lately. Just as he said it, another flash of lightning lit the sky. Thunder pealed behind it, rattling the doors on the Mercedes. You couldn't see out the windshield at all. Rain beat down on the roof like bullets, and sudden gusts of wind rocked the heavy car.

"What's the matter?" she said. "You're not scared of a little storm?"

"Don't you know where we are?"

"We're in the cotton patch. We've been here before."

He felt around on the floor for his jeans and began to pull them on. "We're sitting in about three inches of mud," he said. "In Rick Salter's daddy's field. We're about a mile down the turnrow from the road. You see what I'm driving at?"

"We might have trouble getting out?"

"You're about the smartest sexy girl I know."

She pulled on her clothes, and both of them climbed into the front seat.

"If we do get out of here," he said, "I'm gonna have to take this thing to the Robo-Wash and get it cleaned up quick. My daddy'd shit in his pants if he saw it like it's going to look in a few minutes."

He cranked the car up and turned on the lights.

"Actually," he said, "come to think of it, he probably wouldn't shit in *his* pants. He'd make me take mine off, and then he'd shit in them. That's the kind of guy my daddy is. He's always looking for a receptacle to dump a little bit of himself into."

"Your daddy and my momma might get along just fine," she said, and she'd no sooner said it than she remembered the way her momma had made his daddy blush when Mr. Gautreaux and Mr. Bell came to the house on the Red and Gray business. She began to wonder whether or not, at some point in time, they hadn't gotten along just fine.

Denny shut his eyes, and his lips moved a few times, and then he opened his eyes and pressed the accelerator. The tires spun, the engine whined, and the car began to move, sideways at first and then straight ahead.

The wind hurled sheets of water over the windshield. Denny had the wipers going as fast as they could, but still you couldn't see much, even with the high beams on. The car slewed to one side again, but Denny turned the wheel and fought to hold it steady.

"It's like being in a motorboat," he said. "The same damn sensation."

"I've never been in a motorboat. Not a real one anyway. I've been in one of those kind that you rent to fish in, but not the ones folks use for skiing."

"We've got one," Denny said, gritting his teeth. "If we get out of this cotton patch tonight alive, we'll go skiing. It'll be warm enough before too long."

They got out of the cotton patch alive, and once they reached the road, Denny turned the radio on. The announcer on WNLA said a tornado warning was in effect for all the counties in eastern Arkansas and the Mississippi Delta. Just to make sure everybody listening knew whether or not they were affected, he read the counties off one by one.

"Ever seen a tornado?" Denny asked her.

"No, and I don't want to."

"They can do a lot of damage."

He was squinting, trying to see through the downpour. A car was coming toward them. Water cascaded over the windshield, distorting the other car's headlights, making them flicker and fade, flicker and fade.

"A tornado can pick up what's here and set it down over there," he said. "It can turn anything into something it never was before. I'm talking about an elemental force."

"Like sex," she said.

"Like sex."

They met the other car. Its tires heaved gallons of rainwater over the hood and windshield. For an instant you couldn't see a thing.

"Like fire," she said.

"Like fire." He was squeezing the steering wheel tightly with both hands. "And water."

She agreed that without water you couldn't be anything. Without water you'd be nothing at all.

He let her out at the mailbox. The rain had stopped, but lightning was still flashing off in the west, and the wind was still blowing. Several small branches had fallen off the pecan trees. A fairly large one lay on the roof of Ned's truck. She was surprised that he was home. Normally he didn't come in on Friday nights until two or three o'clock. It was just a few minutes after midnight.

"Bye," Denny said.

"Bye, hon."

"See you tomorrow?"

"What time?"

"Six-thirty?"

"Six-thirty."

"Pick you up?"

"Pick me up."

"Turn you into something you never were before?"

"You've already done that," she said.

"No, you've done that to me. You know what a timid twit I used to be."

"Let's just say," she said, "that we've done it to one another."

"All right," he said. "Let's say that."

She started to shut the door, but he leaned over and stopped it with his hand.

"Hey," he said. "You're great. You're like nobody else. You know that?"

She turned and glanced at the house. The lights were on in the living room. She imagined Ned crouching behind the curtains, watching her as she stood there. She imagined that even over the wind, over the noise of branches raking the roof and the distant rumble of thunder, he would hear each and every word she said to

Denny Gautreaux. She imagined that as he listened, his fingertips would dig into the windowsill, and he would hold his breath, would hold it if need be until his lungs burst. He'd be listening for words and phrases, tones and inflections.

Did she sound like their momma or not?

He was not crouching at the curtains. He was standing in the kitchen, standing right beside the kitchen table. There was a bottle of Old Crow on the table, and the cap was off, and he was drinking whiskey out of a water glass. It was her daddy's whiskey. It always stayed on a shelf in the pantry, and while her daddy never would have gotten onto Ned for drinking his beer, she knew he'd be pissed if he came home and found his whiskey gone.

"Hey," she said.

His eyes were red. "You been letting Gautreaux feel around on you?" he asked her.

Right then she almost told him. She almost said, *He's been doing a whole lot more than feeling me, he's taken everything I've got to give.* She almost said, *I'm like Momma. You can be dead if you want to, but I aim to live.*

"What I do's none of your business," she told him. "And what you do's none of mine. But I'll tell you one thing. You better pour some water in that bottle of Old Crow. Because when Daddy gets home and finds his whiskey gone, he's liable to jump your ass. That whiskey's the one thing he holds dear."

Ned picked up the bottle and sloshed some more whiskey into his glass. He lifted the glass and sipped from it, and then he set it back down.

"Daddy ain't coming home," he said. "Daddy's across the river in Arkansas dead."

The casket was the cheapest kind they'd been able to find. It looked like it was fashioned out of the same material egg cartons were made from. It had cost five hundred fifty dollars at Clarkson's Funeral Home. The space at the cemetery had cost another three hundred and would have cost more except that his momma had said she didn't want to pay for a double plot.

"When I'm dead," she'd told Herb Clarkson, "my body won't do me much good, so I don't care what happens to it. They can cremate it or they can just pitch it in the cotton patch and plow it under."

Mr. Clarkson might have believed her, but Ned didn't, not for one minute. Having her body taken care of had always been her primary concern, and her being dead would not change that. She'd want to make sure her body was treated right after whatever spirit was in it had gone wherever that kind of spirit went. She just believed that with his daddy dead she'd find somebody else to take care of her body, somebody that she'd rather be buried next to.

There were two different chapels in the funeral home, and Herb Clarkson had instinctively assigned them the smaller one. His daddy's funeral was the first of the day. It had been scheduled for nine A.M. The second funeral was set for eleven. The mayor's mother had died, at the age of eighty-one, and as Ned sat in the front pew in the smallest chapel, next to Daze and his momma, waiting for somebody, anybody, to appear, he could hear people out in the hallway already filing into the other chapel to pay their respects to somebody they believed had earned respect. He didn't know or care if his daddy had earned it—probably he hadn't—but he closed his eyes and prayed that somebody would show up and give it, even if they gave it out of charity.

Finally Beer Smith walked in, along with his wife, and a few seconds later Coach Causey led the entire football team in, all of them dressed up in suits and ties. They sat down at the rear of the chapel. The preacher, who had been glancing off and on at his watch and looking worried, nodded at the woman who sat behind the organ, and she began to play "Softly and Tenderly Jesus Is Calling." She played it through twice, and then the preacher stood up with his Bible in his hand and walked over to the podium.

The preacher was an old man. He was completely bald, and it looked as if he'd recently suffered a sunburn: skin was peeling off his head in several places. Ned didn't know his name, didn't know where his momma or Herb Clarkson or whoever it was that had secured his services had found him. He wasn't the preacher who'd been out at Fairview Baptist four or five years ago, when his daddy stopped drinking for a short while and his momma stopped fooling around for an even shorter while and they all went to church and tried hard to behave.

It immediately became clear that just as Ned did not know the preacher, the preacher had never known his daddy. He stood behind the podium gazing down at the casket, on which three or four wreaths had been laid. "Willie Rose lies here," he said, "and yet he doesn't."

Billy, Ned wanted to bawl. *His goddamn name was Billy.*

"I say that Willie Rose does not lie here because Willie Rose does not lie here."

Ned heard a snicker from the back of the chapel and Coach Causey hissing, *Shut up.*

"Willie Rose does not lie here because—as it says in an old hymn that's true, so true—to Canaan land he's on his way, where the soul never dies. Where his darkest nights will turn to day and the soul of man never dies.

"Brothers and sisters," the preacher said, "let's pray."

While the preacher prayed, Ned looked at his momma. She had worn a purple dress to the funeral, the darkest thing she had. She sat there beside him with her eyes shut tight and her lips moving like she was praying too. And maybe, for all he knew, she was. Maybe she was even praying for the soul of his daddy, praying, maybe, that wherever he was now he'd have an easier time than he'd had down here. Praying, maybe, that this time around he'd find someplace where he could rest, where he'd want to stay, someplace where things would be peaceful.

But knowing her, Ned figured she was probably praying that somebody would happen by on the sidewalk outside and notice how good she looked in that purple dress. Praying that after whatever interval such a person would consider decent—two weeks or a month or maybe just a few days—that person would call her up and ask her if she felt like going to Greenville for a drink. And she'd say, *Well, you know my husband just died, so I'll have to think about it,* and then for two or three seconds she would.

Her purse was resting on the pew between them. While the preacher droned on, Ned reached inside the purse. Her checkbook was in there, and the checkbook always had a pen in it. He pulled the pen out and tore off a deposit slip. His momma opened her eyes.

"What?" she whispered.

The checks had her name and his daddy's printed on them. Ned uncapped the pen and circled the name *Billy,* and as the preacher progressed toward *amen* and his momma reached out to grab his hand, he rose from his pew and stepped up to the podium and laid the deposit slip next to the open Bible.

The preacher opened his eyes as Ned laid the slip there, but he never missed a beat in his prayer. And when he'd finished, he looked long and hard at the slip, and then he pulled a pair of glasses out of his coat pocket and put them on and looked at the slip again. And then finally he made of it what he would, probably the only thing he could.

"Those of you who would like to make donations to the family of the deceased," he said, "may deposit money directly to their account at the Bank of Indianola. The number is 33-123-3. I'm sure they'd appreciate whatever you can give."

The team didn't attend the graveside service, but Coach Causey did, and so did Beer Smith and his wife. Otherwise the only folks present were three or four men who worked for Herb Clarkson and were acting as pallbearers and one man that nobody knew. He showed up at the cemetery in a red truck and stood outside the canopy that had been erected above the grave. He didn't have on a suit, just a pair of gray dress pants and a dark gray shirt, and he needed a shave. He was about fifty, Ned would have guessed, and he couldn't figure out what the man was doing there until after the service was over and Ned walked past him and saw the paint flecks beneath his nails.

The man ignored Ned's momma and Daze, but he offered Ned his hand. "I worked with your daddy," he said. "Me and him must have laid on about a million layers of paint in the last few years. He was always talking about you. He said you might not know how proud he was of you, what with him being gone and maybe not being real good at saying how he felt. So I'm here to tell you for him."

He cast one long, unpleasant look then at Ned's momma and walked off.

Afterward Ned couldn't remember much about the graveside service itself. He could remember the man who'd worked with his daddy and everything he'd said and the way he'd looked at his momma, but he couldn't recall what the preacher had said or how long the service had lasted. He remembered the way the ground yawned open beneath the cheap gray casket. Velvet ropes like you might see around the ring at a prizefight fenced off the grave, and directly above the hole stood a rectangular metal frame, with black straps attached to tension rollers on both sides. The casket rested on those straps. At one end of the frame was a foot pedal, which was what Herb Clarkson or somebody else would use to lower his daddy into that gaping hole.

His momma had not cried at the funeral home, and she didn't cry as the preacher stood there under the canvas and said a few final words over his daddy. Daze hadn't cried before, nor did she now, and neither did Ned. His daddy's life was not the sort of life you wept over. You might weep over what his life had not been, and Ned hoped that one day he would, that he'd somehow figure out what it was his daddy had missed out on. Because he believed he was missing out on it too, and if he could figure out what it was, he might find it for himself, which would not help his daddy but might save him.

School ended in May, and he went to work for Carter Bell.

Most days he drove a tractor, working out in the field with Mack or one of the black men who lived on the Bells' place. Like everybody else, the Bells had planted late. By mid-May the cotton had barely broken through the crust on top of the rows. The tea weeds and red vines and Johnson grass had gotten a good head start, and Carter Bell said if they didn't stay on top of things, their asses would all be lost by June.

It was going to be a bad year for farmers; everybody said so. Most had put at least some cotton land into soybeans, but Carter Bell hadn't, and nobody, least of all Ned, had been able to figure out why. Finally, one day when they were sitting on the end of a turnrow, eating lunch in the shade of a tractor tire, Mack told him.

"Daddy's in trouble," he said.

Ned had so much trouble in his own life that he sometimes felt like all the trouble for miles around had been drawn to him, that he was a goddamn magnet. He hadn't seen his momma now for three straight days, and just last night his sister had stayed out till three o'clock. He knew she was out with Denny Gautreaux, and when she came home he told her she was a goddamn fool, that nobody who lived in a house like the Gautreauxs' would ever do anything but use a girl like her. And she'd turned red and said, *So he can use me.*

"What kind of trouble?" Ned said now.

Mack wiped mayonnaise off his chin. "Gautreaux trouble," he said. "Truth is, a lot of other folks are in Gautreaux trouble too, but they ain't been smart enough to figure it out yet."

"What in the fuck is that supposed to mean?"

"Oh," Mack said. "You thinking about your sister. Well, that's not what I mean. Sisters I don't talk about. Same as with mommas and so forth."

He poured himself some water out of their Coleman jug and gulped down several mouthfuls. Then he wiped his mouth on his shirt sleeve.

"What I'm saying," he said, "is that this year's flat-out going to be bad for the farmers—ain't no way around that. Next year may be, you can't say yet, but even if it's not, then the next one will be or the one after that. Problem is, people just won't be able to make it anymore farming cotton and soybeans. Labor costs have gone up too much, the niggers stay stirred up, and everybody's buying polyester. Every year you got to buy the seed, you got to borrow the money to plant, and if it's a dry year you got to irrigate. If it's a wet year, like this one was, you sit around chewing on your nails and drinking whiskey late at night till your stomach starts rotting, and you listen to the weather every hour on WNLA, and every few minutes you go out and look at the sky, hoping you'll see a little band of light somewhere off toward Lake Village. The goddamn Delta wasn't meant to be dry, it was meant to be wet, and Daddy aims to take advantage of that."

"How's he aim to do it?"

Mack ate the last of his sandwich and balled up the wax paper and threw it into the nearby road ditch.

"He aims to farm fish."

"*Fish?*"

"Goddamn right."

"What kind of fish?"

"Catfish."

"Who the hell's gone buy catfish? People want 'em, they'll go catch 'em out of the river."

"Ain't everybody that can get to the river. Say you're some nigger left the Delta for Detroit or Chicago. Probably every day of your life you feel a craving for catfish, but where the hell you gone catch one? Lake Michigan?"

"How's your daddy intend to get the catfish to niggers in Chicago? He ever thought about that?"

"Maybe he don't have it all figured out yet, but you can bet he's working on it."

"Sounds like a bitch of a risk to me."

"Sometimes you got to take a risk," Mack said. "Don't take a risk, ain't nothing good can happen. You liable to lose everything you got. Or you liable not to ever even get it."

They started digging the ponds in early June. By that time they'd had almost three weeks of sunshine, and the land Carter Bell had staked off for them to dig the ponds on—twenty acres of clay and buckshot—was dry and hard. Years of trying to irrigate during drought had taught him how to use a surveyor's transit, so he and Rick Salter's daddy had surveyed the plots and marked them off: four three-and-a-half-acre rectangles that would be connected by crisscrossing levees. They'd slope the bottom of each pond so there was a low point for drainage. Carter Bell had talked to acquaculture specialists, and they'd warned him he'd have to drain the ponds from time to time to rid them of algae and water-borne diseases.

They started at six one Monday morning. Mr. Bell stood near his pickup truck, his hat pulled down low over his eyes, even though the sun was not yet high enough to throw off much light and heat. He was drinking coffee from a thermos bottle, talking to Rick Salter's daddy, who sat on the pickup's tailgate. Ned and one of the black men who worked for the Bells were each driving big

John Deere 5060s with dirt buckets mounted on the drawbars. Mack was on a 4020 with a land plane attached.

Ned and the black man lowered the dirt buckets hydraulically, and the blades took shallow cuts out of the soil. Then they raised the buckets and put the tractors in gear and drove over to the strip of land at the end of the first plot and dumped the dirt there. Later on they'd use it to build up the levee.

Sitting on the tractor, inhaling dust and wiping sweat from his stinging eyes, Ned jammed the gears and worked the lever that controlled the drawbar. It was mindless work, that was the problem, he could have done it in his sleep. It left him free to think. He tried to think about football, to imagine himself making a big goal-line tackle in the championship game against Jackson Prep or throwing an open-field block on a sweep, but the truth was he could make that tackle, he could throw that block, and it would only change things for a while, until he couldn't play games anymore and had to face a life like the one his daddy had lived. It was that sort of life he thought about now. Living from one motel room to the next, from one drink to the next, then coming home and trying to lose yourself in flesh that so many others had poured their own absences into.

At night, alone in his dark room, he poured himself into that same flesh. It never had his momma's face on it, but it was her or someone like her, and what he did to that imagined flesh could not have been called by any name he knew. His fists were clenched and so were hers, their faces were averted, and anyhow they kept their eyes closed. They moaned, but they could not hear each other's moans, only their own, and when it was over they stood and put their clothes on, neither looking at the other, neither willing to admit that the other existed except as a thing that some accident had endowed with a certain set of needs and a regrettable ability to breathe.

Sometimes he felt like he shouldn't breathe, like he didn't deserve to breathe, yet he needed to, and did. There were other things he needed as well, but unlike air they couldn't be gotten through involuntary response. They were things you had to go after, and to go after them, you had to know what they were, and he didn't.

The Bells knew what they were. The Bells were different from him. The black man handling the other dirt bucket was different from him too, different in a recognizable way. How the Bells were different was harder to say. It was more than their having money. It had something to do with their belief that no space was tight enough to contain them. Denny Gautreaux's daddy might put the squeeze on them, but they believed they could wiggle out of it, and so they would. Which was why Ned was driving the tractor right now, with his nose full of dust and his eyes full of sweat, digging a big hole in the ground that would hold a bunch of fish the Bells aimed to sell to black masses in Detroit.

They knew about the pipeline. There were signs along the road ditch warning that it was down there. *Columbia and Gulf Right-of-Way*, the signs said. *Natural Gas. Hazardous.*

The pipeline was buried about eight feet under the ground. It was a thirty-inch pipe, Carter Bell had said, and he told Mack and Ned and the black man that if they happened, for whatever reason, to get too close to it with those dirt buckets, it would blow their sad asses, or whatever remained of their sad asses, from here to Leland, from there to Little Rock and Fort Smith, and maybe beyond.

You could actually hear the gas rumbling. You could hear it down there rolling along, headed toward Belzoni and Yazoo City. You could feel it too, if you stood right on top of it, which was something Ned would sometimes do. He liked knowing so much power was down there, so close to his feet; he liked thinking about that moment when it might erupt, might flow into him, up through his soles and into his blood. He'd burst into flames and they'd shrink from his roar.

He was sitting on the ground near the right-of-way the second or third day they were digging, sitting there in the shade of the tractor eating his lunch, a sandwich he'd made on stale Sunbeam bread. Mack and his daddy and Mr. Salter had gone home to eat, and the black man had too.

The helicopter had no markings—it was just a big fudge-colored thing. The noise it made would not have inspired confidence in Ned if he'd been one of the two men in the cockpit. It sounded like something needed oiling, like friction was involved. Beneath it dust demons danced and died.

The helicopter was flying the pipeline. The man on the passenger's side had a pair of binoculars strung around his neck, but he didn't have them pressed to his eyes. They dangled in the air when he leaned out of the copter, a big man in khaki pants and a plaid short-sleeved shirt, his bullneck plum-colored, spit flying from his mouth.

"Motherfuckers!" he was hollering. "Motherfucking motherfuckers!"

He shook his fist at Ned and shot him the finger, then leaned back into the copter and rummaged around on the floor and came up with something brown in his fist and drew his arm back and let fly.

The paper sack landed a foot or two away.

"Asshole," the man hollered.

He shook his fist one last time and the copter peeled away to the left, rising and turning back in the direction it had come from.

Ned reached out and picked up the sack and opened it. There were two bananas and a Snickers bar inside. He peeled the wrapper off the candy and took a bite.

It wasn't too long after lunch when the man returned. He came in the car with a deputy sheriff named Charlie Pentecost. Charlie Pentecost had been the line coach at the Academy till they fired him. He'd made his defensive tackles grow their fingernails out like a woman's so they could get a better grip on the pass rush, and folks had started saying maybe Charlie might be queer. The sheriff claimed he'd hired him for his size. All his other deputies were built like Barney Fife.

The man Ned had seen in the helicopter got out of the car, and Charlie Pentecost got out, and Mr. Bell and Mr. Salter continued sitting on the tailgate of the Bells' pickup truck. Mack and Ned and the black man cut the motors on their tractors, and for a few seconds nobody did anything else or said a word.

Then Charlie Pentecost pulled off his hat. "Warm," he said. "Ain't it?"

"Hot," said Carter Bell.

"Makes me glad I got out of coaching," Charlie Pentecost said. "Can you boys imagine practicing on a day like this? A jock strap can do terrible things to a man in this kind of weather."

"Jock strap do something bad to you?" Mr. Salter said. "That what it was, Charlie?"

"You guys gone apeshit crazy or what?" the man from the helicopter said. His neck was no longer purple. It had cooled down to a pinkish shade of red. He pointed toward the sign that said *Hazardous*. "There's enough gas down there to keep a herd of elephants farting for the next fifty years. Somebody signed something when the right-of-way was sold. Whoever it was needs to take a look at their paperwork."

"Must've been Carter here," Charlie Pentecost said.

"Which one of you's Carter?"

Carter Bell looked at Mr. Salter and grinned. Then he looked back at the bullnecked man and raised his hand. "Teacher," he said, "it's me."

Mr. Salter and Mack laughed hard.

The man did a passable job of keeping his skin color toned down. "Now, about that paperwork," he said.

"What that paperwork says," Carter Bell said, "is something like this. 'The right-of-way *shall* extend forty feet on either side of said line.'"

"Exactly," the man said.

He did sound like he was talking to a student. He sounded like he nursed moderate hopes that maybe the student was not quite as dumb as he seemed. He wasn't banking on it, but he could at least entertain the possibility.

"Now, if you was to take you a tape measure and stretch it out from the sign over yonder to the edge of this big hole you're digging," he said, "wonder how far it'd be?"

"Twenty-eight feet," Carter Bell said. "Give or take three or four inches."

"Twenty-eight feet," the man said.

He looked at Charlie Pentecost like he thought maybe Charlie knew something he didn't. Charlie crossed his arms over his belly and looked off toward the road and began to probe his jaw with his tongue.

"Twenty-eight feet," the man said again.

"Give or take three or four inches."

"In other words, you knew what you were doing when you started digging a big hole on the right-of-way?"

"Digging a fish pond," Carter Bell said. "It's a fish pond."

"Fish pond?" the man said. "There's not enough lakes and rivers around here? You want to go fishing, and you got to dig you a big fishing hole on top of my company's damn right-of-way?" He shook his head. "That's the illegalest thing I ever heard of."

"No sir," Carter Bell said. "It ain't the least bit illegal. And yes sir, I done checked with my lawyer."

"Not illegal?" the man said.

"No sir. Not the least bit."

"You want to tell me why? You want to explain why words are so damn worthless?"

"Words ain't worthless," Carter Bell said. "No sir. Words are worth a whole lot."

He got off the tailgate, and Mr. Salter did, and Mack hopped down off his tractor, and together the three of them advanced to within two or three feet of the gas-company man.

"'The right-of-way *shall* extend forty feet on either side of said line,'" Carter Bell said again. "'All farming activity to occur within those forty feet *shall* be limited to *normal* farming practices.'"

Carter Bell crossed his own arms now. "Charlie Pentecost," he said.

"Here," Charlie Pentecost said.

Then Mack and Mr. Salter laughed again, and this time Charlie joined in.

"If you aimed to farm fish, Charlie," Carter Bell said, "would you consider it a *normal* practice to dig you a hole? So's that once you had that hole, you could fill it up with water and put you some fish in there that would go on and beget other fish and so forth?"

"Seem to me like it'd be abnormal not to," Charlie said.

"Exactly," Carter Bell said. "And what with all reasonable care being taken to protect the gas company's right-of-way, you wouldn't feel like you'd been trespassing, would you?"

"Not hardly."

"And you'd expect any judge to agree?"

"Judge and jury both."

The man from the gas company opened his mouth, but for the longest time no words came out. Finally he said, "That's the god-damndest kind of talk I've ever heard."

It surprised everybody when the black man spoke up. He was sitting there on his tractor, a few feet away from Ned. He was thirty-five or forty years old. His real name was Tommy, but everybody called him Preacher. He was a good-looking fellow who kept his clothes clean and wore a straw hat and would sometimes jump off a tractor and run and throw himself into the closest road ditch when a cloud bank appeared in the west. If you asked him why he did that, he'd tell you, *Bible say fear God*.

What he said now, in a voice empty of fear but full of resignation, was, "That's *Bell* talk."

It was as if the Lord, rather than Preacher, had just spoken. It was as if there was nothing left to say.

The boat was named the *Barbara S* after Denny Gautreaux's momma, Barbara Sue. The Gautreauxs kept it moored in a boathouse on Lake Fergusson.

The boathouse wasn't much—just a wooden structure that floated on buoys and was anchored to a dock about a hundred yards away from the marina. It was empty except for the boat itself and a rusty tackle box that stood on a ledge a foot or two above the water. Back in the spring, the boathouse had broken loose when the water rose high enough to snap all the chains. They'd almost lost the boat then, Denny said.

The first time Daze went out in the boat, it was a weekday in late June. Denny's daddy had been making him drive a tractor for one of the Morelli brothers, but Denny had torn up a cultivator rig the day before by running it over some tree roots, and now the Morellis had said he couldn't drive for them anymore, not even if Denny's daddy threatened to foreclose.

"So that pretty much means I've got the summer free," Denny said, unsnapping the padlock on the mooring chain.

She was standing on the dock. "I don't understand how anybody could risk pissing off your daddy," she said. "Seems like he owns most of what everybody calls theirs."

"Yeah, he does," Denny said. "But my daddy likes to socialize. He loves to walk into the country club and have everybody holler, *Hey, Russell,* and act like they're happy to see him, even though they're not, and he loves to get invited to those all-night Delta parties. He's got his big toe in a lot of people's asses, but there's a price to pay for him sticking his whole foot in. He's not too eager to piss folks off either."

She watched him check to see how much gas was in the tank. "You tore up that cultivator on purpose," she said, "didn't you?"

He grinned. "Took me several days before I found a tree root big enough to do any real damage," he said. "In the meantime, I plowed down about half an acre of cotton and ran the tractor into a ditch. I was starting to think they'd ignore *whatever* I fucked up."

"You couldn't just tell your daddy you didn't want to drive the tractor? You don't need the money you were making."

"I could tell him I didn't want to do it," Denny said. "But he wouldn't like that. He feels better about it when I try to do whatever he tells me to and fuck it up. He's basically a fuck-up himself. He never could do anything his daddy wanted him to until the day came for him to take over the bank, and then it turned out he was every bit as good at money-grubbing as my granddaddy had been."

"You intend to take over the bank?"

"I intend to get as far away from the Mississippi Delta as I can. But doing that'll be a lot easier, won't it, if I've got access to my daddy's money?"

People who had plans puzzled and fascinated her. She didn't have any plans herself. She assumed that twenty or thirty years from now she'd be getting up each day and going someplace to do something she didn't like, and then around five or six o'clock she'd go back home. Home would be Indianola. It always had been.

"I guess money'll make anything easier," she said.

He screwed the cap back on the gas tank and wiped his hands on the thighs of his cut-offs. He was wearing those cut-offs and a blue Izod shirt and a pair of sneakers that she'd bet had cost more than her momma could earn in a week.

"I want to take you with me," he said, looking up at her shyly. "I want to take you with me when I go."

A fishy odor hung in the air. Out in the middle of the lake, a tug-boat towed a barge south, toward the river. The barge was loaded with lumber, and you could see a couple of guys walking along the sides of it, reaching up every now and then to check and make sure a stack of boards was lashed down.

The lake was muddier than she remembered it from those Sunday afternoon fishing trips with her momma and her daddy and Ned. Denny said that a couple of months ago, during the worst of the high water, the river had washed over the big sandbar that lay between it and the lake, and when that happened the Mississippi had dumped a lot of mud into Fergusson. It seemed like the water was cooler than she remembered it too: she dragged her hand in it as they pulled away from the boathouse.

She sat up front, next to Denny. They motored out past the marina, where a few people sat on the deck under big white um-brellas, people who had the money and the leisure time to eat lunch at the lake on a weekday afternoon. They were women, for the most part, women like Denny's momma. They didn't have to work; all they had to do was figure out the most enjoyable way to spend their time, and eating at the marina was what they'd come up with today.

Denny steered out past the buoys. Then he opened up the throttle, and the boat seemed to rise above the water.

"We'll go up through the bottleneck," he said. "The upper lake's the best place to learn how to ski. Probably won't be anybody up there today."

The bottleneck was a narrow channel overhung with tupelo gum, cypress, and weeping willows. She'd never been in it before—her daddy had always said it was a dangerous area—but she knew it was supposed to be a daring thing to ski through it. Once she saw it she understood why.

It looked like a tunnel, it was so narrow and dark. It couldn't have been more than twenty yards wide at any point, and most of the time it was closer to ten or twelve yards. There was a peculiar odor here, one that reminded her of rotten mulberries.

Sometimes branches actually swept against the boat, making her and Denny duck, and once or twice they heard stumps banging the hull. Near the point where the passage opened into the upper lake, they saw a water moccasin twisted around a limb, its sinuous body two or three inches thick.

"I don't much like it here," she said.

Denny shivered. "Actually, I don't either," he said. "My momma and I just usually drive to the upper lake, and Daddy brings the boat through the channel."

The upper lake was still and quiet and a good bit cleaner than it was farther down. As Denny had predicted, there was no one around.

He cut the motor and let the boat drift into the bank, and when the hull hit bottom, he jumped out and tugged the prow toward a stump and wound the mooring chain around it.

"Come on," he said. "Hop out."

He offered her his hand, and she took it and stepped into the water.

She had her bathing suit on, but she'd worn a tee shirt over it and a pair of her momma's old shorts. The shorts were too long: the water splashed up onto her thighs, soaking the material.

Denny stared at the water stain. It was spreading downward, as if she'd wet her pants.

"Want to go skinny-dipping?" he said.

Sooner or later, no matter what their purpose in being together at a given time, they always ended up with their clothes off. She didn't mind. She looked forward to it. She loved something that happened to her right before Denny put his palms on her breasts, before he pressed his chest against hers and she felt his hardness poking her belly. It was something she couldn't explain, something she knew had no name.

"If I take my clothes off," she said, "and you start touching me, and a water moccasin crawls up our legs and winds itself around us, I won't be able to do anything to shake him off. I just thought you should know that."

Denny looked down at the murky water. Worry lines emerged around the corners of his mouth. He lifted one foot, then put it back down and lifted the other, and then it dawned on him that you couldn't stand in muddy lake water without exposing at least part of your body to a certain amount of danger. He swallowed once or twice.

"Well," he said, "let's get up there on the bank."

The first few times she tried to ski, she couldn't get up. Denny told her to relax her legs and let the skis float in the water until the boat pulled her up. She relaxed until she heard the engine roar and the water began roiling, little waves splashing her face, and then she stiffened. The force of the lake hit her flush between the legs, splayed them, and for a second she always felt as if she were being pulled apart. When that happened, she'd let go of the tether. She'd kick her skis off and, even though she wore a life vest and knew she wouldn't drown, she'd flail the water, beating it with both her fists, gulping down big drafts of Lake Fergusson, until finally her muscles gave out and calmness settled over her and she floated on the surface like a wounded bird.

"You've got to have faith," he told her. "Jesus, you've got to believe you'll get up."

She didn't care if she got up or not. She cared about being at the lake with Denny Gautreaux; she cared about the way he instructed her, about his determination that she succeed. The attention he paid her warmed her, she soaked in it.

"You're having the same sort of problem I had when I got baptized," he said one day. "I was eight and a little overweight. I lacked confidence, you might say."

"No," she said. "Not you."

"The day before the baptism, the preacher and I practiced in his office. He told me not to step backwards when he leaned me back, that he'd baptized three-hundred-pound men and he'd support me, and I did okay during the practice session. But what happened the next day was that when I felt the water rolling over my face, I couldn't help but step backwards. The preacher lost his balance and fell over onto me, and I went into such a panic that I grabbed him by the necktie.

"Everybody out in the congregation was sitting there watching us through the glass front of the baptistry, me holding the preacher under and both of us about to drown. Finally he poked me in the Adam's apple and I let him go."

She was laughing so hard her throat hurt. "Then what happened?"

He put his arm around her, pulled her near. "What else could happen?" he said. "He was risen."

That day, when he hit the throttle and the motor roared and the boat spurted forward, she closed her eyes. The water rolled, but she forced herself to think of her body as something transparent and light, a porous form that liquid could just flow through.

And when she did that, the water—this muddy water that had flowed down the mountains and over the Great Plains, this water that smelled of catfish and sulfur dust and DDT, of diesel and decay and Des Moines—the water flowed through her, and then it was beneath her, the water lifted her up, and like the preacher who'd baptized Denny, she was risen.

It could have been an ordinary Friday night, and if it had been, Ned would have been at home. Or if he hadn't been at home, he would have been in his pickup, driving around drinking beer, or over at Legion Field, running one forty-yard sprint after another, trying to get a little bit faster and, in the process, wear himself out in hopes that he could sleep.

What stopped it from being an ordinary Friday night was that Carter Bell kept them late. They were almost finished digging the last of the ponds, and he wanted the work done—he said it was going to rain tomorrow, he could already feel it way down in his joints.

It was after eight when he said they were through. Sweaty and worn out, they rode back to the headquarters in the rear of Mr. Bell's pickup. After they got out, Mr. Bell drove off to meet his wife in town for supper.

They stood in the gravel driveway. The katydids were starting to sing; you could hear their shrill music.

"I believe I'm gone call Rick and see if he wants to go woman hunting," Mack said. "You want to tag along?"

Ned wanted to go woman hunting, all right, but the woman he wanted to hunt was his momma. He hadn't seen her more than two or three times in two or three weeks. He believed she was staying at somebody's place every night when she got off work at the 7-Eleven. He'd been thinking maybe he'd drive around till midnight and then park near the store and follow her when she left.

But if he said he didn't want to go woman hunting, Mack would start saying he was a fag. Or even if he didn't say it, he would think it. And knowing Mack had thought it but not said it, that he'd shown him mercy, would have been more weight than he was willing or able to bear.

"Sure," he said. "Yeah, I'm up for chasing women."

"Yeah?" Mack said. He kicked a rock into the road ditch and grinned. "Question is, are you up for what'll happen if we catch one?"

He went home to eat and take a bath, and he almost got on the phone while he was there and told Mack no. He'd never know whether or not it would have made a difference if he'd done that. Maybe nothing much would have been different. Maybe what happened that night would have happened soon enough anyway. There was only so much you could keep yourself from knowing. There were only so many situations you could avoid. Especially when you lived in a fish bowl, and all of them—him and Daze, their momma, Mack and folks like that—did, and so had his daddy.

Mack had said he'd meet him in the parking lot at the Academy. When Ned got there, it was nine-fifteen, and the parking lot was empty. He parked over by the flagpole. He made up his mind he'd wait till nine-thirty, not a minute longer, and then he'd go home.

He'd already cranked up and started to back out when he saw the lights of the Caddy. Mack pulled in beside him. Rick Salter was in the Caddy too. He and Mack both raised Miller bottles and made stupid faces. It looked like they were already about half-drunk.

Ned got out of his truck and locked the door.

"You worried about theft?" Mack said when he got in. "Man, a self-respecting nigger wouldn't be caught dead in that shit heap."

The front seat of the Caddy was equipped with headrests, and the headrests were covered by velvety material. Whether or not the softness of that material lessened the pain Mack must have felt when his neck snapped back against the headrest, Ned would never know. Only Mack might have told him that, and Mack couldn't speak because Ned was choking him.

He was choking him, and he could smell Mack's hair, and Mack had used Gee, Your Hair Smells Terrific, the shampoo that smelled like bubblegum.

Ned pressed his cheek against Mack's. Sweat had popped out on Mack's skin. In the faint greenish glow of the dashboard displays, Ned could see Mack's right eye, which was beginning to bulge. He could feel Mack's pulse pounding in his neck.

"Ned?" Rick said, as if he suddenly doubted that the person he knew as Ned Rose and the guy who was choking Mack Bell were the same. "Hey, Ned?"

"Hey," Ned said.

"You aim to kill him?"

Ned took a while to answer. "Not tonight," he said.

Gradually he decreased the pressure. Mack's first breath was a gasp that sounded as if it had started somewhere down in the pit of his belly, as if his deepest need, the need to breathe, had its source there.

"I want you to feel it coming back real slow," Ned said.

"Feel what?" Mack whispered. Tears were running out of his eyes and down his face, mixing in with all the sweat.

"Your life," Ned said. "I want you to feel it coming back."

"Crazy," Mack whispered. "Man, you crazy."

Ned increased the pressure. Mack gagged. He tried to buck loose, but the steering wheel stopped him.

"Life rationing," Ned said.

Measuring life out second by second, breath by breath, one drop of blood at a time—a nickel's worth of living down, a dime's worth. It was easier to total it up that way. It was easier then to tell what, if anything, it all meant and whether it was worth the effort it took to live it.

The main strip began at the intersection of 49 and 82, the crossroads of the Delta. It ran west out past the Skate-A-Rama. Most folks would have said it ended near the billboard that said *Welcome to Indianola,* the words spelled out in white letters two feet high, beneath them the drawing of a cotton boll. At that point most folks turned around and headed back. But some would continue on another two or three hundred yards and take a blacktop road that ran down toward Indian Bayou and crossed it and hit Westside Avenue. They'd drive on past the country club, hang a left downtown at the discount store that declared bankruptcy and changed its name every year or so, then they'd stay on Front Street for one block before turning right, onto Second, which would take you all the way out past the cemetery to Highway 49. Mack called the longer route the Strip Extended, and it was the one he drove that night.

Every couple of minutes he'd glance over his shoulder into the back seat. Ned had considered moving over and sitting behind Rick Salter, but he enjoyed knowing Mack was concerned. Mack had become aware that something could slip up behind you and hurt you bad, just like the tornado had come up behind Ned's daddy and hurt him. That was an awareness that ought to possess everybody. Nobody ought to walk around thinking his backside was safe and secure. Nobody deserved to feel that sure of himself or the behavior of those who came behind him.

It was a hot night, but they rode with the windows down, muggy air blowing in their faces. Mack had an ice chest in the trunk, so every few minutes he'd stop the car and get out and pick up three more beers. Ned drank about half of each one Mack handed him. Then he dropped the bottles out the window, rather than throwing them at stop signs or light poles like Mack and Rick did.

It was a dark night. There was no moon, and even if there had been, you wouldn't have seen it. Clouds had banked up in the west; you couldn't see the stars. Every now and then you'd see a flash of lightning. Arkansas was taking a bath.

It was an off night. Mack said nobody was having a party; there wasn't shit going on. A lot of folks were away on vacation, in Florida or California or Mexico.

It was a night when things were dark and slow, hot and lazy, and there was nothing better for Mack to do, Ned knew, than ride around with someone like him, someone you didn't normally see at parties, except during football season, someone who didn't go to Las Vegas or Miami and wouldn't have known what to do there if he had gone, someone who would have been better off at home except that in a manner of speaking home was like Las Vegas, a place where folks had come and gone so often late at night that it seemed like a desert hot spot.

"Ever notice after you drink three or four beers, it starts to taste like piss?" Salter said.

"You know what Daddy did once to a nigger that used to work on our place?" Mack said. "This was several years ago, when we were still doing a lot of picking by hand. He found out this nigger had been putting rocks in the bottom of his sack at weighing time, so what he did was he drank him a bottle of beer and then he pissed in the bottle and put the cap back on real good and tight and got the bottle cold. And then he went over to this nigger's house and walked up onto the porch and said to him, said, 'Booker, you like a good cold beer?' Nigger says, 'Yes sir,' so Daddy goes back to the truck and pulls out that bottle of pee, and he walks back over there and pops the cap off and hands the bottle to the nigger. And that poor black son of a bitch, he turned it up and took a big swig, and his eyes like to popped out of his head. Daddy says to him, says, 'Got a real rich flavor, don't it, Booker?' And the nigger says, 'Show do, Mr. Bell, show do.' And so Daddy says, 'Go ahead and drink it, Booker. Man picks as many pounds of cotton as you did yesterday, he deserves a little liquid refreshment.'"

Salter pounded the dashboard. "What would we do without niggers?" he said.

"Niggers was meant to amuse," Mack said. "Niggers amuse you, Ned? That nigger amuse you when you hit him on the head?"

"You know I'm holding a bottle right now?" Ned said.

"Say you are?"

"Sure am."

"Just like the one you whacked that nigger with?"

"More or less."

"I ain't a nigger."

"You got a skull, and it's not much different from his."

"Might be a little bit thinner," Salter said. "You know damn well a nigger's skull's thicker than a white man's."

"What I'm saying," Ned said, "is you bring a heavy object down on anybody's head, it's apt to cause him damage. Only question is how much."

"I ain't concerned," Mack said.

"Why's that?"

They were on 82, heading past the *Welcome to Indianola* sign, right at the edge of town. Mack pressed the accelerator down, and the Caddy shot forward. The needle hit 60, hit 70. By the time they crossed the railroad tracks near Heathman, they were doing 110.

Hot air howled in the windows, buffeting Ned's face, making it hard for him to inhale.

"I got your life," Mack was hollering. "Man, I got your fucking *life* in my hands."

Ned lurched forward. Mack's hair was streaming, and it tickled Ned's nose. He laid his hand on Mack's shoulder.

"You ain't got shit, then," Ned said.

There was one carload of girls out that night, but they were all seniors, and every time Mack passed them on the strip and honked his horn, they ignored him.

"What the fuck, Mack," Salter said. "Every damn one of them's probably frigid."

"Frigid means they can't enjoy it," Mack said. "Frigid don't mean I can't."

"That's true," Salter said. "If a man can't find a partner, a victim'll do."

Mack giggled. "Hell," he said, "a little bit of resistance might enhance it."

They'd drunk all the beer. It was almost midnight. Ned was thinking he could tell them now to take him back to his truck. Nobody could blame him for being tired now. Nobody could say he hadn't gone out and hunted women. He still might drive by the 7-Eleven and see where his momma went. He'd bet she drove over to one of those rental houses south of the railroad tracks, either there or the trailer park out behind Weber's Restaurant, where a lot of truck drivers lived.

Only Mack knew why he turned south on 49, away from town. Only Mack knew why he drove down the highway a mile or more and then turned left on a blacktop road that ran east for three-quarters of a mile, through an open tract of land that the city of Indianola was trying to turn into an industrial park. There was no industry yet, just a lot of empty fields that never had produced a good stand of cotton because the land was mostly buckshot.

Johnson grass grew high here. It had taken over the turnrows so that you couldn't really tell where they were unless you looked hard. They were there, though. The turnrows. You'd find a culvert every few hundred yards where tractors and pickers had once entered the fields.

It wasn't a tractor or a picker that Mack was looking out for. It was a car. Not a particular car, Ned decided later on, though he couldn't rule that possibility out either. Who knew what Mack knew?

One thing Mack knew for sure, one thing even Ned knew, was that the Industrial Park was called the snaking grounds. One night last year a senior had driven his girlfriend out here, and they'd screwed in the back seat of his car. Afterward, when the guy got out to take a piss, a cottonmouth struck his naked leg. The girl had the presence of mind to help him into the car, but instead of driving him straight to the hospital, she wasted ten or fifteen minutes trying to get his clothes on, and by the time she reached the emergency room with him, he was hemorrhaging and suffering convulsions.

"Been enough come spilled out yonder," Mack said, "to fill a catfish pond."

"Might get the fish to tasting funny," Salter said.

Mack slowed down. "Somebody's in yonder," he said.

He pointed at the road ditch. There was a culvert there, and you could tell a car had driven over the weeds not too long ago.

Mack turned into the turnrow. His headlights glared off the hood ornament of a white Mercedes parked in the Johnson grass about twenty yards ahead.

For one crucial instant, which was how long it took Mack to open his door and jump out, his headlights still trained on the Mercedes like searchlights that had finally found their target, Ned couldn't move. When he did move, it was way too late. Mack and Rick were galloping toward the Mercedes, yelling and giggling, and when Ned got out he tripped over something, a vine or maybe a root, and sprawled forward.

The ground felt cool. He dug his fingers into it, he pressed his cheek against it, he inhaled its dark, rich odor. He clung to the earth, and for a moment he wished he could return to it, wished he could turn into dirt.

He thought maybe he would never get up. He couldn't see that there was much point in it. He couldn't do anything for her, and she wasn't interested in doing anything for him, or she wouldn't have been where she was, doing what she was doing, where folks could come across her and talk about her, say she was just another of them trashy-assed Roses.

"Good Lord," he heard Mack holler. "Excuse us, Denny. We didn't know you had company."

"Wouldn't have believed it," Salter said. "Would've thought you was out here flogging the dolphin."

"Boxing Buford," Mack said.

"Pounding your peenie," said Salter.

On his hands and knees now, Ned viewed them through the hot white light of the headlights: Mack standing there against a black background, Salter blending into the surrounding darkness, Denny's bare calves protruding beneath the open door.

"Seem to me like that's a mighty tight squeeze for the kind of action y'all been up to," Mack said. "That stick shift could do a man some damage. Could tear a woman plumb up."

Then she began yelling, calling Mack and Rick Salter sorry motherfuckers, horny cocksuckers, dumb sons of bitches who'd never done anything but look at nasty magazines and jack off until their ugly little dicks were raw and bloody.

He couldn't see her, and he hoped she couldn't see him. He began to inch backward, moving on his knees toward the Caddy, hoping he could get behind it and reach the blacktop road. If he could get there without her seeing him, he'd jump up and start running. He'd run all the way to town. He might not even stop there.

"Ned?" Mack's voice rang out. "Your sister's got a mighty dirty mouth. Come on over here, hoss, and tell her she needs to mind her manners. She's got her panties back on now.

"Ned?" Mack hollered. "What's the matter, dude? You done died of shame? Ned? Hey, Ned?"

There were eight or ten days when she refused to acknowledge his presence, to admit to either him or herself that she knew he was alive. These were the days when they established the routine that they'd follow off and on for the rest of their lives, the one that would prevail in all but a handful of moments when passion overruled her and her hatred for him spewed out and she called him by name, both Christian and profane.

Passing him in the hallway, she kept her head down, her eyes following the thin line between two floorboards. If he looked at her, she didn't know it, wouldn't let herself see it. At the breakfast table they ate silently. She washed her dishes, he washed his, or if he failed to wash them she let them stand in the sink or on the countertop until mold grew on them, and then she flung them out the back door, shattering them against the pecan tree. Sooner or later he picked up the fragments and threw them away.

"Daze?" he might say, tentative, outside her locked bedroom door late at night. "Daze? You all right?"

She maintained her silence with a vengeance that fed itself. She did not say his name until good fortune or bad fortune, she would never know which, delivered him unto her, herding him before her like a blank-eyed calf tromping dumbly to its slaughter.

The barn wasn't really a barn, just as the smokehouse wasn't really a smokehouse. The structure was too small to be a barn, it was really little more than a crib with a tin roof on it, and it wouldn't have held more than four or five cows at one time. It had had hay stacked in it when their daddy bought the place, but he'd hauled the hay away. Now the barn was full of junk: old sports magazines that her daddy for some reason had saved, some fishing tackle, several fruit hampers filled with empty beer bottles, lots of discarded household items—broken lamps, a dresser that was missing one leg, two or three old radios that didn't work.

She went there on a Sunday afternoon. Her momma had called from somebody's house and asked her to go and see if she couldn't find an old window fan that she believed was probably in the barn, over against the wall behind the dresser. She said the fan didn't work, but she knew somebody who believed he could fix it. Daze heard a man's voice say something, and then her momma giggled. "He can make most motors run," she said. She told Daze she'd call back in fifteen minutes.

Ned's truck was parked out front. Daze had heard him moving around the house earlier, but she figured he was probably asleep in his room. She'd gotten back last night before he had. Denny had brought her home around midnight. Ned hadn't come in until three or four. She'd been able to tell from the sounds he made that he was drunk. He stumbled into the coffee table, and when he went into the kitchen he dropped a glass and broke it. She imagined he'd try to sleep his beer off today.

The gate swung open, creaking on its hinges. She stepped inside. She was carrying a flashlight because she knew it would be dark in the barn, and she knew too that her daddy and Ned had killed several snakes here. She shone the light down at the dirt, watching where she put her feet, stepping carefully over the fruit hampers, picking her way back toward the rear wall.

She was on him before she knew it. He was in a state beyond knowing. Her scream, she decided later, must have blended in with the screams he was hearing in his mind, somewhere far back behind those clamped eyelids.

His mouth was wide open, and in the beam of the flashlight, which somehow her hand had pointed at his face, she could see into his throat. A thin white film coated his tongue. The fleshy thing that hung down from the top of his soft pallet was red and rigid. The grunts that emerged from his throat sounded so little like the ones Denny made that they might have been coming from a different kind of creature, from a being who had suffered much and enjoyed nothing, who'd struggled every time it took a breath.

"Beat it," she said, and it opened its eyes, its dumb dry helpless dying eyes. "Beat it, asshole. Beat it."

Beat it till it bleeds, beat it till you're dead, beat it till it's just the fucking dust beneath your feet, beat it till it's ashes and you're ashes and we're all ashes, just beat it, you goddamn bastard, beat it.

Going back to work, driving out to Mack's the Monday morning after they caught Denny Gautreaux with Daze, was the second-worst mistake he'd ever make, and he knew it even as he made it. It was like he was saying Mack could do whatever pleased him with regard to Ned Rose; he could think of him as he would a tractor or a combine. He was just a piece of machinery. If you drove it too hard, it might break down. Every now and then it might even dump you on your duff. But it would never drive off on its own. It needed somebody to crank it up and steer it.

He told himself Mack was wrong, had been wrong all along. He'd stood up in Mack's face. He'd watched his own spit trickle off Mack's chin; he'd choked him half to death.

He could tell himself that, all right, but he knew what Mack was saying to Rick Salter. He was telling Rick that you had to let somebody like Ned Rose go crazy from time to time—it was just some trashy thing down deep in his blood. You shouldn't let it worry you because he would never hurt you, though he might hurt himself or others.

It was almost as if they couldn't live without him. It was as if they needed him around for entertainment. The picture show had closed down, they couldn't go to bars in town, and Championship Wrestling came only once a month.

They rode around together every Friday night. Sometimes on Saturday night too. A couple of times Mack made a crack about Daze. He said she was a field Denny Gautreaux loved to plow, said she was a fish he loved to put his hook in.

When Mack made the first crack, they were standing on the side of a gravel road, taking a piss. Ned peed all over Mack's shoe. Mack laughed and said there were more shoes where those came from; he could buy fifty pairs if he wanted to, a hundred.

The second time they were in the Caddy, riding down the highway, doing seventy-five or eighty. Ned swung his beer bottle, fast and hard, and bashed out his window glass.

"Crazy," Mack hollered. "Is he a crazy fool or what?"

"Crazy," Rick Salter said. "There's a certain dead nigger could testify to that."

"Dead niggers," Mack said, "don't testify."

Glass lay all over Ned's lap, lay on the floor beneath his feet. He thought a few shards were embedded in his cheek. He rubbed his face, felt something sticky.

"But a living, breathing white man might," Mack said. "A living, breathing white man might testify."

Ned bent over and picked up a piece of glass and ran the jagged edge along the back of Mack's neck.

"Seem like something cut me," Mack said. "You don't reckon it might could be Ned?"

"Either him or a piece of glass," Salter said.

They were heading west on 82, four or five miles from town. The road was empty as far as you could see.

Mack slammed on his brakes, there was a screeching sound, and the Caddy fishtailed.

Ned pitched forward, flipping into the front seat. His feet smashed into the windshield. He banged his head on something, the transmission hump maybe. Mack's elbow dug into his windpipe.

He pinched Ned's nostrils together and gave his nose a twist, and then Ned felt something warm and damp hit his face.

Mack's spit ran down his cheek, and it was a second or two before Ned realized that the spit would mix with his blood, that his fluid and Mack's were running together down the side of his face, and when he understood that, he began to make a sound he couldn't interpret, a sound that must have surprised Mack as much as it did him, because Mack let go of Ned's nose and raised his elbow.

"Jesus," Salter said.

The sound came again, and Ned was listening to it too, ringing out in the night, this sharp dark piercing sound, he was listening as if it hadn't come from him but from someone else, someone who must have been standing outside the car, across the road in the cotton patch, someone with blood in his eyes, with chains on his legs and welts on his back, standing there howling in this his second century.

It was odd to see Carter Bell in cutoffs. His legs were white and hairy, his thighs as big as Mack's and going flabby. He wore the cutoffs and a blue double-knit pullover with an Ole Miss Rebel on the pocket, and he wore a pair of white tennis shoes that had little drops of green paint on the toes. Ned thought he was probably drunk. He'd looked drunk at ten o'clock, when Ned parked in the Bells' driveway, and he'd drunk three more beers on the way to the lake.

Now he was sitting in the back of the boat, close to the motor, and he was drinking yet another beer, which he'd just pulled out of the big ice chest that Ned and Mack had lugged down the levee to the dock.

"Cool out," Carter Bell was saying. "Cool day for the middle of the summer."

It was a Sunday. The sky was overcast, but for once the weatherman was not saying rain.

"Day like this," Carter Bell was saying, "ain't much to do but go to the lake and get shitfaced. You boys got to be careful, though. You boys best not to break training."

"Aw, Daddy," Mack said. He steered the boat out past the marina. "Man needs to break training from time to time. Man can't break training, he can't break bones."

"Got to break bones," Carter Bell said. "Got to get ahold of them city boys from down at Jackson Prep and see if you can't splinter their kneecaps."

Fergusson was still high, but it looked like a lake again rather than a sea that spread out over the sandbars, all the way to the top of the levee on the Arkansas side of the river. A lot of boats were out today. A lot of folks were skiing, and all those folks were white. But you could see a lot of black people fishing in the shallow water off the banks. Whole families were out there, it looked like, black families that must have come to fish after leaving church. They were standing there or sitting in lawn chairs, ragged-looking lawn chairs, with the nylon straps the people sat on looking frayed. Ned couldn't see them, the nylon straps, but he knew they were frayed, knew that at least two or three of them were about to bust on each chair. Most of those chairs hadn't been bought new. They'd been bought at the Goodwill store, or maybe they'd been discarded, and the people who sat in them today had pulled them out of green dumpsters.

"Lake stinks," Carter Bell said.

The lake did stink. It stank of fish, but it also stank of something else. Ned couldn't say for sure what it was. It had a chemical odor. It smelled a little bit like formaldehyde.

"You know the governor aims to stock this motherfucker with alligators?" Carter Bell said. "Claims he aims to keep 'em from becoming extinct. That kind of thinking's what drove me straight into the arms of the Republican Party."

"Daddy just started back to voting a couple of years ago," Mack said.

"'Fore that," Carter Bell said, "me and my brother canceled one another out. He went over to the Republicans back in '64, and me and him just agreed not to vote. Now I have to drag my sorry ass to town. But what can you do? Can't just turn your head. Bad enough when some son of a bitch is throwing tax money at the niggers. Aim to let him pitch it at baby 'gators too?"

They were here for an unspecified purpose. Mack had said something about teaching Ned to ski. Mack had said come, and Ned had climbed into his pickup.

Two pairs of skis lay on the floor of the boat, back near Carter Bell, but nobody said anything about wanting Ned to use them. They rode up and down Fergusson, just cruising, the throttle down low, Ned up front beside Mack, Mr. Bell in the back, drinking beer and telling stories.

He told one about a waitress who worked at Weber's Truckstop. Jane, he said her name was. He said he'd overheard her talking to another waitress the other day.

"I was coming out of the bathroom," he said. "You know where it's at, Ned? Over there by the Coke machines. Well, the women's bathroom's back there too, and then there's this little area between the hallway and the kitchen—used to be a coatrack back there—and that's where they were standing. Jane tells this other waitress, says, 'The last time Bert Kenney come through town, he tore me.' Other one says, 'You mean—' and Jane says, 'Damn straight.' Says, 'I went down to Dr. Betts and he looked at me, and he said, "Honey, why don't you quit messing with fellows like that and find you a man who'll treat you good?" And I told him, I said, "Hell, he was treating me good when he did this."'"

Mack let out a stream of high-pitched giggles. When he quit laughing, he looked at Ned and said, "Didn't your momma used to work out there at the truckstop?"

"No," Ned said, "my momma never did."

"Truckers," Carter Bell said. "Can you imagine letting a man that smelled like diesel get between your legs?"

Ned looked over his shoulder at him. Mr. Bell winked. He leaned back in his seat and tried to balance his beer can on his belly. The can fell off, soaking his lap and thighs.

"Motherfuck," he said.

He leaned over and stuck his hand out of the boat into the water rushing by.

He scooped some up and sloshed it onto himself. He rubbed his hairy white thighs with it.

"Not no point going to the lake," he said, "unless you aim to get wet. Person needs to kick back and relax. You don't relax enough, Ned. You been working mighty hard for me, and don't think for a minute I don't appreciate it. But you do need to kick back, boy. Sure do. And to tell you the truth, I do too."

As if to prove that he intended to kick back, he pulled his shirt off over his head. His belly was enormous, a wide white expanse. There were purple stretch marks on either side of his navel.

He crossed his legs and locked his arms behind his head. "Hell yes," he said. "Man needs a little time to float and forget."

Evidently what he needed to forget had something to do with Russell Gautreaux. It had something to do with Russell Gautreaux, with addition and subtraction, credit lines and interest payments, assets and liabilities.

The white motorboat approached them, skimming the surface. Russell Gautreaux manned the wheel, a silly-looking captain's cap on his head. Denny was sitting in the seat beside him, his smooth face dark and sullen.

"Daddy," Mack said, "I hate to tell you this because it's gone ruin your whole day. But here comes Mr. Gautreaux and Denny."

Carter Bell shaded his eyes with the back of his hand, even though there was no glare today. "Shit," he said.

He bent. The sides of his belly sagged over his hips. He grabbed his shirt and pulled it back on and looked down at his cut-offs, making sure his fly was zipped.

"Next thing I know," he said, "the son of a bitch'll surprise me in my own goddamn bathroom, wanting to slap a lien against one of my turds."

"Can you all believe this?" Russell Gautreaux said. He waved at the sky. "It's cloudy, but it's not raining. Does that beat all?"

"That beats all," Carter Bell said.

He had not stood up. He was sitting back there with his big legs crossed, hoping to hide the beer stains on his cutoffs.

"You all out here skiing?" Russell Gautreaux said.

"Looks like it," Carter Bell said. He nodded at the skis that lay on the floor of the boat. "If I saw somebody with them in his boat, I'd say he was out here skiing."

"Reason I ask," Russell Gautreaux said, "is that I don't see anybody up on the water."

"We're just having us a little refreshment right now," Carter Bell said. "We're just floating and sipping suds and talking. Kicking back's what I call it."

"Kicking back's a fine thing to do," Russell Gautreaux said. "Seems like you've been kicking back a good bit lately."

"Say it does?"

"Seems like it. Seems like I called you three or four times last week, and your wife kept telling me you'd gone fishing or something. And, hell, I don't know—did you ever call me back?"

"Don't seem like I did, does it?"

"Doesn't seem like it," Russell Gautreaux said. He pulled off his captain's cap and wiped some imaginary sweat off his forehead. "Thank God," he said. "I was afraid you'd called me back and I hadn't gotten the message, or I *had* gotten it and forgotten to get back to you. At least I don't have that on my conscience."

The two boats bobbed in the water, their hulls scraping against one another every time a wave from a passing speedboat rippled the surface.

Ned would not look at Denny Gautreaux. He hadn't seen him for several weeks, at least not in the flesh, though many times he had closed his eyes and seen Denny's bare legs sticking out of the white Mercedes.

"If you ask me," Russell Gautreaux said, "it's practically sinful to mix business with pleasure. I don't know how you feel about that, Carter, but that's a belief I've always clung to, just like my daddy did and his daddy before him. Things are changing now, I know that, but the way I look at it, a man still needs time to be with his friends and his family. He needs time to relax. As a general rule, I say let him have it. I say whenever possible, keep business and pleasure separate. What do you say to that?"

"Your boat," Carter Bell said, "or mine?"

"Mine's fine."

Carter Bell stood up, and the boat rocked sideways, and Russell Gautreaux ordered Denny into the boat with Ned and Mack. Denny stood in the back of the Bells' boat and watched the boat his daddy and Carter Bell were in until it was so small you couldn't see it. It looked like Russell Gautreaux aimed to motor all the way down to where the lake opened into the river.

Water lapped at the sides of the Bells' boat. A big wave rocked it, and then the lake got still again.

Denny sat down in the rear of the boat. He crossed his legs. He was wearing a pair of white tennis shorts, white crew socks, and a purple tee shirt with a pair of crossed tennis rackets on the pocket.

"You want to ski, Denny?" Mack said.

"No."

"You want a beer?" Mack nodded at the ice chest.

"No."

"Nice day, ain't it?" Mack said.

"It was."

"But now it's not?"

"Now it's not."

"How come?" Mack said. "What happened to make the day stop being nice?"

"I got up. And then I saw my daddy. And now I'm seeing you two."

"You don't like us? Me and my old buddy Ned?"

"Let's put it this way," Denny said. "I can see the virtue in a water moccasin. A water moccasin's good at doing what a water moccasin does. But as far as you two are concerned. . . ." He made a face.

Mack got up out of his seat and walked over to the ice chest and raised the lid and pulled out another beer. "Want one, Ned?"

Ned didn't answer. He was looking straight ahead, through the windshield, but he wasn't really seeing whatever lay out there, at least not well enough to differentiate one thing from another. He saw a solid brown wall. That was all.

"Swear to God," Mack said. He walked back to the front of the boat and sat down next to Ned. "Stuck for fuck knows how long in a goddamn boat with two folks that just can't seem to act civil. Wonder what the connection between the two of them could be? They're bound to be linked up somehow."

He turned his beer up and swigged from it, and when he'd finished it he threw the can into the lake.

A big fight had started on the dock near the marina. You couldn't tell how many people were involved, but you could see that several guys were going at it. A few shouts and curses crossed the water.

Finally a clot of bodies toppled into the water, and that seemed to put everybody in a better mood. People started climbing up onto the dock, pulling off their shirts and wringing them, and it looked like some of the same guys who'd punched each other were laughing and shaking hands.

"I just love to make up," Mack said. "Anybody can get pissed at somebody else, but it takes a man to say he's sorry."

He ran his tongue over his lips.

"I can do that," he said. "I can say I'm sorry."

If only he'd said what he was sorry for. If he'd opened up his bag of transgressions and poured them all out, each one wrapped differently and bearing a name tag, there would have been plenty for both Ned and Denny. There would have been a few items for each by himself, and there would have been a few that had both their names on them. Knowing they'd been wronged together, and hearing the one who'd done it admit the blame, might have made a difference.

But Mack never said what he was sorry for, so in a minute Denny said, "Sorry for being sorry."

Mack had turned the motor off to save gas. He cranked it now and opened up on the throttle.

"Hey," Denny said. "Come on. My daddy's expecting us to be here."

Mack headed toward the upper lake. Or, to be more precise, he headed toward the narrow passageway that connected the lower lake to the upper lake. The bottleneck.

They were traveling fast.

"Son of a bitch," Denny said.

The boat was bouncing off the surface; Ned's hair was in his eyes. Mack leaned into the wheel, his jaw locked. They crossed the prow of another speedboat. The guy who was steering it gave them the finger. Cold spray hit Ned in the face.

"Goddamn it," Denny hollered. "Turn the boat around."

Denny was on his feet. Ned glanced over his shoulder at him, and Denny was moving forward, picking his way past the cooler, past a pair of orange life vests, the skis.

"Sit down," Ned said.

"Turn the fucking boat around!"

Like any good ski boat, Mack's had a lot of power, and it was so responsive it could almost turn around on itself. He spun the wheel and the front end of the boat reared up, it actually rose, so that for a second you couldn't see anything except the boat's nose, which was pointed upward at a twenty-five-degree angle.

Coming down, the hull slapped the surface, jolting Ned out of his seat. Looking over his shoulder, he saw Denny sprawled out on his back. The life vests had broken his fall.

Mack made a tight circle, bucking his own wake, the boat bouncing up and down, the motor groaning, the muddy water churning, sloshing over the chrome handrails and into the boat.

Mack came out of the circle full throttle. Denny stayed down, lying there on his back, as if he knew it was stupid to risk getting up.

The trees in the passage drooped down into the water. Stumps bumped the hull, now and then a branch raked it. The water here was greenish. In some places a thin, slimy film lay on the surface.

You could hear frogs croaking, and you could see cottonmouths and water moccasins wound around trunks and limbs. You could almost hear them slithering. You could imagine what their sinewy bodies might feel like, the way they'd tighten just before some icy impulse made them strike.

Denny was off his back now, squatting in the middle of the boat. It was clear he didn't want to stand. He must have been thinking that his head would present a good target for anything that decided to drop down off a limb.

"Ain't much point in trying to duck them old moccasins, Denny," Mack said. He'd slowed down now—he didn't have any other choice unless he wanted to tell his daddy that he'd gouged a hole in the bottom of the boat. And he wouldn't want to tell his daddy that because his daddy was in another boat right now, getting enough bad news to last a while.

"One of them old cottonmouths decides to munch a bunch of Denny," Mack said, "he'll just skydive right in here. Won't be shit you can do, Denny, except hope and pray he don't like your flavor."

He cut the motor. They sat there in the passage, hardly moving at all. The sun had come out now. Shafts of light cut through the green canopy, suffusing the passageway with a moss-colored glow.

"You had your fun for the day, Bell?" Denny said.

"I was having plenty of it till you and your daddy showed up."

Denny rocked back and forth on the balls of his feet. Two fingers on his right hand kept tapping his knee. "So why don't you turn around?" he said. "Soon as my daddy gets back, I'll get in the boat with him and you can go back to having fun. Maybe you and Rose can ride around Greenville and throw beer bottles at old ladies or whatever it is you do for kicks."

"Ned?" Mack said. "You want to ride around and throw bottles at old ladies? That your idea of fun?"

The air was green, and the water was too. Things grew uncontrolled here. For all Ned knew, faint green fuzz might have sprung up on the back of his neck. He put his palm there, but he couldn't feel a thing.

"*My* idea of fun," Mack said, "would be to ride around and throw Denny at old ladies. Scrap by scrap, bit by bit. A clump of dick hair at this one, his left nut at that one. I'd turn you into dog food, Gautreaux."

A cypress tree stood no more than four or five feet from the back of the boat. On the lowest branch, a snake reared its head. The mouth opened, the tiny tongue probed the air. The snake's body, wrapped around the branch, was at least eight feet long.

The shiver must have started in Denny's feet. You could see it running up his legs, into his stomach and chest. He hugged himself.

"I need to pee," he said.

"So pee," Mack said.

There were molded plastic seats at the rear of the boat on either side of the motor. You could have stood on one of those seats and shot your stream out over the motor, but to do that you would have had to stand within a few feet of the cypress tree where the snake lay curled around the limb. You could see Denny considering—and then rejecting—the possibility. He looked at the side of the boat where Mack was sitting. That was next to the bank, just a few feet from another tree. No snake was visible in that tree, at least not to Ned's eye, but it would not have been unreasonable to suppose one might be there, somewhere higher up.

Ned's side of the boat was nearest open water. Denny cleared his throat and wet his lips and stood up, glancing into the sky, into the greenish mist that had filled the air, and then he took a step toward the edge of the boat and unzipped his tennis shorts.

Ned had seen Denny naked in the locker room, but he hadn't known then everything he knew now. Back then, Denny's dick had just been a dick. Back then, Denny's body had just been full of blood, whereas now it was full of significance.

It was funny, Ned thought, as some impulse—the same kind of cold-blooded surge that compelled a snake to strike—urged him into motion. Denny had been one thing, and now he was still that one thing, but he was also something else to Ned, he meant more. And because he meant more now, Ned spun him around, he threw his arms around Denny, embracing him. Denny hollered something and their eyes locked and Ned felt Denny's hot piss against his belly. And then Denny reeled backward, he was falling, and Ned was pushing him, shoving him over the side.

"Way to go, Ned," Mack hollered. "Way to give the little butthound a bath."

Denny was foundering, beating the water with his fists, his hair a thin wet curtain that hid his eyes. He groped toward the side of the boat, but Mack had already cranked it, and the boat moved forward four or five feet.

"Come on," Denny hollered. "Let me in there, Bell."

"Moccasin man," Mack said. "He's the moccasin man, ain't he, Ned?"

"Let me in the fucking boat!"

He reached for the side of the boat again. "You better let me in there," he yelled. "My daddy's gonna take that boat and everything else you've got."

"You little fucker," Mack growled. He gave the boat gas. It shot forward ten or twelve feet.

Denny must have realized that the only way he'd ever get out of the water was to swim over to the bank and climb out. He began to pull himself toward it. And as he swam, knowing full well that when he got to the bank he stood a good chance of disturbing a nest of water moccasins, he began to lose his symbolic value. In Ned's eyes he was turning into Denny again, into a boy who was scared of plenty but who kept on moving forward, kept pulling himself onward because that was all he knew to do.

There was a shudder followed by a sudden roar. The boat spun around on itself, and Ned almost lost his balance. Even as he caught the handrail and hung on, he could imagine what Mack would say.

We were trying to turn around and pick him up quick. That water's crawling with moccasins. I didn't know I had the outboard cocked the other way.

He gave thanks for the roar of the motor. There must have been a terrible thudding sound—the kind of sound you'd never forget, a sound that would make you scream in your dreams—when the prow of the boat cracked Denny Gautreaux's skull, and the water ran together with his blood.

1996

The sound was not the one Daze expected. Rather than a ringing bell, she heard a beeping noise, the kind of noise she associated with digital clocks. At the bar there was a microwave oven for heating up frozen po-boys, and it made a similar sound when the second count reached zero.

She rolled toward the source of the noise. Warm flesh blocked her way. She opened her eyes, and the noise stopped.

Hair grew in patches on Beer Smith's back. A big purple birthmark covered part of his left shoulder. She'd seen the top portion of the birthmark before, when she rode behind the driver's seat on the bus in high school. It had been visible above his shirt collar.

"Good morning," he said.

He didn't turn over to face her. She wondered if maybe he couldn't.

"Good morning to you too."

You could hear the sounds of traffic on the highway. She must have been hearing those sounds last night without knowing it. There were different kinds of quiet. Quiet didn't always mean the absence of noise. There was no noise in the house she lived in, not until Ned came home and went to bed and started moaning, but she had never thought of that house as a quiet place.

"Out yonder," Beer said. One hand rose and gestured at the window. Then the hand fell. It slapped the bed. "Out yonder they're saying he don't just sell beer, he's turned into a dirty old man. Except you can't turn into one, they'll be saying. You either are one or you're not, which must mean he's always been one. Your car's standing out there under the chinaberry tree. Just as brazen as you please, where everybody can see it."

She laid her hand on his hip. She thought he might flinch, but he didn't.

"I slipped out there last night," she said. "After you fell asleep."

"Cars and trucks were going by."

"One right after another."

"You was in your drawers, I imagine."

"I was naked," she said. "I slipped out there and I got me a can of spray paint and I walked over to my car and wrote 'Harlot' on the driver's-side door. Just so everybody would know."

"You did, did you? And what'd you write on my pickup?"

"I didn't write anything on it. All I did was draw a picture on the windshield."

"Picture of what?"

"It was kind of phallic."

He puffed himself up and blew out a big stage sigh. "Thank God," he said. "Had me scared you'd drawn a picture of a dick."

He rolled over then and lay on his back. Naturally, like she'd been doing it all along, like she was used to waking up with a man she felt close to, she let her head rest on his chest. The hair there was wiry; it tickled her nose. His armpits smelled hearty, like a pot of chicken soup.

He ran his palm over the top of her head. "I used to lay around like this in the morning with my wife," he said. "It make you feel strange to hear me say that?"

"No. It'd make me feel strange to hear you say you didn't lay around with her."

"What about last night? How you feeling about that?"

"Good," she said, but good was not all of it. Good was how she'd felt when she'd opened her legs and he'd lain between them and, before beginning to move, had run his palm along the side of her face and told her that as much as he wanted to make love to her, what he really looked forward to was the afterwards part, the lying and holding and whispering, the falling ever so slowly asleep. That was what he needed, he said, even more than he needed the other. And that was what she needed too.

But in those seconds last night when she'd known she would have all of it, she had thought of all the other nights. She'd had nothing on those nights except the company of her own body, the familiar feel of the sheets against her skin. And those nights added up to a lot of dark hours.

Now light was everywhere, it poured into the room through the slit in the curtains. It was daylight, nothing more, but this morning it possessed the qualities of a liquid. And she was scared the daylight would wash the nightlight away.

"Damn town'll be talking," he said. "Lord God, how the gossips'll make them old phone wires sizzle."

She pressed her cheek flat against his chest. She could hear his heart beating. Right now it sounded strong.

"I don't care," she said. "For all I care they can take out time on the radio."

"That wouldn't bother me none neither. Truth is, I'm feeling real good right now."

"Me too."

"Kind of like to feel this way again."

"So would I."

"Say you would?"

"Yeah."

"When?"

"Tomorrow. And the day after that."

He ran his fingers through her tangled hair. "But what about Ned?"

When he said her brother's name, she remembered the way Beer had looked last night, the lines around his mouth growing deeper and deeper as she sat in his living room drinking whiskey and telling him what she believed she knew.

"Why?" he'd said. "Why would Ned have anything to do with that? It was an accident, pure and simple. Accidents happen."

"Some accidents happen," she'd said, "because somebody wanted them to."

So he'd asked why Ned or anyone else would have wanted to make the Gautreaux boy die. And then she'd told him about that Friday night, how they'd caught her straddling Denny in the Mercedes, her pants off, her blouse pulled up around her neck. Ned had been with them, she said. Ned knew. He'd probably known right then what he'd do, and when the chance presented itself he took it.

"Why would Mack have gone along with it?" Beer said. "Wasn't he the one driving the boat?"

"His daddy was in trouble with Denny's daddy."

"Everybody was in trouble with Denny's daddy back then. Including me. Most folks still are. That don't mean they'd have anything to do with killing his boy."

"There's another reason Mack would have gone along with it," she said. "Mack Bell's one sick son of a bitch. Ned's like a monkey to him. He finds Ned entertaining. Always has."

She hugged herself.

"It must have been a lot of fun," she said, "to watch Ned shove Denny into that water."

Then she described the scene she'd watched so many times in her mind. The film stock was black and white. There were lots of shadows on the screen, a grayish haze over everything. The sound-track was blessedly absent.

When Ned reached for the wheel, she said, Mack probably started to resist. It was his boat, and he wasn't about to let Ned drive it, though he would have let somebody like Rick Salter, or maybe even Denny himself. They were folks who felt at home with the wheel in their hands, who knew how to steer an expensive car or boat.

Then he realized Ned was about to erupt, and it was always fun to watch trash catch fire. So when Ned grabbed the wheel, Mack sat still.

Denny was thrashing the water. Not swimming, just thrashing, beating up a muddy froth. He wouldn't have had the presence of mind, she said, to swim toward the shore, where the water quickly became so shallow that the boat would've grounded itself. He might have saved himself if he'd done that. But he'd panicked, and his panic had left him a stationary target. And a boat like Mack's would turn around fast.

Mack would have been the one who decided what they'd say, how they'd claim it had been an accident. Even then he must have known what he was buying. He'd own Ned forever.

"It was Ned that told me," she'd said last night. "I was in the kitchen when he came in. At first I didn't pay him much mind. I think I was looking at a magazine, *Redbook* or something like that. I think I was, but I can't say for sure. He tried to put his hand on me. He came up behind me, and he tried to lay his hand on my shoulder, and when I felt it, I just reached up and knocked it off.

"And then he was saying that Denny had been standing on the side of the boat peeing while they were moving through the bottleneck, and he'd lost his balance and fell in, and there were snakes everywhere, and Mack tried to turn around and pick him up, and the boat hit his head, and then Denny was dead.

"Can you imagine that?" she said. "Sitting there hearing that Denny was dead? Hardly anybody knew he meant anything to me. His daddy had seen me in the car with him once or twice, so he knew we were going out together, and some of the other kids did, but that was all. When Judy got killed, Beer, they called you."

"She was every bit as dead," Beer said. He might have said more, but she cut him off.

"Ned got to tell me himself. He got to stand there and act like he was broken up over it, when the truth was he was just thinking Denny would never have me again. He was thinking maybe nobody would, and then both of us would be different from Momma and Daddy."

Beer was sitting right beside her on the couch—his hand lay on her shoulder. But he looked at her from a vantage point far beyond the place where she was.

"Well," he said, "you can keep on hating him for it, or you can let the hating go. If you ask me, choices like that usually come down to a question of cost. And letting go'd be a whole lot cheaper—for you as well as him."

Now, the morning after she'd done the sort of thing her momma had loved to do, Beer Smith was saying, *What about Ned?*

She looked around the bedroom, which was tidy in a way she could not have predicted. Last night, when she'd walked ahead of him into the room, the bed had been neatly made, and when she crawled beneath the covers, she found the sheets clean and crisp.

Dirty clothes were not piled in the corners: his pants and shirt lay folded this morning on the armchair that stood by the door, and her dress lay on top of them. Somebody had folded it too, though she didn't believe she'd been the one. There was no dust around the baseboard; the white globe that shielded the ceiling light was not full of dead bugs and mosquitoes. It looked like somebody had recently mopped the floor, but as far as she knew, he had no cleaning woman.

His life was tidy because like hers it was missing almost everything that mattered. What he needed was the same thing she needed. Some way to clutter things up, to make his days and nights less neat, a way to violate the lines he'd laid out for himself.

She propped herself up on her elbows and looked at him. "What *about* Ned?" she said.

"How's he gone feel about this when he finds out?"

She spoke without thinking, but when she heard her own words, she knew they were true. And for some reason it didn't matter at all that there'd been a time when these same words would have constituted a lie. This time, thank God, was not that time. Sometime between last night and now, that time had passed on.

She heard herself say, "I believe he'll be glad."

Ned sat in his pickup truck, watching the night shift stream out the gates at the Southern Prime processing plant. A couple hundred women, all of them black, all of them wearing white smocks and white hairnets. Blood stains spattered the smocks.

They been standing on the kill line since eleven o'clock last night, and you could tell it. Most of them walked with their heads down, and it looked as if it was all they could do to keep putting one foot in front of another. A few of them headed for the parking lot, but a large number walked off down the blacktop toward Indianola, two miles away, or set off for Highway 49.

One of the last to pass through the gates was Larry's woman, Leota. She was walking with another woman, talking fast and making lots of hand gestures. They stopped at the edge of the parking lot. They talked for a couple more minutes, then the other woman walked off toward town, and Leota headed for the highway. Ned waited a good fifteen minutes before he cranked up and turned into the road.

He caught up with her right where he wanted to, just north of the Sunflower River bridge, on the gravel road that cut a swath between two of Mack's fields. Cars didn't travel that road very often—it was not in good shape—but he knew a lot of farm hands walked on it because it was the fastest way to get home on foot from Indianola.

She'd pulled her shoes off and tied them together and slung them over her shoulder. She was walking on the left side of the road, and she didn't turn around like a lot of folks would have as soon as she heard the engine. She didn't even turn her head when he pulled right up beside her. She just kept walking.

"Want a ride?" he said.

She stopped then and looked his way. He pressed the brake down and held it. She let her eyes rest on his face for a few seconds, then they traveled down his torso until the truck door blocked the view. Then back to his face.

"What kind of ride?"

His hand gripped the door handle. He was close to jumping out of the truck and slapping her face. You could tell she knew it too. You could tell that if he slapped her face, she aimed to slap his. And not just once.

He sat there squeezing the handle. "You wield much influence with Larry?"

She rolled her eyes. *"Wield?"* she said. "What do that word mean?"

He looked back over his shoulder at the road behind. It was empty.

He took his foot off the brake pedal. "He's costing his boss a whole lot of money," he said as the truck began to inch forward. "And his boss ain't the nicest man around—fact is, he's one of the meanest. You care anything about Larry, you better suggest he move someplace else. Dee-troit might be nice."

In his sideview mirror he could see her cupping her hands around her mouth, getting ready to holler. He pressed the accelerator, hoping he wouldn't hear whatever it was she aimed to yell, but the words still reached him.

"Ain't nothing different in Dee-troit."

Daze was gone when he got home.

She was gone, and the house was empty, and it was just seven-thirty in the morning. He parked his pickup truck, got out, and walked into the house; he walked down the hall toward her room and opened the door.

Her bed was made up. A few bottles stood on her dresser. One contained cologne, another was a roll-on deodorant. Her brush lay there too. Several clumps of hair remained caught in the bristles.

The clothes she'd probably worked in—a pair of jeans and a purple tee shirt—lay across the armchair near the foot of her bed. Her sneakers stood side by side underneath the armchair. A pair of panties lay on the floor.

The panties were white, just like his underwear, but made of nylon. It crossed his mind that she might have had a colored pair somewhere, over there in one of her drawers, and she might have taken this pair off and put the colored pair on, and he knew colored ones were supposed to be more sexy.

As a child he'd often slipped into his momma and daddy's room, and he'd gone to his momma's chest of drawers and pulled out her panties, her bras and slips and hose. He'd rubbed them between his fingers, touching the material lightly, and he'd run the really soft stuff, the nylon panties and sheer silky stockings, along the side of his face. He hadn't known why he was doing it, he just knew he liked the way it felt. And then at a certain point he'd understood why he was doing it, and then not too long after that he'd stopped doing it, and a little bit later he'd even stopped remembering having done it.

But he remembered it now. He remembered the way this kind of material made you feel when you touched it, like you'd crossed some invisible line between what was fine and what wasn't, like you yourself were as naked as the skin the material was meant to hide, that everything which normally stayed inside you was outside you now, out in the open where everybody could see it, and you wanted them to, but there was no one nearby.

He bent and picked the panties up and laid them on the bed.

She drove in by herself and parked her car where she always parked it and got out and walked over to the lounge and unlocked the door. Light pooled on the bare concrete floor. It was cool inside the bar, and the air felt damp.

You could do something a thousand times, a million times, and then you could do the same thing again, in a new frame of mind, and the act itself changed. It stopped being what it had been and became something else. Knowing this, she wondered as she often had whether the little day-to-day endeavors that everybody lived by meant anything in themselves.

Her daddy had lived by changing his surroundings every few days; her momma had lived by changing men. Every day of his life, Ned did what Mack told him. She opened up the bar almost every morning. Once inside, she did the same things each day that she'd done the day before.

She was doing the same things now. Washing down the bar. Turning on the Mr. Coffee. Washing up those glasses that had been left out last night. Turning on the TV.

Normally what she did dulled her, bored her. But now, for the first time in ages, she'd started the day off someplace new, just like

her momma and her daddy used to do, and everything felt different. It all felt new.

The truckers were there around noon, chalking pool cues, wiping
sleep out of their eyes. They could sink an eight ball in the corner
pocket just about as well asleep as they could awake. Which was to
say not very well at all. Truckers had to be the worst pool shooters
in the world. They were always knocking balls off the table, and the
hard little things would bounce once off the concrete and then roll
across the floor and smack against the bar. She'd seen and heard it
happen more times than she could count.

They were telling jokes this morning, jokes about sex and jokes
about wrecks, and one joke in which both subjects figured.

"Dude flips a rig off the side of a mountain," one of them said.
"Wakes up sometime three, four days later in a hospital bed, and a
doctor and four or five nurses are standing over him. Doctor says,
'Mr. So-and-So, we got good news and we got bad.' Says, 'The
good news is that despite all your injuries, we managed to save your
genitals.' Dude says, 'Thank God.' Doctor says, 'The bad news is,
them little items are under your pillow.'"

One of them knocked over his beer bottle, he was laughing so
hard. He looked at Daze, expecting her to give him a dirty look and
fling a wet rag at him like she had the last time he'd knocked over
his beer, but instead she stepped around the end of the bar and
walked over and picked his bottle up and wiped the beer up herself.

"One day," she told him, "you're liable to hurt yourself laughing at one of Charlie's jokes."

She handed him the empty bottle. He stood there looking un-
settled, a two-day-old growth of stubble on his face, his eyes flick-
ing back and forth between her and Charlie as if each one of them
was a road and he didn't know which one to take.

When he left he called her Daisy and tipped her five dollars.

Ned parked in the gravel lot right beside her old LTD. On the far side of her car stood Beer Smith's pickup. His dog was lying under it, near one of the front wheels. He lifted his head as Ned went by.

Ned pushed open the door to the lounge. He used to come here from time to time; he'd sit on one of the barstools and do his best to make conversation with Daze, but she wouldn't have any of it. She'd just stand there with her back to him, pulling bags of potato chips off the snack rack and clipping them back on, as if rearranging them required all her attention. There was a mirror behind the bar, and every now and then she'd look up at it, and their eyes would meet. He was usually the one who looked away.

Today she was standing there smiling.

She was smiling at Beer Smith, who was sitting on a barstool and telling her a story that must have been entertaining. She was looking at him as if he was the only other person in the room, though he wasn't. A bunch of guys were back at the tables, shooting pool and drinking beer and telling dirty jokes.

She wasn't aware Ned was there either, at least not until one of the guys playing pool, a big blond-haired fellow named Dave who was a foreman on the kill line out at Southern Prime, hollered, "Hey, Ned. Hear y'all had you some nigger trouble last night."

She looked up toward the door then, and as always when she saw him, her face began to harden into the stiff plastic mask he'd been looking at for so long. But today something miraculous happened. Somehow she arrested the process. You couldn't actually say she smiled at him—not like she smiled at Beer anyway—but the skin over her jaws relaxed, and those deep lines he was used to seeing around the corners of her mouth never quite formed.

"Hey, Ned," she said.

He couldn't quite find his voice, so he just nodded at her.

"Hear y'all had you a little fire drill," Dave said. He was standing there resting on his cue stick.

"Where'd you get your information from?" Ned said.

"Around and abouts."

"Yeah, well, I wouldn't place too much faith in rumors."

"Ask me," Dave said, "y'all ought to turn two or three of them niggers into fish feed." He was grinning. His teeth were the color of a school bus.

Ned said, "Truth is, I ain't asked you."

Dave's smile crumbled. He ran his hand up and down the cue stick a time or two, as if he were thinking about putting it to a different use than the one it was designed for. Evidently he decided that wouldn't be too smart. He finally mumbled something under his breath and bent over the table.

Ned watched him muff a shot, then walked over to the bar and sat down beside Beer. "I could use a good cold one," he said.

Beer said, "Draw your brother a beer. On the house."

She stood a mug under the tap and began to fill it.

Beer tilted his head back toward the pool tables, where Dave was racking the balls. "Something go wrong out at Mack's?" he said.

Ned kept his voice down. "Got a little hot out there last night. Somebody set a fire in the backyard, and while we was all going nuts over that, they dumped a couple gallons of Toxaphene into one of the ponds. The fish were in the sock. Every one of 'em was dead in thirty minutes."

"Damn," Beer said. "He call the sheriff?"

He could feel his sister's eyes on him. "Naw," he said.

"How come?"

He didn't answer.

"He ain't planning to administer Southern justice, is he?"

"I don't know what he's planning."

Daze laid a tab on the counter and stood the mug on top of it. A small amount of foam ran over the sides. She reached over with a rag and wiped the foam up. Her hand brushed Ned's, and she didn't draw back as she had for so long whenever they accidentally touched one another.

"Well," Beer said, "I hope ain't nobody fixing to get hurt." He lifted his mug, finished his beer, and got up off the stool. "Bull's out yonder in the parking lot," he said. "Don't want to let him get too hot. I'll see y'all later."

Before he walked out, he clapped Ned on the shoulder, almost as if he aimed to brace him up.

For a while neither of them said anything. He sat there quietly with his hands wrapped around the sweaty mug, and she stood there on the other side of the bar, just a few inches of hardwood between them, which wasn't much when you considered everything else that had separated them for so long.

Ned picked up the mug and took a sip. "I've always liked that man," he said.

"You have?"

"Yeah. I always have. He came to Daddy's funeral. Remember?"

"Of course I do."

He set the mug down. His courage was about to fail him, as it had on that last ride he'd taken with his daddy, as it had again the last time he'd seen his momma. It had failed him when he didn't have the spine to walk out of that little country store or stick his hand out and pull Denny back into the boat. There were a lot of things to say now, and he'd said them in his mind a hundred times, a thousand, but right now all he wanted to do was change the subject.

"How's that old car of yours running?" he said.

If she thought it was an odd question for him to ask right now, she didn't let on. "Like the piece of shit it is."

"Day's coming when you gone have to cave in and get you something else."

"I know it. It's just that I've had it so long I hate to give it up. Even though it's worse than worthless."

"I could help you find something. I been looking, off and on."

"You have?"

"Yeah. I been looking."

"For anything in particular?"

"Just something good and sturdy. Something you might like."

"Well," she said, staring him right in the eye, staring at him so intensely that he couldn't have broken the visual embrace, even if he'd wanted to. And he didn't. "I think I'm ready," she said, "to let that old thing go."

He felt as if he couldn't breathe, but it didn't matter. Air was the last thing he needed. "Say you are?"

"Yeah," she said.

She picked up the rag and began to wipe the counter. She'd wiped up most of the spilled beer, but there was a thin film of moisture there she hadn't quite gotten rid of.

"Ned," she said, "I'm ready to let it go."

Larry Singer stood shirtless in tall Johnson grass, down close to the water, right next to one of Mack's John Deeres. His bronze back glowed. Rivulets of sweat ran down his shoulders. He'd just disconnected an aerator from the drawbar on the tractor. Hearing the noise of the truck engine, he turned around and shaded his eyes and watched as Ned cut the engine and got out of the truck.

Heat waves rose off the levee, and the pond water shimmered. It was one of those days when you felt like you were seeing everything a little more clearly than you usually saw it. The lines were cleaner, the colors sharper. Objects looked bigger than they normally did.

Ned shaded his own eyes. Larry nodded at him, then turned and heaved himself onto the tractor seat.

Ned began to walk down the bank toward the water. Larry cranked the tractor, gunned the engine. He threw the tractor into gear.

"Watch out, now!" he hollered.

Ned stopped walking. Larry drove forward a few feet, stopping the front wheels just inches from Ned. The odor of diesel fumes assaulted his nose.

"Wonder what it's gone take," Larry hollered over the noise of the engine, "to get Mack Bell's attention?"

"Oh, I believe y'all done got his attention."

"What make you say so?"

"This and that."

Larry shook his head as if Ned had just committed some childish misdemeanor. "That's just like white folks," he said. "Wanting to say it and not say it. You people's got a problem with your presentation, Ned."

He turned the wheel, backed the tractor up, turned the wheel again. He repeated the operation two or three times until finally he had the front of the tractor aimed at the pond.

He let the engine idle quietly. "Reckon what a tractor like this cost?"

"A brand-new one?"

"Yeah."

"Close to sixty thousand dollars."

"Damn. Them implement companies making a killing."

He sounded as if the workings of the free-enterprise system had just become clear to him. But they hadn't. He'd understood free enterprise a long time. He understood it better than most folks.

"Everybody involved in this business making a killing," he said. "Except the people that do all the work."

"Way it is in any business."

"Yeah, but that don't make it right."

"Naw, it don't."

"So sometimes," Larry said, revving the engine, "a person got to take corrective action."

While Ned stood there watching, he drove the tractor down into the fish pond.

The water rose over the front wheels, then reached the level of the fan belt, and the fan hurled silver sheets into the air. The engine began to make a chugging sound.

He kept driving forward until the water level was about two-thirds of the way up the rear tires. He stopped the tractor, then, but left it running, churning up the muddy water.

He jumped down into the pond and sloshed over to the bank. Grinning, he gestured at the tractor with his thumb. "Out yonder," he said, "we got a merger of the natural and the mechanistic."

Ned couldn't help but smile. "Yeah. I reckon so."

"Gone add a little diesel flavor to the fishes, while at the same time creating some more business for them good folks at John Deere."

"Pump a little money into the local economy."

"They ought to invite me to the chamber of commerce."

"They liable to," Ned said. "Or then again, they liable to invite you someplace else."

"Say they might?"

"I wouldn't put it past 'em."

"Well, I may bring a few of 'em along with me. Truth is, I ain't got nothing to lose by taking that little trip."

"Look like you got you a girlfriend that's pretty stuck on you."

"Could be." Larry put his hands in his pockets and cocked his head. "Something I been wondering about you," he said.

"Say there is?"

"Yeah."

"And what's that?"

"You not a bad-looking guy. How come you don't have *you* no woman?"

The water around the tractor was brown and roiling. Brown water belonged in a pond. Tractors didn't. Catfish and snakes and alligators did. People didn't. People ought to be where he and Larry were now, their feet firmly on the ground, their lungs sucking in that blessed fresh air. That was the natural order of things, and anybody that upset it would have to pay for fucking it up.

Ned said, "I ain't entitled to no woman."

For a moment Larry was speechless.

"Damn, man," he finally said. "You even weirder than most white folks. And that's saying something."

"Yeah. I imagine it is."

Larry started past him, tromping through the Johnson grass, but before he'd taken more than two or three steps, he changed his mind. He stopped and looked at Ned.

"Hope it don't never come down to me having to hurt you, Ned," he said. "That ain't nothing I got no urge to do."

It was just something said at the edge of a fish pond on a stifling day, something said and heard over the noise of a diesel engine that was about to drown out, over the sound of sloshing water. But saying it changed something, and hearing it changed something else. And looking at Larry, Ned could tell he knew it too.

"Thought you said I was a zero. Seem to me like you said that. Or was I dreaming?"

"Maybe I did say that—fact, I know I did. But I'm here to tell you something else, man."

"Yeah?"

Sweat ran down Larry's smooth, hairless chest and onto his stomach. His navel glistened. "Every nigger got a heart," he said. "And every zero got a middle."

The store wasn't there anymore.

But if you knew what you were looking for, and God knows he did, you could tell where it had once stood. Grass grew in clumps around the concrete blocks the joists used to rest on. A concrete slab, cracked into three or four pieces now and badly overgrown, marked the location of the gas pump. Underfoot, ground into the dry buckshot, lay a soft-drink cap, bleached white by the sun. There was glass in the dirt too—from shattered windows and display cases, the occasional broken bottle.

He stood there at the edge of somebody's cotton field, his eyes trained on the spot—maybe fifteen feet away—where the counter must have been. A few feet to the left of that spot—ten feet at the most—stood the soft-drink box that had been turned into a beer cooler.

Ten feet.

He'd opened the lid, peered inside, found something less than he was looking for. He'd opened his mouth, said a few words, heard the man's reply, then started gathering up the beer cans and making the first of six trips to the counter. And by the time he got through doing that, the man behind the counter knew what the two folks waiting outside—over there, right where that pickup truck stood now—had already figured out.

He wasn't what he was supposed to be. He was an imposter: a boy who'd chosen this place, and that moment, to impersonate a man.

What remained of the sun was about to disappear behind the roof of the house when Ned turned into the driveway. Climbing out of his pickup, he wondered how many times he'd pulled up here under the shade of these pecan trees and gotten out and gone inside to find out what Mack expected of him. It had to be at least once a day, he figured, and most days it was two or three times.

Multiply two by 365, and you got 730, and multiply 730 by 22 or 23 and you'd get a figure that was truly too big and awful to think about. There had been a first time—the night after the opening football game his sophomore year, when Kyle Nessler made Mack give him a case of beer—and there would be a last time. The question was when.

Mack's truck was here, and so were Rick Salter's and Alan Morelli's and one that Ned figured belonged to Fordy Bashford, since it displayed a Humphreys County license plate.

The house was quiet—all the shades on the windows had been pulled down. Ned walked across the yard and knocked on the door.

"Who is it?" Ellie said.

"Ned."

He heard her turn the deadbolt. She opened the door and stepped aside to let him in. He saw his face reflected in the polished hardwood floor. The reflection must have always been there, every time he walked through this door, but for some reason he'd never noticed it until now.

Ellie had on black shorts and a tight black tee shirt that displayed her nipples in relief. She smelled like whiskey, and her pupils looked dilated.

"They're out there," she said.

"Yeah, I know they are."

He started down the hall.

"Ned?" she said.

She was close to him now, and the odor of whiskey and sweat was coming off her. She probably wouldn't live to be too old. If pills and whiskey didn't kill her, Mack might.

She grabbed his wrist. Her palm was wet.

"You probably think I'm just as hollow as a cane pole," she said, "and you may be right. But I've always liked you. I wanted you to know that."

A week ago he would have done his best to get away from her after she said a thing like that, but a week ago seemed like a lot longer than seven days. The way she was standing there now reminded him of the girl from Florida that he and Mack and Rick had left standing alone in the woods so far from town. He didn't know why he thought of that girl right now, but he did, and he didn't aim to make that same mistake again.

So he reached out and put his arm around Ellie's thin shoulders and pulled her close and said he liked her too, exactly as he might have said it more than twenty years ago, in a corridor between classes at the Academy, if there had ever been anybody back then to say it to.

Mack and the others were sitting on the screened-in patio. They'd all pulled lawn chairs up around a white plastic table. Each one of them balanced a tumbler on his knee or held it clamped between his legs. A gallon jug of Jack Daniels stood on the plastic table. The jug was half-empty.

He stood there in the dark. Listening.

"'Dixie,'" Rick Salter said.

"What about it?"

Salter was drinking the whiskey straight—no ice, no water. He turned his tumbler up and took a big swallow. "Just take 'Dixie,' for instance," he said and set his glass down.

"Take it where?"

"What I'm saying is just look what that song represents to us as opposed to them. I'm a Mississippi State man, same as you are, Fordy, and let's face it, 'Dixie' *is* an Ole Miss song. But to me it's more than that. Man, I can't hardly hear it without getting a big old lump in my throat."

"Talk about it, Rick," Mack said. "Say what it does to you."

"Man, it brings *smells* to my mind."

Mack reached for the jug. "What kind of smells?"

"Morning in November when I was a little bitty boy. Momma's cooking bacon. I'm waking up and smelling that smell, and I get up and walk over to the window and raise it, and across the road I see them old fields full of cotton. The niggers are already out there pulling them old canvas sacks, and my momma and my daddy and both my granddaddies are still alive, and the world's all right."

Salter reached up and rubbed moisture from his eyes. "That's what 'Dixie' means to *me*," he said.

Mack poured himself about two inches of whiskey and set the jug back down. He made a sour face. "I guess we all know what the song means to them," he said.

"Means chains," Morelli said. "Means shackles."

"Means the overseer's whip," Fordy Bashford said.

"Means a stinking shack with cracks in it," Salter said.

"Means George Wallace," Mack said, "and Ross Barnett."

"Jefferson Davis and Robert E. Lee."

"Theodore Bilbo and Byron de la Beckwith."

"Medgar Evers and Emmett Till."

Ned stepped around the corner, onto the patio.

They all looked up at him then, as if by mutual consent, all their eyes rolling toward him at once. They had him in their sights now; they could see a manlike object.

"Have a seat," Mack said. He gestured at the single empty chair. "We been waiting for you."

Songs about the road kept playing in his head.

His daddy had died on the road, and if you looked at it a certain way, his momma had too. Looking at it that way, everybody did. Death on the road was no disgrace, though dying was always a failure of sorts.

Mack drove. Ned sat beside him. Salter and Morelli and Bashford followed in Salter's pickup, their lights glaring off the sideview mirror. They had the jug of Jack Daniels with them; he'd seen Bashford tote it out the front door. It crossed his mind that all of them, Mack included, were about half-drunk, that they were moving around in a numb-lipped fog. It also crossed his mind that you could wreak a lot of havoc numb-lipped.

The Johnson grass that grew along the road ditch kept whipping his door. Every now and then Mack would steer the truck out of the ruts, and the tires would heave up a hailstorm of gravel.

"They've cost me a lot of money," Mack said. "I don't watch out, they'll cost me a lot more. You can't let the word get around that the kind of shit they've been up to works. Somebody fucks with you, you got to fuck with them."

"Yeah. You can get a rhythm going that way."

"Rhythm?"

"Tit for tat. They fuck with you, you fuck with them. They fuck with you again. And so on. You see what I mean? Seem like sooner or later, it's all got to stop."

"It's fixing to stop tonight," Mack said.

"He's apt not to be in that house by himself," Ned said. "He's apt to be in there, if he's nearabouts at all, with Booger and God knows who all."

"That's Booger's tough luck."

"I imagine they got the door shut good and tight."

"They'll open it for you."

"What makes you so sure?"

"Far as they're concerned, you're damn near one of 'em."

The night stank of pesticides and dust. Ned had been smelling those odors all his life. Same as Larry. Neither one of them had been able to escape those smells by taking off for the Bahamas as Mack had. "They know I'm not one of 'em," he said. "Especially after I went in there and run Q. C. and his family off."

"They just figure I made you do it."

"They do, they figuring wrong. I ain't a John Deere. You don't drive me."

Mack looked at him as if for once in his life he'd said something interesting. "Naw, I don't," he said. "I just pay you. Which is one reason—though it ain't the only reason—you gone do what I say."

They rode on in silence for a couple of minutes. Ned could feel the butt of the 9-mm. against his skin. He'd walked over to his own truck while the others were standing out in front of Mack's house, working the action on their shotguns and boosting one another's spirits. He'd reached in, grabbed the gun, and tucked it away inside his shirt before anybody saw him. It was there now, hard and cold, and before too long he'd have to deal with its presence.

"What happens," he said, "after he opens the door?"

Mack gestured with his thumb at the gun rack. His shotgun was up there, a Remington Wingmaster that packed enough punch to fell a grizzly and had done just that a few years ago when he had gone hunting in Alaska. "When he opens the door," he said, "he'll wish to hell he hadn't."

"And the sheriff'll just obligingly conclude it was an act of random mayhem?"

Mack laughed. "I'll tell you what it is," he said. "It's a drug-related killing. Sheriff'll find a little coke on the premises, just enough to convince him this is one bunch of drug dealers going after another."

Nobody would be around tomorrow to tell the sheriff otherwise. Not Larry or Larry's woman or whoever else happened to be in the house tonight. In the end it wouldn't matter whether Ned went up to the door and knocked, whether he did what Mack wanted him to. If he didn't, Mack would just find another way to bring it off.

"Yeah," Ned said. "I reckon it'll all work out just like you planned it."

"Seem like I hear a little note of disapproval."

Ned moved his right hand so it lay in his lap.

"You didn't seem to have so many scruples when you smashed that old nigger's brains out that night," Mack said. "What's happened in the meantime? You done seen the light?"

For most of his life he'd been looking at everything but the light. He'd seen that black man staring at the television set, even after the bottle hit him, as if he were still capable of making sense of what he saw. He'd seen his daddy's body going into the ground in the cheapest box his momma could find. He'd seen his momma's skin draw up and turn so green it began to smell of death, and he'd seen Denny Gautreaux lying limp in the water like a gutshot bird.

He didn't know if he'd seen the light or not. But one thing he did know: you only had to see the light once.

Mack stopped the truck about a quarter of a mile down the road from Larry's house. It was pitch dark tonight. You couldn't see a thing except the single bulb burning above Larry's front door. He sat there looking at it, trying to remember if he'd ever noticed it before.

Salter and Morelli and Bashford would be getting out of the pickup behind them, Bashford and Morelli carrying shotguns, Rick toting a pistol Ned knew he wouldn't use. Rick was willing to hire his dirty work done, but he liked to keep his own hands clean. It was a pretty trick if you could pull it off. Most of the time you could, as long as you took care to buy yourself a Ned Rose.

Mack put the truck in park and cut the engine.

"Me and them'll slip down the road," he said, "and hide on the other side of the levee. Wait a few minutes and then drive on down there and stop—they've seen you driving my truck before. Get out and just go up to the door and knock. You may have to do a little hemming and hawing, but sooner or later they'll open up. When they do, you take a dive."

He opened his door and got out, then reached back in for the shotgun. In the darkness his face looked gray, like dried paste that at any minute might start to fleck away.

Ned's right hand was gripping the 9-mm.

"Leave that pistol in the fucking truck," Mack said. "They got a goddamn porch light on. You think they'll open the door if they see you coming across the yard with that?" He shook his head. "Sometimes I wonder if your brain cavity ain't plumb empty."

"Sometimes I wish to God it was."

"I reckon if I was you, I might think that way too."

Ned raised the barrel and aimed it at Mack's chest.

"Put that fucking thing down. Don't you point that thing at me."

For more than twenty years they'd been traveling down the road toward this instant and this place. For most of that time, Ned hadn't known he was on that road, and Mack hadn't either. Even now Mack didn't know it.

"How many orders you reckon you've ever given me?" Ned said. "Lifetime, I'm talking about."

"What's got you wanting to tabulate everything?"

"I'm trying to see what I add up to."

"You gone add up to nothing if you don't put that gun down."

"Naw, I'll add up to nothing if I do."

He couldn't see Mack's eyes too well, but he knew they were cutting back and forth between the barrel of the pistol and the gun rack where the shotgun lay cradled.

"You ever wonder how it'd feel to be me?" Ned said. "Ever think much along them lines?"

"Naw, I never."

The safety was on the left side of the butt. It clicked dully when he released it.

"Or Larry. Ever think much about what it'd feel like to be him?"

The trigger teased his finger.

"I bet even now you'd rather be yourself than him or me. Even with what's about to happen."

When Ned said that, Mack ducked his head and began his lunge, throwing himself forward, grasping for the shotgun. It seemed to Ned then, as his finger squeezed the trigger and his right hand roared, that Mack had always been lunging at him, that all of Mack's weight, the mass of what he was, had been hurtling toward him since the day he was born.

"Remember when there used to be a stoplight here?" Beer said.

They were sitting at the intersection of 82 and Beaverdam Road, waiting for a break in the morning traffic. She needed to go home and get some fresh clothes. He had said he would drive her.

"That light's been gone for about thirty years," she said.

"Has it been that long?"

"I think so."

"Makes me want to quote a country song."

"Which one?"

"I reckon almost any one would do."

"Yeah," she said, "I guess so."

She believed Ned would be home when they got there, his truck parked out front where it almost always was at eight-thirty on a weekday morning. Instead someone else's truck was there.

It was an old, rusty-looking thing with bad dents all over it and a couple of hoes jutting out over the tailgate. It must have belonged to the man who was sitting on the front steps.

He was a young man, late teens, early twenties. He wore a pair of faded jeans and a tee shirt and a pair of work shoes that had mud encrusted on them. He stood when they pulled into the driveway.

If Beer thought it was strange to find a black man on the front steps at eight-thirty in the morning, he didn't say so. He just said, "Looks like somebody's waiting for you."

Her heart began to beat faster. "Looks like it."

They got out and walked across the yard. The man made no move to meet them halfway. He just stood there waiting. Long before they reached him, she knew he had something important to say.

"My name's Larry," he told her. "I work with Ned."

She felt Beer's hand touch her elbow. His touch felt firm but not insistent. It was as if he just aimed to remind her he was there.

The sun was in her eyes, so bright it almost blinded her. She offered her hand to the black man. After a moment's hesitation, he took it. His palm was warm and soft.

"I'm Daisy," she said. "Ned's my brother."

THE OXYGEN MAN

DISCUSSION POINTS

1. Though numerous writers live and work in the South, not all are considered Southern in the tradition of, say, William Faulkner and Flannery O'Connor. Yarbrough received his higher education in Mississippi, sets much of his work (including this novel) in that state, and has been called "one of the best writers to come out of the South in many years." Do you think *The Oxygen Man* draws from a distinctly Southern Gothic mythology, one in which the very air exerts a tormented, spiritual pressure? Or should it simply be considered a work of Southern regionalism, documenting the reality of a particular social landscape?

2. In literature, snakes are commonly symbols of evil and of lost innocence. Would you say that the many snakes in *The Oxygen Man* are symbolic? Or are they really just snakes, doing the things that real, poisonous snakes do?

3. Most adult brothers and sisters don't go on living together in their dead parents' houses. Another author might have chosen to tell us, right off the bat, that Ned and Daze's relationship isn't like that of most siblings, and might even reveal, at once, some background for, and explanation of, the peculiar blend of regard and disregard they have for each other. But Yarbrough takes his time, offering only incidental clues while gradually uncovering Ned and Daze's history. What are some of these clues? When did you start noticing things were seriously awry between Ned and Daze?

4. After Daze sees her parents making love in the smokehouse, she finds real dignity in the act. Yet elsewhere in the novel, sex is shown in a cruder light. How does this disparity shape Daze's own sexuality? What are some of the other dichotomies that provide texture, and tension, in this book?

5. Ned and Daze's parents are responsible for much of the sorrow and disarray in their children's lives, and yet their love for each other is clear, as is their resistance to racism. Do you find them credible? Do you have sympathy for them? Why? Why not?

6. "[Y]ou could be dead while your heart was still beating. . . . You could die over years or decades," Ned thinks while listening to his

father enthuse about his work as a housepainter on pages 186–187. Why do you think Ned has this thought at this moment, rather than at another? Exactly what do you think he means? Do you agree with him? Would Daze?

7. Much of the novel has to do with race relations, while its way of jumping between the early 1970s and mid-1990s provides a look at what changes, if any, have occurred during that period. Are there changes? What are they? Are you surprised by how big or small they are? Would a novel set in the north, or in a larger southern city, paint a different picture? How else does Yarbrough's technique of shifting between decades affect your reading experience?

8. On the sweltering day when the men are seining the pond, the white men keep their shirts on but the black men take theirs off. Discuss the complicated hierarchy of power implicit in this event. Who's better off here? Now, take a moment to examine Larry's interesting role in the novel and in the lives of the people around him. How would you describe it?

9. Yarbrough has named the novel for Ned, and indeed, Ned is the book's most complicated figure. In what moments did you see him most clearly? When did you begin to expect that Ned might exchange his passivity for a more aggressive stance?

10. If you were the adult Daze, would you be able to forgive Ned his role in Denny Gautreaux's death? If you were the teenager Ned, would you have tucked in his sleeping mother on the couch, being so tender and so careful not to wake her?

11. Despite the book's many tragedies, Daze keeps going. Ultimately, do you find this novel uplifting or despairing? What did it teach you, about yourself or other people?

Author's Note

It's been more than seven years since I wrote the first sentence of *The Oxygen Man*. I'm going to resist the urge to pretend that I knew exactly what I was doing the whole time I was working on the book, because the truth is that I didn't. Writing a novel—for me at least—is always an act of discovery. What I can say with certainty is that one morning in the spring of 1993, I turned my computer on and found myself writing a scene about a man and a woman. The man had just come home from work. The woman was eating breakfast, so that meant the man had some sort of job that required him to work at night. At first I thought they were husband and wife, but before too long I realized that they were brother and sister. Something was wrong between them. I wrote the rest of the novel to find out what that "something" was.